A VAIN AND INDECENT WOMAN

the scandalous life of
Joan of Kent

Colin Falconer

For Loz and Jess,.

PART 1

1.

Arundel castle, March 1330

They call my little Joan the most beautiful woman in all England. Well, every father thinks that about his daughter. That she is special, and prettier. But I never had the opportunity to boast. My name is Edmund of Woodstock and I am the son of a king and the brother of a king and the grandfather of a king.

I was twenty-nine years old when I died.

Died; I use the term loosely. I was murdered, but within the dictates of the law and with the full approval of the king, even though he was barely eighteen years old at the time. But let's not use his age to make excuses for him, it does rather grate on me. I am ashamed to say he once had my slobber on his boots, after I begged him for my life. He wasn't moved then, so listening to people apologize for him now doesn't move me much.

But thinking back to that last day, if I had known it would be the last time I would hold my daughter in my arms, then I would have held her longer, hugged her closer, kissed her more, there would not have been that wasted, rushed goodbye we shared that morning.

But look, that is all history now, as they say.

As she walks towards me, into the light, I hold out my arms and see her smile in tender recognition. In the years to come the chroniclers will call her vain and indecent, a woman of slippery ways. But to me she is, will always be, my little Joan; if I had lived I might have saved her so much pain.

Perhaps.

But that is all in the past and no matter what they say about her in life, now she is mine again, at last.

* * *

It is a cold, grey day in March. My wife, Margaret, clutches little Joan in her arms and holds her out to me for a kiss but I am pressed for time, the wind is blowing the rain indoors and there has been some trouble with the horses and it has made me late to depart. I give her a hurried buss on the cheek and that is it. She puts her arms around my neck and tries to cling on. She is fresh out of bed and smells warm as straw.

I disentangle myself with a frown.

I do not know then that it will be the last time I will ever see Arundel Castle or my family again, not in this life. So I do not even look back, I keep my head down to the wind as we ride away. I have been summoned to attend the Parliament in Winchester and I think not to be away too long. That black-bearded bastard Mortimer says I must attend.

He called the former King's favourite, Hugh le Despenser, a tyrant when he replaced him. Now we find we have replaced a wolf with a mad bear. Is there no reasonable king in all England?

Yet somehow, I still believe I will see the danger before it arrives. Why should I think that when it is clear to me, to everyone, that we have no inkling of what is in our Lord Mortimer's mind? Shortly after I arrive in Winchester I am arrested by the king's officers and charged with treason. Imprisoned on the Wednesday, dead on the Monday. You cannot complain that justice is not swift in our new England.

When the king's warrant is served, I think well, perhaps a fine, banishment from Parliament, an early retirement. I do not realise until the very last that Mortimer's judges want me dead. I go to the king, I know he is just his mother's lapdog, but even then I do not believe he will let this stand. It is still down to him to sign the warrant of execution.

Yes, I know, I have heard people say that my young king dared not go against his mother or against Mortimer, that he feared for his own life. Nonsense, I say. Isabella would never have allowed Mortimer to harm her son. The truth is, he is just a little boy frightened of his mother, damn his eyes. And so, I have to die.

But I grovel to that beardless lickspittle. I offer to walk barefoot to Canterbury with a rope around my neck as atonement for trying to save his father - his father. I weep. There is snot all over the king's fine carpets when I am done. All I can think of is little Joan's arms around my neck and I long to return to her.

Don't let it end this way. Give me one more day, my king.

Well, you all know what good that did me.

So, hands bound, I am escorted outside Winchester Castle to wait in the freezing cold in just my shirt while someone tries to find someone to swing the axe.

As I stand there shivering, the rain soaking through the linen, I think about my wife and what she will do when she hears about my misfortune. I have let her down. She is almost to term with our third child. There is little Joan, my son Edmund. I will never see either of them grow.

What will become of them now?

They tell me they cannot find the public executioner; he has fled, unwilling to lop off the head of one of Longshanks' sons. Well at least someone shows some restraint. And so I must wait there from Lauds almost to Nones while they look for someone who is willing to do the deed. I should be gratified that it takes so long but I find I am short on feelings of appreciation.

After all, with the former king's favourite, my lord le Despenser, they were practically queuing up to do the job.

Oh, where is this executioner? Let us be done with this. I am cold, I am despairing, I do not wish to think any more about my wife and my little ones and what Mortimer and that damned Isabella will put them through.

Finally, they find a willing soul in one of the dungeons. I am told that he is a latrine cleaner who is under threat of execution himself for doing murder and has been offered a royal pardon if he will do the deed. Heartening news.

It seems it has come to this; death at the hands of a man who shovels shit for a living. What will my family think when they hear this?

My father was the Hammer of the Scots.

My wife had warned me. *'You're too eager to do everything the king asks. He has made a fool of you.'*

She was right, women are always right about these things. What she referred to is this: years ago I had duped a rebel baron into surrendering to the king's mercy. I got scant gratitude from Edward for it. He never did heap appreciation on me. But he was my brother - my half-brother anyway – as well as my king. I was doing my duty.

How could I have known then that the miserable wretch I took in would become the queen's lover and champion and rise to become the most powerful man in England? Back then Roger Mortimer was just another belligerent who refused to bow to the king's law, but somehow he got out from under and found his way into the queen's bed.

Clever bastard. We all misjudged him. We all misjudged her most of all.

I suppose he was hardly to forget what I had done. I was naïve to think that I could just blend into the tapestries when at last he had me in his power. I still believe the king my brother lives but perhaps, as Margaret always told me - *Edmund, why do you care?*

It is too late now to say that in future I will pay more attention to her counsel. There will be no future now, not for Edmund of Woodstock.

My executioner staggers as he makes his way through the gates, I suspect he is drunk. Perhaps they have given him a jug of brandy wine to fortify him for the task at hand. I tell my man to bid him try and do the job properly and I see a little purse of money change hands but it makes no difference in the end. I am sure the poor fellow does the best he can but though he is not new to murder he is new to wielding an axe. His aim is terribly off and it is a long afternoon for both of us.

Let us not linger on that part of the story.

I am back at Arundel Castle the next day - without the ghastly remains of my mortal body - when the king's yeomen, Nicholas Langford and John Payn, ride up the avenue of beech trees to the gatehouse to perform their unenviable commission. My wife staggers when she sees them and only the intervention of one of her ladies keeps her from falling. Langford reads from a scroll that he has produced from his tunic, informing her of my arrest and trial on charges of treason against the Crown, and tells her that I have been executed for same. This time her lady is not strong enough to support her and she sinks to her knees wailing. I can do nothing but stand on the stairs, invisible and insubstantial, and see the results of my own artless faith in God's justice.

I am a man of principle and my principle was to remain loyal to my king.

But the king is dead, or in exile abroad if you believe the rumours, and so my wife and my children are left unprotected to face the consequences of my foolishness. Look at the shock on little Joan's face as she watches her mother wailing on her knees, gasping as if she is drowning in the air.

Joan does not understand what has happened but when she sees her mother in such distress she starts to jump up and down, both feet, like she is skipping rope. The poor mite, she does not yet have four years and there is no one to calm her. Edmund, barely a year older, just stands his ground, stricken. He is now the man of the house.

Langford and Payn look at each other and shuffle their feet. They didn't want this commission and I don't blame them for not knowing how to behave. Payn nods for Langford to continue and he does so, reading the rest of the warrant over my wife's screams; the servants are to be dismissed, just two allowed to remain; the bailiffs are required to confiscate the jewellery and anything else that is of value. All lands, goods, titles and moneys are forfeit to the Crown.

Which is to say, forfeit to Mortimer.

My wife is still wailing on the floor. Did I mention she is nearly at term with our third child? My ethereal hands cannot raise her, a servant girl gets on her knees and puts her arms around little Edmund but there is nothing anyone can do for Joan. I once saw a cat, after it was scalded with a spilled kettle of boiling water, in less panic.

She is running in circles now, screaming, her eyes wild.

'Help Joan,' someone says.

This is all my fault. I am dead now and there is nothing I can do for them, any of them, I can only watch on.

Margaret is placed under house arrest, and is allowed just two ladies-in-waiting. Our Arundel Castle is placed in the hands of another of the king's yeoman, Roger Ashe, and will never return to our family again. Everything is sold off and the proceeds sent to the Treasury. Even her first husband's stepson demands the return of her dower lands. Margaret is kept under house arrest, and a month later she delivers our third child. Thomas is born under armed guard.

Poor Margaret, at a stroke she has lost her husband, her position, her wealth and her possessions to a woman she once served faithfully for many years as lady-in-waiting and to her own cousin, that black-bearded bastard Mortimer. Edmund, Joan and the new baby have all, at a stroke, lost their inheritance and their good name.

It's all gone. My houses in Westminster, Castle Donington in Leicestershire, two manors in Gloucestershire, another manor in Woking, two more in Derbyshire and one each in Nottinghamshire, Rutland and Wiltshire. And that was just what Mortimer and Isabella took. Sixty more manors and fourteen farms went to their lackeys.

Margaret can look forward to the Tower and it will be the abbey and the convent for the children. This is why I turn my back to the light, why I cannot move on to my own peace. Instead I cry to the moon and moan around the walls of the castle at night, looking on, helpless, haunted and desperate.

What have I done?

Only little Joan still sees me, she holds out her arms to me and cries. She is scolded for talking to phantoms.

I have missed my chance. I cannot hold her now.

2.

Eltham Palace, eight years later

B ut in time there are better days than these.

I am still here, watching on, watching over her, as my Joan sits in the window seat overlooking the court, reading tales from the days of King Arthur. They are popular now, these stories, Edward has even talked of recreating a Round Table, and his knights and nobles like to think of themselves as Galahads reborn.

And little Joan; she is not so little now; she will have twelve years in a few months. Already her beauty is translucent. With her white hair and porcelain skin, she seems as fragile ethereal as an angel.

She sits on the sill, one leg drawn beneath her, the book held in her right hand. From her little window she has a view of the whole yard between the armoury and the Great Keep. There are thuds and grunts coming from the yard below. The young princes are drilling, as they do every day. My John is part of the prince's household now, with William of Salisbury and a handful of other noble sons. One day they will perform their own acts of chivalry and daring, if they learn their lessons well.

John looks as if he has spent all his time in the kitchens eating the cook's lemon tarts. But under all that padding he is as thin as a poker. He needs all this padding too for he has not aptitude for this, not like the Prince, who has the speed and natural aggression of a born fighter.

John backs away as the Prince - Ned they call him in the yard - comes at him, perfectly balanced, hardly breaking sweat. John puffs, red in the face, fending off the Prince's padded wooden sword. Ser Henri Beaumont, the grizzled master-at-arms, shouts encouragement and instructions. The other boys crowd around, cheering. John is all in. They have been at this for a while now and I sense that Ned is just toying with him. I do not think he means to be cruel; it is just that he knows his superiority and wants it to seem that my John has put up a good fight

At last John goes down, he makes a show of trying to get up but Ned is on him, his padded sword at his chest. John tries to crawl backwards out of range and Ned looks to the master at arms to end it, which he does, calling time on the combat. He holds out a hand to John and pulls him back to his feet. "Well fought, Master John,' he says and then looks at the young prince and claps him on the shoulder.

The master calls to one of the squires to help get the boys out of their armour. It is enough of the sword drills for the day, now they are to the butts for archery practice.

The prince looks up at the window and he sees my daughter there and gives her a wink. Did anyone else see that save me and Joan? She flushes red in the cheeks and turns away.

Her mother is calling for her. She shuts the book and hurries down the corridor to meet her. 'The Queen wishes to see us straight away,' Margaret tells her. 'No, you don't need to change your gown. You look presentable enough. Come now.'

Yes, they live in the royal court now, guests of the man who once had my snot on his silver buckled shoes, the same *seigneur* who signed my death warrant. I am pleased to tell you that it was partly my doing that Joan can read romances at summer windows in fine castles instead of singing vespers on chilblained knees in a draughty convent. My death – judicial murder, some called it – persuaded many fine gentlemen in the court that they had lost their taste for Roger Mortimer and Queen Isabella and so helped young king Edward take power in fact and not just in name. Mortimer admitted at his trial that he had invented my supposed crime and my name was mentioned frequently in the judgment.

Perhaps it is from guilt, but I prefer to think it is just her good nature; Edward's queen, Philippa, took them in, made my wife and children part of her household. And so they are saved; though it is little satisfaction when you watch your wife cry herself to sleep and hear your daughter's prayers to you by her bed each night, and cannot answer.

Little Edmund crossed over to meet me very soon after. This was too much grief for Margaret, I watched her toughen like leather. In the intervening years she has set herself the task of winning back everything that was taken from her. She says she does it all for John, the slip of a boy I have just seen battered to the ground by the young prince. But there is no laughter to be found in justice; it is a joyless task, isn't it? But she sets herself to it with a will.

I watch Joan hurry across the court after her mother, wondering why she is summoned so urgently. I could tell her; Edward has decided to pursue his war against France in person and is to proceed to the Low Countries in a search for Allies. He intends to take his household with him. The Queen wants company for her two young daughters and so she will take my Joan with her. Margaret and John will stay behind. Only John matters to Margaret now, or so it seems.

But there are others, not so indifferent towards her. A pair of eyes follows her as she glides across the quadrangle. I see what is on the young prince's face plain enough, though no one is watching but me.

It is longing, pure and simple.

Oh, come on now, Ned. They'll never let you marry my Joan. You are too precious a prize to waste on the landless daughter of a former traitor.

Never.

* * *

Joan is presented to the Queen by her mother and told that she will be leaving England for the Low Countries that summer with the royal house. I stand in front of Margaret as she leaves the Queen's chambers. No, I tell her. No, you cannot do this, you cannot send her off alone at such a tender age. But if she hears me, feels me, she makes no sign, walks right through me without breaking step. John, you see, is the strong one who will restore the family's fortunes and reputation. He's all that matters.

She thinks.

So Joan, with the two little princesses chattering in her wake, boards a cog at Orwell in Sussex for the crossing of the little sea to Antwerp. She does not look afraid or even excited; she looks as she always does, serene.

It makes for a spectacular leave-taking, the fleet heading out to sea on a blue day, the flags at stern and masts displaying the royal arms and the banners of royal Edward's favourite saints, George, Edward and - such irony - Edmund.

What Edward covets is nothing less than the French throne. When Isabella's last brother died - her brothers, unlike her, were not blessed with a gift for survival - he became the closest living male relation. But the French are not going to give an Englishman the throne, rightful claim or not. The only thing he will get out of this is an endless war. You can't negotiate with a Frenchman; I speak from bitter experience.

But his mother keeps goading him. Any evil that befalls England from this is down to her, in my opinion. Isabella can be - no, is - relentless.

Joan spends that afternoon in her cabin with her cousins and their maidservants. But the rocking of the ship upsets them and all but my daughter is sea sick; so just on dusk she escapes all the retching in buckets and supplications to God, and climbs the gangway to the deck to breathe in some fresh salt air.

I watch over her as she stands at the rail, the planking shifting beneath her feet, a lantern swaying above her head with each jolting wave. She looks so fragile; you would think the wind could pick her up and send her soaring into the grey and lowering sky like parchment. But she seems to be enjoying every moment. She clings to a halyard and leans over, peering ahead, at the foam of the bow wave and the run of whitecaps.

Where are her ladies, Lady Saint Omer and the Duchess of Salisbury? What if she should slip and fall?

'Not thinking of jumping?' She turns around. It is the captain of the guard, a knight named Thomas Holand.

Joan gives him an appraising glance. 'Did they send you to keep a watch on me?'

'They don't need to send me. Looking out for the welfare of the royal household is my commission.'

'You don't need to worry about me,' Joan says.

He smiles at that. 'How old are you?'

'Thirteen.' Wait. Why does she lie? She is not yet twelve!

'Thirteen and fearless. That's good.'

'Don't mock me.'

'I do not mock. I mean it. Where are your ladies? Shouldn't they be attending you?'

'They are all in the cabin with their heads in buckets.'

'But not you.'

'I have been in worse storms.'

My Joan. She takes my breath away with her bravado. Need I mention this is her first time on a ship of any kind; and second, this is not a storm, it is just a heavy sea, and there is a difference between a bit of chop and surviving a tempest.

Something alerts me; I watch her more carefully now, how she smiles at him, touches her hair, toys with the locket at her throat. She is flirting with this upstart! I cannot believe my eyes.

I know this man, this Holand. His father was a traitor. I never liked him even though his decision not to appear on the field at Boroughbridge turned the battle decisively in our favour when we crushed the Earl of Lancaster's rebellion. How long ago was it? It must be almost twenty years ago now. It always seemed to me that the senior Holand's duty was to the earl not to us. I suppose you shouldn't judge the son by the father, but they even look alike.

I hurry below decks and start banging on doors, trying to rouse the Duchess and Lady Saint Omer to look to their responsibilities but they are groaning and rolling around in their cabins with the rest of them now. There is bile slippery on the floor, down the front of their dresses. No help there.

When I get back up to the deck Holand is still there, whispering to my Joan, and she is letting him whisper. And she is still playing with her damned hair.

I tried to warn Margaret, did I not? You simply cannot trust royalty. If this was one of the princesses they would not be allowed up here alone, they would have three barons and a squadron of archers at their backs. Am I the only one who sees how many romances young Joan reads, how all this talk of chivalry and white horses has turned her head? And Holand, he is what, twenty-three, twenty-four? A grown man with that look in his eye. He looks the part, does he not, in the king's colours, with his fine golden beard and deep-set eyes and the wind in his hair?

At last - at last! - the Queen thinks to send the Duchess of Salisbury on deck to look for Joan and, finding her with Holand, she merely scolds her mildly and reminds her that it is getting late and she should be in her cabin. She thanks Sir Thomas for his good service and they return below decks.

Not a moment too soon. I do not like the smile that plays around this young man's lips after she is gone. Twelve years old! Does no one else see what is happening here?

Happily, on arriving in the Low Countries, Edward does not stay long behind the high grey walls of Antwerp Castle. He and the Duke of Brabant head down the Rhine almost immediately to fight several inconclusive skirmishes with the French. Edward takes his knights with him.

War is dangerous work. I wish the Crown well in its endeavours, but I shall not mind if Sir Thomas Holand meets with sharp misfortune.

3.

Gravensteen Castle

The forbidding grey fortress of Gravensteen had once belonged to Louis de Nevers, the count of Flanders. The count fled to France when the shopkeepers took over here. No, I cannot believe it either, but this is a country ruled by men who owe their wealth and position to their facility for buying and selling wool.

They do things very differently in the Low Countries.

The castle is largely unused now and so they have decided it will be Edward's home while he is here. If Edward will not use it, then his army will; there are barracks, stables and tilt yards, ideal for warriors with time on their hands. The king has so far little to show for a summer's campaigning and now he is nuzzling up to potential allies who bat their eyes at him and then give him a price, like whores down at the docks.

Meanwhile Valois, the dauphin of France, has refused to engage. He knows Edward has no money. He doesn't have to defeat him on the battlefield, he just has to wait him out and let him spend himself to death.

Which he proceeds to do. After fifteen months aimlessly burning French villages and pillaging for the sake of it, Edward returns to the Low Countries with nothing. But one must not look anything but glorious, especially when one is hoping to persuade allies to come into the fold, and so Edward's return is spectacular. Stands are hastily erected for the ladies and nobles, so they take their ease while they admire the returned flowers of England.

The steel points of their pikes and lances wink in the pale winter sun as the army approaches. A rider with a kettle drum takes the van, pounding out a deep-throated marching rhythm, *boom, boom, boom*. Now the heralds join in, with trumpets.

Edward rides ahead of his army through the streets and squares of Ghent, magnificent in his gold cloak, the Earls of Salisbury and Derby behind him. The horsed soldiers wear ringmail over their leather, they have on gauntlets and greaves and their steel helms are spit-polished. Their cloaks billow behind them, they carry red and gold banners with lions rampant.

It doesn't look like failure. It looks like a victory march.

But it's failure. You have my word on it.

And there is my Joan in the viewing stands, biting her lip. Why does she search these serried ranks so eagerly? Surely not. But it has been eighteen months and it seems Thomas Holand's absence has only fevered her imagination more. It is these books she reads, I think she believes herself Guinevere and he is one of Arthur's champions. Now he sees her too and he glances up briefly but gives no sign of fond feeling.

Well, he cannot afford to.

Our Thomas, her Thomas, he looks so heroic and so handsome, doesn't he? What woman could resist him?

But she is not a woman.

She is a girl and he has no right.

* * *

Look how beautiful she is. They have braided pearls into her hair, and with a final flourish her maidservant places a gold circlet on her head, it has a small pearl pendant that hangs down in the middle of her forehead. She is dressed in a blue silk gown with slashed sleeves, revealing yellow silk beneath. She is a vision.

But look at her bodice, it is too tight and laced too low. I would not have allowed it. I suspect that Edward's intention is to put the goods on show.

She arrives at the van Artevelde manse in a litter. Jacob van Artevelde is Chief Shopkeeper, the Brewer of Ghent they call him here, though he actually made his fortune from his weaving business. He is the most powerful of the five merchant princes who now control Ghent, itself the largest city in all this part of Europe outside of Paris.

It was van Artevelde who led the insurrection against the Count of Flanders and he is the power in this country now. He even has his own private army that guards him wherever he goes. He lives in very fine style even though he has no noble blood.

As the royal party arrives, a servant flutters down the steps and opens the curtains on the litter. He offers Joan an arm for support as she steps out. Her maid servant Anne fusses over her, straightening her gown and fixing the pins in her hair.

I suppose the manse is a great deal more imposing than she had imagined. It is the first time she has been to a commoner's house and I can see she is shocked at its luxury. Edward might privately call him a shopkeeper, but van Artevelde lives very much like a prince.

There are liveried guards and an army of servants, and the great hall is almost as large as that at Woodstock. Inside is a dizzying crowd in silks and jewels and brocades. Joan hears people talking in several different languages.

Everyone turns to stare as she enters on the arm of Lady Salisbury, her fashionable sleeves trailing on the floor behind her. It has been raucous until this moment; now it falls silent, for just a heartbeat, perhaps two. I am so proud of her, for she looks utterly regal. She does not even stare at the young bucks in their short jackets proudly displaying their codpieces and buttocks. Not a blink or a blush.

Lady Salisbury introduces her to the local dignitaries; there are even a few lords mixed in with the wool traders, though not many, as well as two of the Queens' own brothers, for she was born here, of course.

There is a blast of trumpets and Jacob van Artevelde leads his procession into the Great Hall. He has Katherine van Artevelde on his arm, she is much younger than her husband, elegant in velvets and silks, and wears enough jewels to make a Pope look like a vagabond.

I watch as Joan bows to van Artevelde and his commoner wife, it seems that over here money not only buys good clothes but it can be used to negotiate for respectability as well.

I could weep.

* * *

Joan is escorted to her seat alongside the princesses, Bella and Jeanette, all round eyed and aghast at being in a commoner's house. Bella is still only ten years old, and little Joan - Jeanette - just seven. They both grapple to understand what is going on.

Well, we all do.

Van Artevelde sits on the high table next to Edward, who treats him like fellow royalty. He has recently fawned to Jan of Brabant as well, but at least he is a duke. The merchant's seat is just as fine and well cushioned as the king's, the arms of England and those of Van Artevelde hang on the wall behind them side by side. There is a part of me that is secretly pleased by the turn of events. I have forgiven Edward for signing my death warrant - well, almost - but seeing him grovel to shopkeepers would be cheering for the heart, if I still had one.

The banquet is a lavish affair and some of those gathered there privately wonder where Edward got the money to pay for it all. The answer is this: he got it from his guests. They are loaning him money so that he can impress them with how rich he is. No, it doesn't make sense, does it, but then you and I, we are not the King of England and we are not trying to win the throne of France.

Bella is a doe-eyed little creature who makes up for feeling so young by gathering gossip and repeating it to anyone who will listen. I very much hope that she grows out of this in time.

'You see that girl there?' She nods breathless in the direction of a rather plain girl in a dress of green silk. 'That is the Duke of Brabant's daughter. My father is arranging for her to marry my brother.'

Ned's upcoming engagement is common knowledge about the court but Joan does not want to deflate her by telling her so. 'Does Ned know?'

'Not yet.'

'He won't be well pleased.'

'Well, it's not up to him, is it?'

'I should like to at least like my husband a little.'

'Mother says one day I will marry a royal prince and live like a queen in another country, like she did.'

'I suppose you will.'

'Who will you marry?'

'I don't know. My mother will tell me when she has found someone suitable.'

'I imagine my father will decide that for you. I wish he wouldn't. If we both live in other countries we shall never see each other anymore, will we?' Already her child's mind has leaped ahead to all possibilities. She is a strange child, Bella; she is precocious, even for a princess, and has grown very fond of Joan, treats her like the big sister she never had.

I see Joan look over Bella's shoulder and her eyes go wide for a moment, and there is the suggestion of a smile before it is quickly disguised. I follow the direction of her gaze and see him standing against the wall, talking to two of van Artevelde's guards, but looking directly at my daughter.

Thomas Holand.

No one sees the look but me. And then he turns away.

* * *

They have Isabella between Bella and Bernardo Ezi, the Gascon lord of Albret. I wonder if this is what Edward has in mind; his son will bring him the Brabant and his niece will win him Gascony. In marriage as in battle you must look to your tactics and deployments and get them exactly right. The food arrives; they bring out the venison, dressed as a swan, and I have to concede, it is artfully done.

But food does not hold much fascination for me any longer, as I am sure you will understand, and besides my attention is focused on this Gascon. I do not like the look of him, all dark eyes and dark hair and dressed in black sable. His lips are too full, his eyes linger too long on my daughter's bodice. She is a child, what is there to see? His eyes are insolent. He is supposed to be there to judge if she is a suitable wife for his son, not to eye her up like a chambermaid.

Even before they serve the sweetmeats I see his hand slip onto her leg out of sight below the table. Out of sight to all but me, or so I think.

I watch Joan's face. The colour rises to her cheeks, though the smile does not leave her face. Such poise. I should be proud.

I should also have a long-pointed dagger in my hand so that I could come back to life and slide it into this bastard's kidney.

It is Holand, of all people, who comes to her rescue. After the trenchers are removed and the dogs are squabbling over scraps he asks Joan to accompany him for the first dance. He escorts her into the middle of the hall, away from that old lecher, and they join the other fine couples to the music of lute and drum for a slow *basse*. Later the music lightens for a galliard and he shares her with the other young gallants and then fades discreetly into the background.

I should be grateful to him.

I am merely suspicious.

* * *

That night, when she is once more in her chambers, one of her maidservants brushes out her hair. When she is done, Joan thanks her and takes the silver brush from her hands. You may leave me now, she murmurs. She tiptoes into the nursery and leans over the high bed to blow out the candle but changes her mind. Instead she falls to her knees on the carpet and joins her hands.

'Oh papa.'

It is a whisper, no more. Bella and Jeanette are in their beds and asleep and she does not want to wake them. The nurses, too, are in their trundles and will not like to be disturbed. I move closer, and the candle flickers in the draught of my passing, but Joan seems not to notice.

'Oh papa what am I to do? Did you see them all tonight, looking at me as if I were a horse at the market? Did you see that disgusting Frenchman with his hand on my knee? What will happen if Edward sends me to Gascony? Am I to be wife to both father and son?'

I want to reach out and hold her. But I can provide her neither protection nor comfort now.

'Help me. Give me strength to defy them.'

To defy them? What is she saying?

'I will not be part of my uncle's horse trading. I will marry for love as you married mama. I will not spend all my life in misery in some distant castle, look at what happened to the dowager queen, how they treated her for all those years. They turned her into a bitter and vengeful old woman. That is what will happen to me if I do not find a way to resist them. I would amuse these Gascons for as long as a battle, perhaps as long as a campaign, and then my usefulness will be done and I will spend the rest of my life in some dusty sewing room, pawed at dinner by my husband's father and then die young on the birthing bed. Can you not see it?'

She is right. I can see it. She is just not quite thirteen-years-old and already she is wiser than me. And how does she know that her mother and I married for love? Who told her that?

Yet she cannot do what I did. I am a man and it was my second marriage and I had the freedom to defy convention, I even thumbed my nose at my brother the king, perhaps the only time I ever did.

She is a young girl without a father to speak up for her.

'Resist them.' Where does she get such ideas?

'I cannot see out my life as a neglected wife in some foreign castle, never seeing my mother or my brothers and sister again. You would want better for me.'

I want to answer her: Of course, I want better for you, but kings being what they are, even if I were alive I do not think I could help you with this.

I watch a tear track its way down her cheek in the candlelight. 'I will make my own marriage and marry for love,' she promises the darkness.

There is nothing I can do to steer her from the dangerous course she proposes. I am just a ghost, a memory, as substantial as vapour, as dew.

So where is her mother? Back in England, occupied with lawyers and the king's agents, poring over contracts, taking inventory of every single sod of land that Mortimer and Isabella stole from us, securing the future for our son. But she should be here.

Joan needs you also, Margaret. Do you not know what is happening to our daughter?

'I will not bend my knee to them, father. I will defy them, as you did.'

Oh, but Joan, my Joan, this is not true. Defy them? When they pronounced my sentence, I went on my knees to your uncle begging for my life, sobbing like a child. Did they not tell you that?

She climbs into bed next to Bella and lies there on her back, staring into the dark, her eyes unblinking. I can see her plainly for there are two bronze candlesticks, as tall as a man, at the foot of the bed, and two lighted wax candles, thick as saplings. The young princess insists on keeping them burning through the night, for fear of the dark and the night phantoms. In their faint glimmer Joan looks like as pale as porcelain.

'I will make you proud of me,' she murmurs before she closes her eyes.

I could not be any more proud of you than I am already, my little mouse. But have a care to what you are proposing here.

I feel a shiver run through the dark night, like a breeze whispering through a filmy curtain. I think we may have all misjudged you, little Joan.

4.

I slip away into the river mist. Already the water in the horse troughs is frozen over and the guards patrolling the walls stamp their feet, trying to keep warm, their breath freezing on the night air. They huddle around the braziers, beating their bodies with their arms.

I leave them to their thankless duty and drift on through the shadows. I know who I am looking for and soon I find him, slipping like a ghost himself along the long passageways and into the private chambers of one of Lady Brabant's ladies-in-waiting. She is married, the wife of some minor Flemish noble. It is not this that troubles me, being a man's wife does not mean she is well disposed to him or that he is overly fond of her.

What troubles me is how practised Sir Thomas Holand seems at this game. He slides so easily through the door, off comes his cloak and off comes the lady's chemise in one silky movement. In no time she finds herself naked and expertly feasted on.

I must concede that he knows what he is about, a silky charmer this one, so handsome, a king's knight with a golden beard and a cow's lick that falls over one eye.

Get away to the war, Thomas Holand. And get away from my daughter.

My Lord Salisbury, he of the one eye. The Scots have the other one, they say it is lying at the bottom of some peat bog, glaring after the man who took it, a laird with a red beard and a war hammer who bested the Earl during the siege of Dunbar and bashed in his helmet. Now the grizzled old veteran wears a patch to cover the hole where it had once been.

This evening he is taking his ease in the rooms they have given him in Gravensteen castle, a dark and draughty place even for a ghost.

He has Holand sit down and a servant brings them brandy wine and throws another log in the fire. I watch Holand's face, see how he covets the life that the earl has; look at his tight smile, the way his eyes linger on the fat jewelled rings on Salisbury's fingers. I know what he is thinking: he would like servants and rings too. Perhaps he covets the eye patch as well. As events unfold, it would certainly seem so.

'The king is on his way back to England,' Salisbury tells him. 'They don't like our little war over at home and he yet hopes to persuade them to be more malleable. If they do not acquiesce to his demands, I fear he will look for another Parliament that pleases him better.'

'A famous victory would change all their minds.'

'It would, but to achieve such, we need to raise a proper army.'

'And for that we must have cash and friends.'

'In my opinion, an Englishman won't find either in this part of the world.' Salisbury drains his glass and calls for more, his one eye glaring at Holand over the table as if it is his fault the Flemish barons have proved so faithless. The wine leaves dark stains in his beard. '

'Are you ready to go to war again?'

'We shall have another campaign this summer?'

'It seems we have a new ally.'

'Another Flemish shopkeeper?' Really, Holand should watch his tongue, he'll need the king's favour very soon.

But Salisbury does not take offence. 'You have met Lord Albret?' he says.

'One of those puffed-up minor nobles.'

'This puffed-up noble holds the key to the Aquitaine. Edward has paid him handsomely to shift his loyalties to us. For my part, I never trust a man whose loyalties have to be bought.'

Salisbury suddenly realises what he has said. Was this not exactly the allegation laid against Holand's father? The two men find other things to look at besides each other; Holand stares out of the window at the last sunlight reflected on the Scheldt, William watches a spark fly in the hearth.

Someone has to finish Salisbury's thought: Holand decides it might as well be him. 'Money is never enough.'

'No. That is why the king will offer him extra inducement.'

'What might that be?'

'His niece, Joan.'

Look at Thomas Holand; his face is immobile. If he feels anything at this news, he does not show it. 'The Gascon favours the match?'

'Why not? Joan has royal blood. Bit hard for the girl, though, having to spend the rest of her life with that pack of wolves. I like her, it would seem a shame.'

'But that's politics.'

'Yes. If you are the king of England, you cannot afford to worry about whether your niece is lonely. Her feelings are weighed against the hope of the French crown.'

The earl and Holand talk some more about the coming campaign, Holand is one of his most trusted and capable commanders. Edward's priority, Salisbury says, is to end the French command of the little sea. Their huge fleet, which consists mostly of galleys under sail, could easily penetrate even England's shallow harbours and was ideal for raiding or ship-to-ship combat. The French had captured two of Edward's finest ships, *Christopher* and *The Edward*. They were pirating the Flanders wool trade and raiding the south and eastern coasts of England whenever they chose.

'Edward intends to convert our merchant cogs into warships by building wooden castles at the bow and stern, and place crow's nest platforms at the mast so our archers can use their bows against the enemy from above.'

'Will it work?'

'We will see. But our cogs are bigger, so we can carry more men, and the high freeboard will make them better in close combat.'

'When?'

'We are assembling a fleet at Orwell now. By summer we will be ready. Once we have control of the little sea, we will not need these shopkeepers and petty tyrants so much.'

They drink the rest of the brandy wine and Holand takes his leave. He goes downstairs to the kitchen and orders a bowl of ale and downs it alone in the garden, leaning against the buttery wall. He curses at the sky and punches the bricks, making his knuckles bleed. But it is not the war that makes him rage so.

Is he cursing for Joan's bad luck?

Or for his own lost opportunity?

5.

Saint Bavo's Abbey, Ghent

The royal women are kept away from the hurly-burly of Gravensteen; the rough manners of the infantry, their curses and bad manners and pissing up walls; the noise they make when they are put to practice by the sergeant at arms; the foulness at night when they drink and dice and sprawl with camp followers. Instead the royal women are housed in the gentler refines of Saint Bavo's Abbey, with its frost-crisp lawns and blood-red holly berries scaling the crumbling walls.

Joan is restless there, confined to needlework and prayers and Bella's childish gossip. No one watches her properly, as I have noticed. Lady Salisbury and Lady Saint Omer are more concerned with currying the favour of the queen. Philippa suffers greatly through her last trimester and the whole household is attuned to her every groan and murmur. No one has time for Joan or the princesses, not when the queen's veins are troubling her and her back is breaking. They fuss around her with possets and creams and cushions.

Joan walks alone in the garden. I follow her, and see what the others cannot, or will not. These days I am a zephyr, a murmur, an uneasy feeling one has when alone. Joan turns, thinks she is being followed, then shrugs and moves on.

I see him in front of the arbour ahead of her, huddled in a cloak. The marble benches are too cold to sit on, so he stands by a frozen black fountain, staring gloomily at his own reflection. She has not seen him yet.

He catches her in an unguarded moment, but does not reveal himself, watches her silently, like a wolf waiting to pounce. I can see the play of thoughts on his face.

I want to take her by the arm and drag her away.

She walks with her head down and is almost on him by the time she sees him. She gives a little gasp of surprise.

'I did not mean to startle you, my lady.'

She puts a hand to her breast, as if he might see her heart fluttering if she does not. 'Sir Thomas.'

He bows and kisses her hand. This is neatly done. He looks the part in the velvet, the golden lions of Edward on a red field emblazoned on his chest. My Joan is still enraptured with stories of Arthur and his knights and I fear she has mistaken Holand for one of them. Yet he must be ten years older than her; this is not right, his smile is far too bold.

Yet under his pleasant demeanour Holand is exhausted from his exertions of the night before; yet another wife, another shedding of linen chemises in the dark.

'What are you doing out here?' Joan asks him.

'I was sent here with the rest of my men to guard your majesties.'

Joan looks around the brown bare garden for her enemies. Finding none, her eyes alight on a lusty peacock, prowling the frosty lawn for an unchaperoned peahen even at this time of year. 'All appears to be safe here.'

He knows she is teasing him and takes it in good grace. At that moment the peacock approaches a hen and shows her the full fan of his glorious tail feathers, red and gold, rattling them in the pale winter sun. Even in winter it is indefatigable, much like our Holand. How can the hen fail to be impressed?

'Walk with me,' Joan says, and he falls into step beside her.

They pass under the rose arbour, the stems are gnarled and brown and bare. Her cloak catches on one of the thorns, obliging him to free her. He stands close and their breath mingles in soft white clouds.

'You are well caught,' he says.

'That is the trouble with roses.'

'The trouble with thorns, at least.'

'What is taking you so long?' She turns and looks up at him. Their faces are close, just inches away. His fingers are surprisingly clumsy, he appears distracted, but finally he frees her. She thanks him with an impudent smile and carries on. He follows, less sure of himself now.

'How do you find it here, my lady?'

'It is all very fine, my ladies see that I am well cared for.'

'And yet?'

She smiles because he has not allowed her to pass him off with such a practised answer. 'Yet I am homesick. I miss my brother and sister, I miss England.'

'And your mother?'

'Yes,' Joan says, as an afterthought. 'I miss her too. And what about you, Sir Thomas? What do you miss?'

'There is nothing to miss, I fear. This is my life. I am accustomed to strange castles and sleeping in whatever hard cot they show me. If there is no bed, then I sleep on tables or in the straw.'

Or with another man's wife. But I am being uncharitable; he is a knight, and all knights do that.

'You have no family of your own?''

'I will have to serve in many more campaigns and try to earn favour at many more tournaments before I can afford a wife and a household.'

'And yet Holand is a famous name.'

'Famous for all the wrong reasons.'

'I am sorry. You must educate me about your family history, I do not know it.'

He straightens his shoulders. Her frankness has taken him by surprise, I think. People either know the answers already or are too discreet to ask such questions of him. 'My father's liege was the Earl of Lancaster. When the Earl rebelled against our present king's father ... this was before you were born, my lady ... he failed to take the field with his men. It was a decisive moment in the battle.'

'Is that not a good thing?'

'His loyalties, even if misguided, should have been to the Earl. His honour was besmirched. Even the king thought so and threw him in prison.'

'For failing to rebel?'

Holand shrugs his shoulders. He is uncomfortable discussing these matters of honour. He has had to live his whole life with this stain, and now Joan, in her innocence, wants to interrogate him about it.

'Where do your loyalties lie, Sir Thomas?'

'I am the king's man entirely. Yet I still see that look in people's eyes.'

'Look?'

'Of mistrust. My father's crime is one not easily forgotten.'

'Then you are fortunate I do not know the story, so there is nothing to forget.' Another winning smile. Where did my baby girl learn to charm like this? 'But it must be difficult for a man to be without a wife,' she says and looks frankly into his face. 'I have noticed certain ladies watching you.'

'My lady?'

'At the banquet. There were many secret glances, and if I noticed them, I am sure you did.'

Holand looks as surprised as me. When exactly did she see these secret glances? I did not think she was attuned to such things. She is growing up quickly, too quickly.

'I am sure you are mistaken.'

'I am sure I am not. There must be many ladies who should like to be the wife of such a handsome knight.'

'As I said, a wife will have to wait until fortune serves me better. Until then, I am here only to serve the king.'

'I am here to serve the king also, did you know that? He is going to marry me to some Frenchman, or so I am told. Do you know of Lord Albret?'

'The Gascon? Does he not already have a wife?'

'His son is in want of one, apparently.'

'If this is true, then it is a fine match. You will lack for nothing, I am sure. And I would consider the young Albret a very lucky man.'

'Would you?' Joan says, now flirting shamelessly. 'Why?'

The muscles in his jaw ripple as he tries to think of the correct repost. 'Because he would find himself married to the most beautiful young woman in England.'

There is silence. God's teeth. There, it is said.

A look lingers between them and the silence increases. His knuckles are white around the pommel of his sword. Why does she not tear her eyes from him and stop this? She knows this is not seemly.

And as for me, what can I do? I would fly back up the stairs and drag the king himself out here if I could; I would shout to Lady Saint Omer, leave the queen, for the love of God, she will not bear the child for another moon. Instead come and see what is going on under your own noses!

It is then, at last, that Lady Salisbury comes hurrying down the path, calling Joan's name. Holand and Joan tear themselves apart; I have seen bricks prised from walls with an iron bar more easily.

But they are separate and at ease when Lady Salisbury appears; she is alarmed to see her there with a handsome young knight of the King's guard, as well she should be. 'What are you doing out here, my lady?' she says to Joan.

'Just enjoying the crisp morning air,' she answers, and I am disappointed to see what an accomplished liar my daughter has become. Nothing of her former ardour shows on her face. The colour is gone from her cheeks and she is once again pale and innocent.

'Well you must come and join your ladies inside. Bella and Jeanette are wondering where you are and desire your company.'

Joan smiles and thanks Holand for his gallantry and parts from him without a backwards glance. I watch his face. Something has changed for him now. As he stares after her he sees the glimmer of possibility, though of course he is much more delighted at the prospect than I am.

* * *

The King has ten years on the throne now but he is still a young man, good looking like his father, with a thick fair beard and generally a good disposition towards everyone but the French. He even liked me and he was the one who signed my death warrant.

He paces the room by the windows. His expedition to the Low Countries has not gone well, his only successes have been in the bedroom, where he has sired one son and hopes for another soon. But he could have done as well at home. The purpose of crossing the little sea was to gain allies for his war against the French, but so far all he has done is bankrupt the Exchequer.

He has formally assumed the title of King of France and if the French would believe it, then his job would be done. But the French, as always, are proving contrary.

He is embarrassed by his lack of credit and in a bitter mood with the Parliament, who have failed to advance him more funds. He is like a man at a game of dice, desperate for a loan from his friends, convinced the next throw will make them all rich, but all he gets is grumbling and sour looks. He cannot even afford to pay his daily living expenses. He is forced to rely on the good graces of the shopkeeper.

He is becoming desperate. Up and down the long carpet he goes, head down, hands behind his back. For her part the Queen cannot pace, for she is close to her confinement and her back is paining her. This will be her fifth child. She is at the heir-producing stage of her life and she is finding it wearing. Her ankles swell, and she looks puffy about the face and she tires easily.

I should not have liked to have been a woman.

But she is a sweet thing, this Philippa, plump and plain but you know where you stand and her smile is kindly to everyone. I have not forgotten that she was kind to my wife and children when she became queen, she was the one who persuaded Edward to take them in.

It was her dowry that paid for the ships with which Isabella invaded England; the king, then still a lad, had been told to marry whoever he considered the least ugly of the Duke of Hainault's daughters. I think he chose quite well; it seems to me that he has grown to love her.

I have come in at the middle of the conversation. He is telling her of his idea to marry Joan off to the Duke of Albret's son, Arnaud. This will bring Gascony into our side in alliance against the French, he tells her. I think by now he is so desperate he would sell his own mother to the French for ten bowmen and a promissory note.

Well, we should all like to sell Isabella back to the French, but I do not think we would find takers.

'Joan is fast growing into a woman,' Edward is saying, 'and a beautiful one. I am pleased we brought her with us to Antwerp. Her presence has not gone unnoticed here.'

'But does it have to be Albret?'

'You can think of a better alliance for us?'

'I feel like we are throwing her to the wolves. You know that man's reputation.'

They are talking of Albret père; Bernard, Lord of Albret, head of a leading and powerful Gascon family, the one with the wandering hands. He had been persuaded to support Edward's cause soon after his arrival in Antwerp, having formerly been an ally of the French Crown. He will bring much-needed cash and many friends and allies, and Edward is eager to offer him inducements to keep him on his side. In effect, our Edward is reduced to bargaining with whores with beards.

'It is the son we are wedding her to, not him,' Edward says.

'She is such a fragile thing.'

'She knows her duty.'

'Well you must do as you think fit,' Philippa says, which means she does not approve and thinks he is wrong.

'I need Lord Albret.'

'Yes, but can you trust him?'

'That is what Joan is for.'

'You think she will be enough to keep him loyal?'

This is not what he wants to hear, these doubts, even though she is right to voice them. He wants her to tell him that he is brilliant, that he has found the perfect solution to all his problems. Instead she smiles placidly, her hands resting on her swollen belly.

In his mind Edward's hand hovers over the pieces on the chessboard, his fingers rest briefly on Joan's head but now move on. He will try another move first. He decides instead to go back to England, and harangue the Parliament, get them to squeeze a little more juice from the dry lemon that is England.

6.

Joan is restless. Sometimes we meet in her dreams, and what I have to say to her leaves her listless and disturbed. I am the voice of her doubts.

She is too good-natured to toss and turn in the bed, knowing it will disturb little Bella, so she swings her legs out and goes to stand by the window, peering down into the courtyard below. She sees a familiar figure down there, hovering outside the chapel; it seems her new soul mate cannot sleep either.

The maid is not asleep on the trundle at the foot of the bed where she should be, and Joan can guess where she is. She creeps down the stairs, hears a furtive snuffling in the scullery, two shadows pressed against the wall. The cook is getting full value from all those lemon tarts he gave Joan's maid. A prince gives a woman jewels; but when you are a poor man, sweetmeats have to suffice.

Joan is quickly getting an education about life, here among the nobility. She turns away, ties the thick ermine cloak around her shoulders, and slips out on her tiptoes, padding down the stairs in her bare feet.

Joan, put on shoes your feet must be freezing, I want to shout at her.

Still, never mind her feet. There are greater dangers down there in the dark.

There is ice on the cobblestones and the cold stone makes her wince with pain. Her breath freezes on the air. She hurries across the court, careful not to slip, and pushes open the heavy oak door that leads to the chapel.

It is gloomy inside. Two candles burn on the altar and a sacristy lamp illuminates a mural of the blessed saviour. Holand is on his knees but as soon as he hears her he is on his feet in an instant, a soldier's instincts. His hand goes to the dagger at his belt but when he sees it is her he relaxes his fighting stance and hurries over, alarmed.

'Joan, what are you doing here? You should not be out here alone. Where is your maidservant?' He looks down. 'Where are your boots?'

'I saw you from the window,' Joan says, ignoring his concern. 'I had to talk to you.'

'Your feet! You will freeze.'

Thank you, Holand, that is what I think also. Tell her to get back to bed before she catches a chill.

Instead he has her sit, takes off his cloak, and wraps it around her. Joan pulls her knees to her chin, so that she is now snug inside his leather coat. 'What are you doing here at this late hour?' she asks him. 'Should you not be in an alehouse with the rest of your men?'

He seems shaken by the directness of her question, the frankness of her gaze. Of course she knows about alehouses, Holand, about drunkenness and about much worse. She is innocent but not that innocent, not anymore.

'I came here to pray.'

'I did not take you for an overly pious man.'

'I am a good Christian.'

'I am sure. But you are not a monk, or so they tell me.'

'You have been asking about me?'

'I have been discreet.'

Holand, accomplished seducer of women and trollops that he is, looks quite undone by Joan's wide-eyed candour. He stumbles over his answer. 'I came here to ask for God's favour,' he says.

'Has he not favoured you enough? You are handsome, strong, brave and high born.'

'I am also poor.'

'Poor?'

'I am the second-born son and so my older brother Robert has inherited everything. I am landless. As a knight, a man can make a living from ransoms and booty, but it is an uncertain life and unless I find some profit in the king's war or in a tournament, I must survive on two shillings a day, which is all the king pays.'

'Is that so bad?'

'Lady Joan, do you understand what it is to be a knight in the king's service? For this campaign I needed to buy four *destriers*, a quilted *gambeson*, a tunic of mail, a surcoat and a breastplate, as well as armour for my arms, shoulders and legs. There is also a helm with a visor, for battle, and I must have at least one page in my service to look after it all. Forty pounds a year it costs me, and I have an annuity of twenty-six pounds. I was in debt before I even left England. My mother had to borrow almost four hundred pounds to pay for my brother and I to come to this war and we must pay this back before we even start to turn a profit.'

'I see.'

'But you do not see. I wish for a wife, and heirs to carry my name. More than this, I want them to say their name with pride, not as I have had to do, waiting for the sneer, the dark looks, the muttering behind my back whenever I announce myself. That is why I am here. I pray for fortune and redemption, not only mine, but my entire family's.'

'But do you not wish for love, also?'

'Should I love, my lady, I should have to keep such fond affection to myself, as I have explained, a knight cannot afford to have both love and marriage.'

'So your heart is unmoved by common passions, then?'

'I have found that passion is not at all common, and my heart is not in any way cold. Just restrained, due to my circumstances.'

'A pity, then.'

'I think so, for I have felt it almost leap from my chest in recent times.'

'What fortunate lady could evoke such a response from such a fearsome knight?'

'I think you know,' he murmurs.

Have my ears deceived me? Did he really say this? Had I substance I should like to murder him, even in such sacred surrounds. I see the effect his words have on my daughter. Does he mean it, or is it a moment's inspiration? He is clever on his feet, our Holand, in love as in fighting.

Can we trust this man?

Joan has already made up her mind. She lays aside his cloak and stands on her tiptoe, - her frozen tiptoes - and touches his lips with her own. Then she runs out of the chapel, the door swinging wide behind her. Holand stands there a long time, staring after her, wondering what this all might mean for him.

I think it is now, in this very moment, that he starts to plan.

* * *

I must to England. From Flanders I allow myself to be carried with the wind across the grey sea. Below me, around me, I see foam whipping off the whitecaps, a line of English cogs wallowing in the swells, their square sails headed down the Thames to Saint Katherine's Dock.

In London there is snow piled along the river banks, black ice and mud in the streets. I moan with the wind along the labyrinth of alleyways, past the taverns and tenements. It is too cold for many to be about, there are slim pickings for the purse-snatchers and cutthroats tonight. As I pass the great abbey I see a black-robed monk hurry across the cloister, hood pulled up around his face. He thinks he sees something and stops to look around, but it is too cold to linger.

And so to Westminster, past a startled scullery maid who screams and drops the dishes she is carrying. In the morning she will swear she saw something on the stairs and they will laugh at her and she will get a scolding for denting some of the king's best serving bowls.

In the palace, the walls are damp and chill, the tapestries faded. I glide along a hallway, down winding spiral stairs, across a dank courtyard, see a candle burning at a shuttered window high above. Here is my Margaret at her desk, it is cold in her rooms despite the roaring fire, she blows on her fingers as she hunches over her letters and accounts. John is asleep. So should she be. It is late.

She looks tired, my wife, and careworn. There is grey in her hair now.

I brush a hand across her shoulders and she shivers and gets up to put another log in the grate. She rubs her eyes and looks over her shoulder, as if she expects to see someone standing there.

Me, perhaps.

But I am not there, I have slipped away to my son's room, watching John as he sleeps. He is Margaret's favourite but not mine. I love him of course, but Joan is the child I always carried in my heart. I do still.

When I get back to Margaret's chamber she is sliding a knife through Lady Salisbury's seal and reading her latest letter. The missive is to inform her of how her daughter fares in Flanders. She writes that the king is considering a marriage bargain with the Lord of Gascony. Margaret puts a hand to her breast in surprise. But surely she must have anticipated this?

She lets the letter drop to the floor.

I know what she is thinking, for I am of the same opinion; the king has betrayed us a second time. He likes to be seen as a man of grace and favour but when it comes to important matters - his cousin's marriage, for instance, his uncle's warrant of execution - it is all about what is best for Edward. But what else can you expect from a king?

'Oh Edmund, why aren't you here?' she murmurs.

Oh, but I am here, my love, I am here in the draughts and the noises in the night, the creaking of doors that were never open, the flickering of the candle flame. And if you could hear me, I would say this to you: I wish you would leave all these papers and take yourself to France to look out for our daughter. But of course you won't, will you? You are so afraid of being poor again. Twice now you have known impoverished widowhood; once with your first husband, that fool Comyn, and the second time with me. It was that second time that beat you down so. You never loved Comyn; and you didn't lose everything you had, you weren't threatened with a lifetime of incarceration, they didn't threaten to take your children away and give them to the Church.

So you will weep for Joan but you will do nothing to help her.

You were a good wife to me and did nothing in the past for which I should upbraid you. But if I was here now you would feel the lash of my tongue.

Why has Margaret never remarried, I wonder. Is it because she loved me so much that another would just not do? My vanity would like to think so. Or is there another reason, more prosaic? Could it be that she has had enough of men, and another husband who meddles in politics - and what man cannot, if he is high-born? - would put all she has regained at risk. While she remains a widow, she keeps control of everything; if she remarries, the power would return to her husband. So perhaps it is not love that makes her chaste, she has simply become hardened by experience.

A door slams. Margaret jumps to her feet, peers into the corridor, startled. The passageway is empty, or so it appears. She crosses herself, and goes back into her chamber, turning the key in the lock. But even when she is in her bed, she leaves a candle burning.

The wind moans around the eaves. It sounds like a man crying.

7.

Joan wakes screaming, it is enough to startle the dead. And that is exactly what it does. Her father is there first, of course; I am always there first, I scarcely leave her side these days. Finally, her maidservants rush in. Joan is sitting up in the bed staring at the blood on her nightdress and on the sheets between her thighs.

Lady Salisbury is sent for and she rushes in, folding Joan into her arms, like her mother should were she here. 'Don't let the servants tell Edward,' are Joan's first words to her.

She knows what is happening, but it is still a shock for her. I do not stay to see how Lady Salisbury helps her, I hurry outside and follow the maid as she rushes to the kitchen for hot water and towels. But of course, while she is there she whispers the news to the scullery maid who will in turn tell the cook. Her gossip will find its way to the queen's ear within the hour and from there it must surely find its way to the king.

It means his prize is ready for the offering. Perhaps he will make sure she is chaperoned a little better from now on, that one of her ladies is always on hand, or at least a maidservant.

Well, you would have thought so, but Edward has other things on his mind and the queen is about to give birth to their third child. I am the only one that worries. I am the only one who sees what is going on.

* * *

Joan gets angry with her maidservant, Anne, for hurting her as she brushes out her hair. It is not like Joan; but then she has never had these cramping pains in her stomach before, 'the curse of Eve' as Lady Salisbury likes to call it. Bella takes the brush from her and sends her from the chamber before the poor girl breaks down in tears.

Everyone thinks it is just the time of the moon that makes Joan behave this way. No one else but me knows about her secret; no one.

'Thank you, Bella,' Joan says and closes her eyes as her young cousin finishes brushing out her hair. Bella smiles at her in mirror, then leans in close and whispers something in her ear. Joan flushes scarlet. 'How did you know?'

'One of the servants told me.'

'Does everyone know?'

Bella makes a face.

'Know what?' Jeanette says.

'Nothing,' Bella tells her sister. 'You wouldn't understand.'

'Why not?'

'You're too little.'

Jeanette pouts. Joan would never have stood for being spoken to this way, even when she was seven, but then she never had a big sister to boss her.

'Now you can have a husband and have babies, like the Queen,' Bella says, as if this is something she knows all about.

Joan puts a hand to her middle and winces.

'Does it hurt very much?'

'They say having a baby is the worst pain in the world,' Bella says. 'When Mother had Lionel, I heard her screaming from the other end of the castle.'

'Did she scream when she had me?' Jeanette asks.

'You were the worst one of all,' Bella tells her. 'Mother screamed so loud with you, they heard her in Scotland.'

Jeanette's bottom lip quivers.

'We are going to be sent away to stay with the two shopkeepers,' Bella tells Joan.

'With Lord and Lady van Artevelde? Why?'

'I don't know. I hope we don't miss the birthing. Papa is certainly going to miss it, he's going back to England to try and get more money from the Parliament. They are all rogues and ungrateful scoundrels in the Parliament, I heard him tell Mother so.'

But I don't think Joan cares a great deal about Edward or the rogues and scoundrels in Parliament. I do see a look pass across her face though when Bella tells her about the van Arteveldes. Is she scheming already? Once I would have thought it unlikely.

But I am not so sure anymore.

* * *

34

Fires blaze in the twin hearths at each end of the queen's rooms, but still there is a chill edge to the room.

The queen is vast. Can there be but just one child in there? The poor woman. She puts a hand to her back and winces as she sits in her favourite chair by the hearth. 'So, Joan. I have been neglectful of you lately. Are my Ladies Salisbury and Saint Omer treating you well?'

'Indeed, your Grace.'

'Your maidservants are satisfactory? My little chatterbox doesn't bother you too much? I swear she could talk at the bottom of a moat with a mouth full of pebbles.'

Joan smiles. She is rather fond of the queen, as am I. She has a kind heart, Edward would not be the king he is without her.

'The van Arteveldes are very taken with you. They have offered that you can stay with them for a while, perhaps show you a little of the town, provide more entertainment than we can here. The princesses also. Would you like that?'

'That would be most pleasant,' Joan says. Of course she will say that, my daughter is always perfectly agreeable until you cross her.

'A change of air from this stuffy place,' the queen adds and gives Joan a resigned smile. She is easily tired these days.

'Of course the king would like you to pay attention to all you see and hear while you are there.' Philippa seems almost embarrassed to say it. This would be Edward's idea; it is not something she would think of.

Joan is not obtuse. She understands the Queen's point without having her spell it out. She smiles and bends the knee and leaves.

So, it seems Joan and the royal princesses have been artfully recruited to spy on the Brewer of Ghent.

How quaint.

* * *

Katherine van Artevelde takes the three girls under her wing; she has a brood herself, a gaggle of daughters and two unsmiling sons. Joan and Bella and Jeanette are quickly settled in the guest house of the grand manse with their maidservants and in the following weeks she takes them on a tour of the gardens of Ghent, shows off her husband's weaving factories, and has them all climb atop the belfry of the Saint Nicholas church above the Kornmarkt to enjoy the vistas.

'Of course you know why you are really here,' Katherine says to Joan in a quiet moment when the younger children are out of earshot. They are on a barge on the Scheldt, she is pointing out the weavers' houses crowding the river.

'I was told it was at your invitation.'

'Alas no, it was your king's suggestion,' she says.

Joan is confused and says so.

'Is it not true that the queen asked you to spy on us?' Katherine says, though not unkindly.

Joan looks panicked. 'I don't think she did.'

Katherine laughs delightedly and puts an arm around Joan's shoulders. 'Oh you will never be a very good spy, if you look like that every time someone asks you a question.'

Joan blushes at being caught out in her little lie. 'I go where they tell me to go,' she says.

'Of course you do.' She moves closer. 'But wouldn't it be fun to do what you wish to do now and then?'

Joan smiles, and so does Katherine. Suddenly they understand each other, these two.

The younger children crowd around again and no more is said, Katherine's vague promise of assistance in her wilfulness must wait for another day.

But every night at vespers Joan kneels and prays not to God, but to me, her father, to help her. Let me lead a good life with a man I love in it, she says, which seems a humble ambition for a princess. But I do not know if she can have even that.

I feel so helpless.

People are so afraid of ghosts. It is the living they should fear.

* * *

Thomas Holand wakes in the middle of the night and as he rolls over he feels the warm body of some nobleman's wife beside him. He is not done with her yet, so he nudges her awake. Let us not sit in judgment of him, she is after all feeling neglected, and Holand is a knight who cannot afford a wife, so no honour is besmirched here. At the end of the pounding and the grunting and the thrusting he lies on his back and looks out of the window and look wistful.

As we have seen, he is well-versed in the secret arts of the bedchamber and there are enough wives and scullery maids who appreciate him for it. But he will not be a handsome chevalier forever, he knows this, in the future there will be wounds and the natural degradation of age. He does not want to be still campaigning for the king's meagre coin in ten years from now.

Well I believe this is what he is thinking. If such considerations have not passed his mind, then he is a fool.

But does he love my Joan?

And if he does, how will he get away with this?

He slips from the bed and puts on his clothes while the wife pretends to sleep. When he is gone she smiles and closes her eyes.

I follow Holand down the narrow stairs to the castle kitchen, where the servants snore on the straw. He kicks one of the dogs that tries to bite him. The fire is almost out and it is cold. He finds some bread and cheese and ale and takes it into the garden. He wraps his cloak tighter about his shoulders and sits down on a water trough with his feet on the cobblestones to eat his supper.

Some men might envy him his life, but they would not be men like Thomas Holand. Every day he carries a burden, it weighs heavy on him this burden of his past. He cannot forget that his father was once so well favoured by the Earl of Lancaster. He gave him two castles and twenty-five manors and made him rich beyond his dreams. Then came Boroughbridge.

Holand is bitter that life has turned out this way for him, for if it were not for his father's lack of marrow he should be sleeping in a feather bed and this bowl of warm ale would be a silver cup of wine. He should have his own wife and not have to borrow another's.

He goes to the barracks room and lies on a narrow cot with just a threadbare blanket to keep him warm. He puts his hands behind his head and stares. He says one word: 'Joan.'

But how does he say it? With wistfulness, with longing? Or is he merely answering the riddle he has set himself. And the riddle is: how do I get myself out of this mess and find a better life?

* * *

Edward paces the bedchamber, wearing out the carpets. Philippa sits at her table while her handmaid brushes out her hair but she cannot stand the pacing and snatches the brush out of her hand and sends her out.

'Edward, what is wrong?'

'Everything is wrong. I cannot trust any of these so-called allies of mine.'

'Well of course you can't. You have bribed every one of them for their allegiance, how can you trust a man whose only interest is your money?'

'Then what would you have me do? If I am to wage war against Valois and the French then I need an army, I need men who have power and influence here.'

'You do not ...'

There is silence. Edward stops pacing. 'Go on. Say it.'

'You do not have to do this.'

'The throne of France is mine by right!' he screams and throws his goblet into the fire. The wine sizzles and steams.

She turns away. Edward hangs his head. It is not seemly to have these tantrums in front of his pregnant wife. Philippa is his stalwart, she does not merit such disrespect. 'What am I going to do?' he repeats, regaining his composure.

'They will not hand you the throne. They do not want an Englishman as their king.'

'It doesn't matter what they want, I am their sovereign by divine right!'

'You may indeed have divine right on your side, but I would remind you, husband, that the Pope now lives in Avignon, so if you ask Valois he will say that God resides in France and so does divine right.'

I try not to take pleasure in this little scene. It is not easy. There is a certain satisfaction to be had from watching those who once destroyed us now destroying themselves.

A man doesn't have to be alive to savour it.

You see, it is Isabella who still drives her son to take her father's throne. Though she has been retired now to her country estates for some years this is still her war. It will bankrupt England and perhaps even kill her son one day.

And though Isabella left France when she was just twelve-years-old still she will not let it go.

'How much longer will you crawl to men like Brabant?' Philippa says, perhaps the only woman or man in the world who can speak to him so directly.

'I crawl to no one.'

A lie. Of course he crawls, ever since he came to the Low Countries he has done nothing else and it is a bradawl to his pride, every day it sinks a little deeper in.

I watch Philippa struggle with herself. Oh please, your Grace say it to him: *This is your mother's doing.* But she won't, she is too kind, too loyal, too much the good wife and queen.

And so they lapse into silence. They seldom argue, these two, it was a marriage made at the bargaining table between Edward's mother and the Count of Hainault yet I believe one might now call it a love match. People scoff at such things, but it happens.

'I am sorry,' Edward says at last, still staring into the fire. 'You know that I value your advice and your counsel.'

'I hate to see you tormented like this.'

He turns from the fire and slumps onto the end of the bed.

'I have no choice but to return to England. I must persuade the Parliament to give me more money.'

'Will you be back when the baby comes?'

He avoids her eyes. 'I don't know.' He reaches for her hand. 'I will be back as soon as I can.'

'What does van Artevelde think of this?'

'He is only worried about getting what he says he is owed. I have run up debts here, and my Lords Salisbury and Derby are to stay behind as surety.'

The trouble is, you see, he had expected a better reception here. The count of Hainault is his father-in-law, and many of the merchants in Flanders have made their fortunes from the wool trade with England. He brought his wife here to remind them all of their dynastic connection to the English throne but these shopkeepers aren't concerned with dynasties or bloodlines, they only care about ledgers and accounts.

'That it has come to this,' she says.

'I still wonder if marriage might not be better than money. It binds tighter than gold, they say.'

'You are still thinking of Joan?'

'Through his men and influence the Lord d'Albret could deliver us the Aquitaine. His son is not an unpleasant boy. Why not?' He sighs. 'Why do you look like that?'

'She would have to leave her family, her friends, everyone she knows and present herself to a complete stranger in another land.'

'That is her duty, she was raised to it. My mother did it.'

'Your mother was Isabella.'

'What does that mean?'

'It means she was made of sterner stuff than Joan.'

Well, that gives me pause. Is that what she thinks? I suppose it is what everyone thinks. Joan has done well. If you can make people underestimate you, you are halfway there.

'He has a reputation, Lord Albret. You know this?'

'I shall not give up this match, I am decided. I need d'Albret. He may be a liar and a lecher but I will make him *my* liar and *my* lecher.'

'I urge you to think more on this.'

'I have thought about it long enough. I have to do something. If there is no money coming from the Parliament then I shall have to build alliances somehow. You are right, I am tired of bowing and scraping to shopkeepers for money.'

A sigh. 'Why don't you just give this up?'

'This enterprise is too far gone to abandon it! How can I give up now and still be king of England? Everyone will think I am weak.'

'The throne of France has possessed you, not you it.'

'That is not the way I look at it.'

'Yet it is one way of seeing things.' She gets up and sits next to him on the bed, puts an arm around his shoulders. Her tone softens: 'Do whatever you must, I will always be here at your side, you know that.'

He puts his hand on hers. 'I don't know what I'd do without you.'

'I don't want you to ever find out.'

He kisses her. She is no beauty, but he loves her truly, and if Edward has a redeeming feature - and this coming from a man that he condemned to death, so no small praise here - if he has a redeeming feature, it is his love for his wife.

I leave them to their sweetness and return to prowling the corridors, shutting doors that are open, frightening the dogs and scaring chambermaids with a cold and ghostly hand on their bare shoulders.

Marry d'Albret's son? He cannot do this to my Joan.

But what can I do to stop him?

8.

Joan and the princesses have been given their own quarters in the van Artevelde manse, they each have their own parlour and bedchamber, it is a relief for all of them not to wake in the middle of the night to Lionel squawking in his cot.

But the days are long and tedious. There is little to do here in the middle of winter and most days Katherine van Artevelde and her daughters join the royal princesses and sit by the windows on the south side, where there is most light, to busy themselves with their needles.

Today Joan fingers the threads in her sewing basket, her mind elsewhere. Her stitches are crooked and this is not like Joan, her work is usually exquisite. Finally, she sighs and sets it aside. Bella is chatting away airily, does not seem to care that no one is listening.

Jeanette is staring out of the window at the clouds, her lips are moving, perhaps she is singing to herself. Such a dreamy girl, only half of her belongs to the world. I have noted lately that there is a shadow that follows her. I do not know yet what it means.

Katherine addresses most of her conversation to Joan, being the eldest, and she is mostly quiet but pleasant. A well brought up princess.

But I suspect the shopkeeper's wife sees through her. Indeed, it seems to me she is the only one that is not fooled by my Joan, she senses the deep disquiet that Lady Salisbury and Lady Saint Omer do not. They have been her guardians for the last eighteen months and they know as much about her as they do the secrets of alchemy.

Perhaps Katherine is more adept because she only sees what is in front of her, not what she expects to see.

'Joan, you seem preoccupied,' she says to her finally. 'Is something amiss?'

Joan smiles, but I can tell she is alarmed. She is not accustomed to candour. 'No, I am perfectly content.' She gives Katherine a broad smile to reassure her. Poor Joan, it hurts when she smiles.

She picks up her needlework again and takes elaborate care over another stitch. She is making a shawl, embroidered with her family emblem, a white hart with a crown.

Katherine lays her own works aside and turns to the other girls. Bella is still talking; something about a scullery maid. 'I should like you all to leave us for a while. You may go to the kitchens and ask the cook to give you all one of the lemon tarts she baked for us this morning.'

The children cannot believe their good fortune. The Van Artevelde girls rarely enjoy a break in their routine and they are slow to make their escape, but Bella and Jeanette immediately throw their work aside and run yelping towards the stairs like a pack of puppies.

Joan continues with her own work, but I can see her thinking furiously, the crease at the top of her nose worked into a furrow as she tries to anticipate what Lady Katherine might want with her.

'So, tell me about your handsome knight,' Katherine says when they are finally alone.

'My lady?'

'I have seen the looks you have given him on royal occasions and the looks he has given you. I know you think that no one has noticed, and you are mostly right, but it would seem to me that having royal blood makes you blind. Come girl, I mean you no harm, I want to help you.'

'Help me?'

'Please don't repeat back to me everything I say, or we shall be here all afternoon. Don't pretend to me that you are in any way as dense as the rest of the English women here. You say little, but you see everything, don't you?'

Joan's eyes go wide. No one would dare talk to her like this at court.

'You have heard the rumours about how the king wants to match you with Albret's brat, no doubt. Is that what you want?'

'I have no choice. I am a royal princess, I must do as the king commands.'

'Perhaps.'

'Perhaps?'

'You know, when my husband took power from the Duke of Nevers, our life here changed forever. Men will do anything for power, yet it seems to me that when they have it, it only brings more burdens than they had before. These days we cannot go anywhere without an armed guard. So, his latest impulse is to secure what we have won with fortuitous marriages for our children. But I have stood up to him, I told him, this we will not do. My father did not force me to marry Jacob, for instance, I knew he was a good man and when it was suggested I consented readily. But he was my father's second choice, I refused the first.'

'You refused?'

'Of course.'

'That is not possible for me, I have a duty to the Crown. The queen herself married our king in exchange for an army and she has been very happy.'

'She did not have to marry a Gascon.'

'They will put me away in a convent if I defy them.'

'They will do no such thing.' Katherine moves closer. She brushes a lock of hair from Joan's face. 'You are such a pretty girl. What would you do if you did not have to obey the king?'

'I would marry Sir Thomas Holand.' There it is said and without a moment's hesitation.

Katherine stares at her for a long time and then she says: 'Then perhaps that is what you should do.'

'But I cannot, it is impossible.'

'Is it? Why?'

Joan is just a child still, until now she has not understood what might be gained by boldness and determination. But I believe in that moment she is transformed; hope is held in front of her like a blazing chalice. She raises her eyes from the floor and smiles. 'Defy the king?'

'Defy everyone.'

'Will you help me?'

'Perhaps. I am not afraid of England. Edward needs us; we do not need Edward.'

'I can be my own mistress?'

'If you have the courage, if you have the strength.'

'Oh, I have both!' Dear God, did she just say that? I remember the day I left her, when I rode away to die, how she clung to my neck: no, daddy, no! I realise now that she was not upset, not at all; she was angry at me. She probably still is. I had never thought of that until now.

'What about Lord van Artevelde?'

'Jacob?' Katherine pats her hand. 'I am his wife. You let me worry about him.'

I wonder why Katherine is doing this. Because she loves Joan? Or because she can? In the days that follow, I trail her about the house, looking for clues. I see her order the servants about, check the pantries, visit the stables where she steps around the dung checking that the grooms are not idle, keys jangling from her girdle.

I see the way she looks at her husband, as he bends over his books, how she listens to him laughing with his cronies behind closed doors.

Ah, I see it now!

She is doing this because she is a woman; and she is tired of men.

You see? I would never have divined that when I was alive. I am learning.

* * *

Philippa sits on the royal bed, the maidservants have plumped cushions all around her, the queen's hands rest on her belly. Their child will arrive soon. She looks tired and impatient. It must feel to her that she spends all her life carrying a child. Her face is puffed and red.

One of her ladies is reading her a tale of King Arthur's court while another plays the lute. A brazier warms the room. It is tranquil. A mist of rain falls gently in the garden. Everything is damp, sodden. The sky is the colour of pewter.

The peace is shattered without warning. She hears Edward coming, roaring at the servants as he crashes about down the stairs. She winces and sends her maids out of the room. They are not fast enough, one of them has to step back as the door flies open and Edward strides in, raging again, as he so often does these days.

I feel for the queen, having to navigate this man on a daily basis. I feel no such sympathy for Edward. In my opinion he has brought this on himself. Or rather, his mother has.

He tears off his gauntlets, throws them aside, one of them lands on the lute and produces a discordant note. He snatches up the wine and splashes some into a goblet.

His fury today is reserved for the Pope. Benedict is stalling on the dispensation he needs for Ned to marry Marguerite, Brabant's daughter.

'You seem surprised,' she says.

'There is no reasonable impediment to their marriage.'

'Except that the King of France does not want your son to marry a daughter of Brabant.'

'You mean the Dauphin does not wish it! *I* am the King of France.'

'So your mother says, that is why we are here. But we are still to persuade France of that.' She speaks slowly, patiently, clearly. 'When do you leave for England?'

'The day after tomorrow.'

'It will be a rough crossing this time of year.'

'I don't care about the crossing, I will swim through a tempest if I must. The Parliament still refuses to send me the money I need and something must be done. If they will not come willingly by the nose then I shall have to apply the stick to their tail.' He stares at the dripping leaves in the garden below. 'I wish you could be there with me.'

'And I wish you could be here with me.'

'Everything will be all right, won't it?' he asks her. He refers to the birthing. It sounds as if he is seeking her reassurance, as if she could know what God plans for her.

She smiles fondly. For all his bluster, Edward is a good husband and a good king, something no one ever said about *his* father. She has been lucky, he really didn't care if Edward would turn out to be either when the contract was signed.

'Just hurry back to me.'

'I will,' he murmurs, the bombast gone out of him now. She is good for him, Philippa. Whenever he works himself into a rage her serenity heals him again.

'Husband, will you not take Joan back with you? It is eighteen months now since she has seen her family.'

'I still need her here. Have you forgotten?'

'Will you give her no say in who she marries?'

'Why? I had no say in such matters, and neither did you.'

'What if we had hated each other?'

'But we didn't.' He sits beside her on the bed and takes her hand. 'Perhaps she will be lucky as we were.'

She squeezes his hand. 'I hope so.'

You see? It is as I said. Edward gives no thought to my daughter's welfare. These people were the ruin of me and they will yet be the ruin of the rest of my family.

The only other option here is Sir Thomas Holand.

And we are not sure what we think of him yet.

9.

The ladies Salisbury and Saint Omer are so deep in conversation they do not see Joan standing by the door, on her way to vespers. They are gossiping, thinking no one can hear them. I can tell you this from my short lifetime spent at court and in politics; everyone can hear you in a castle, even the scullery cat collects secrets.

'Poor girl,' Lady Salisbury is saying. 'Apart from a handful of maidservants she will know no one. Edward is prepared to exile her for a tilt at the French crown.'

'What is this Gascon boy like?'

'Armand? They say he likes to paint and sing on the lute. A beautiful boy, he has his father's looks and spends too much time looking into mirrors. But harmless enough. Scant consolation for the girl, I would think.'

'I wouldn't like to be trapped in a castle with Lord Albret.'

'You don't think he would try and share her with his son?'

'Well, you know. He is French.'

This is not what a father wishes to hear, and my daughter does not appear to be overjoyed either. By the look on her face, by those white lips, by those blazing eyes, it would seem to me this has only made her more determined to defy them.

'What does her mother think?' Lady Saint Omer asks.

'Her mother doesn't care a fig about her. She is only concerned with her son and making sure he gets his inheritance.'

'It's a shame her father is not here to protect her.'

'You think he would?'

'He married for love. Margaret was a widow with no money. I do not think he would have much sympathy for what is going on here.'

This much is true. When I married her, Margaret was a childless widow whose husband died at Bannockburn in another of my step-brothers calamitous Scottish adventures. She claimed they had never shared a bed. When I asked for the king's permission to marry her, Edward told me it was a poor match, that Margaret had no lands and a small dowry and it took some persuasion to have him finally give his blessings to our marriage.

'I wonder what it is to be in love,' Lady Saint Omer says.

'Have you never had a lover?'

She looks startled by this question. 'Of course not. Have you?'

Lady Catherine looks wistful and does not answer her directly. 'Could you imagine having a husband and a lover that are the same man?'

'I imagine it is impossible!'

'It is nice to think it though.'

'Well Joan's father is the only man I know who tried his hand at it. I wonder if it would have lasted.'

'They never had the chance to find out, did they?'

'His daughter won't either. Do you think Edward is set on this?'

'I suppose it depends whether Parliament gives him the money he needs.'

These two tattle on like this for what seems like an eternity, even to a restless and sleepless spirit like myself. Joan hears every word. If there is a doubt in her young mind about what she should do, I think this settles it for her.

She closes her eyes and I would wager I know what she sees; a knight with a forest green tunic and a lazy smile. Her lips part in longing. She breathes his name. Oh, it is like one of those romances she likes so much to read.

My daughter is clearly in love.

10.

I find Joan in the chapel, at a *prie-dieu*. She rocks back and forward on her knees, but no prayer will come. What does she ask for? What can be her petition when she already knows what God will say?

The candle flickers: *Joan, I am here.*

'Papa, what am I going to do?' she whispers, and though it makes my heart fill to think she would choose to pray to me over her Lord, I wish there was something I could do. I would have chosen an easier path for her than this.

'I wish you were here to tell me what to do,' she murmurs. It is cold in the chapel and she shivers.

Do it, Joan. Defy them. Look what they did to me; you owe them nothing and you owe your country nothing. If you trust Edward, he will let you down. Kings all demand loyalty but they are all faithless bastards in return, every one of them.

I put my arms around her, feel her tremble. Not yet thirteen years old and she is alone and about to stand against God, her mother and her king. I only pray she is strong enough for what is to come.

11.

Joan stares into the mirror as Anne brushes out her hair, watching Lady Salisbury's reflection. She and the rest of the royal ladies are still here at Saint Bavo's Abbey, these cloisters and grey walls have been their home since Edward went on campaign last summer.

'Look at how beautiful you are growing,' Lady Salisbury says.

Joan returns her attention to herself. I think she is surprised at the young woman who stares back at her. Although she is still snake-hipped, she no longer looks out of place in the wide sleeved pale green overgown that she wears for the feast tonight.

Her golden hair frames a face of exquisite beauty; her girl's body is taking on the shape of a woman. As a child I called her dumpling, as an endearment; but she is no dumpling now.

Her curls have grown out as her hair has grown long. Every head will turn as she enters the hall tonight. Edward is putting her on show, he is a shopkeeper himself the bastard, with a merchant's instinct for displaying his wares.

They are to go to the castle for the feast Edward has arranged to fete all the local captains of trade and visiting nobles to his cause, one final attempt to woo them before he leaves for London.

Anne finishes dressing her; a *crispinette* for her hair, glittering with pearls, and a matching necklace. She stands back for Lady Salisbury to make a final inspection, which she does. She looks at her in the glass, puts her hand on her shoulders.

'How can Lord Albret resist?' she says.

'The king's mind is set on this?'

'It is a fine match, Joan, a fine match.'

'Does my mother know of it?'

'I have told her, in a letter. No doubt the King will speak with her further on his return to England.'

'Will she consent to it?'

'My dear, it is the king's wish, your mother cannot refuse. She knows he would not do something that was not in the best interests of England or of you.'

This is such a bald lie that it shocks me. Lady Salisbury speaks this nonsense with a smile, she blathers whatever it is politic to say at the time.

'My Lady,' Joan says to her, 'the King is doing what is best for the king. More than that I could not venture.' If I were alive I would have stood and applauded her.

Lady Salisbury's smile vanishes. 'My dear, what a thing to say.'

'What is marriage like?' Joan asks her.

She is off kilter and starts to stammer. 'It is ... a woman cannot be safe until ... until she is married to a good man with estates and wealth and position.'

'And all that has made you happy, Lady Catherine?'

Their eyes lock in the mirror. It is Lady Salisbury who looks away first, such close scrutiny makes her uncomfortable. 'Well, of course.'

'You love Earl Salisbury then?'

'What has love got to do with it, my dear?'

'My mother loved my father.'

Did he, she wants to say. That is not what I heard. But she cannot.

Instead: 'We should hurry. Our escort will be waiting for us.' She hurries Joan out of the door. That will teach her to engage my thirteen-year-old daughter in conversation. Already she is no match.

12.

The Great Hall at Gravensteen is ablaze with banners and flags, the tables covered in white linen, no borrowed coin has been spared. Musicians play on lutes and drums in the minstrel's gallery above the screen, but they can scarce be heard. The din inside the hall is like a minor battle.

The women are dressed in velvets of green and burgundy, everywhere the swish of silks, emeralds and rubies catch the reflection of a thousand candles. Knights and nobles mix with fat Flanders shopkeepers, a sight I had never seen in England and it still pains me to witness even after all these months here, though such matters are no longer business of mine.

Edward does not do much feasting or dancing, for tonight is not for merry-making; this is politics, pure and simple. Resplendent in his purple, he moves around the room, whispering in alcoves, murmuring behind screens with wealthy peat barons and merchant princes of Ghent and lords from Brabant and Gascony.

Joan dances, and dances gracefully, but her attention is somewhere else, she looks for Holand among the household knights, always aware of where he is and which lady he is dancing with.

When she rejoins the Ladies Salisbury and Saint Omer their eyes meet for a moment and then Holand withdraws from the hall and she watches carefully which door he takes. She waits a moment then tells her guardians she is tired and is feeling unwell and they smile knowingly for they assume that it is to do with her time of the moon. Joan takes her maid Anne with her and they leave the hall.

But not everyone is blind to her subtleties. One pair of eyes at least follows her as she takes her leave; Katherine van Artevelde sips her watered-down wine and smiles.

Joan hurries along the cloister. The garden is uninviting, an icy drizzle settling on the grass and the yew hedges. Down in the garden she sees some rich Flanders wife hurrying from the privy with her maid, but it seems that no one else is out here. Then she sees a shadow under one of the beech trees.

She rounds on Anne.

'Do you know what's good for you?' she whispers.

'My lady?'

'You have a keen sense of self-preservation, yes?'

The girl is suddenly terrified: the look on her face.

'You will wait here for me. I am going down into the garden and later you will tell no one, no one, what I have done. Do you understand?'

Anne nods.

'Because if you do tell someone, I will tell Lady Salisbury that her husband has had you up against the scullery wall and she will dismiss you instantly from service out of spite. She is like that. Do I make myself clear?'

I am truly shocked. Blackmail! Where did my daughter learn this? She is just thirteen-years-old. I at once admire her spirit and resourcefulness while I abhor her morals. I must face it now; my little Joan is gone, her innocence is just a memory. She is a woman now and she intends to fight for what she wants.

'Well?'

Anne is certainly convinced. 'Yes, my lady,' she says and backs away. 'Not a word.'

'Again, so I can be sure you have understood. What will I do if you tell anyone about this?'

'You will tell Lady Salisbury that I have ... that I ...'

'Good. You do understand.' Joan smiles and kisses her on the cheek. Then she picks up her skirts and rushes down the steps to the garden.

I follow.

* * *

Joan puts up the hood of her fur-lined cloak against the rain and joins Holand under the beech tree. Without a word he takes her hand and leads her towards the stables. They shelter inside from the rain. The horses stamp in their stalls, there is a strong smell of straw and dung and damp.

She pulls back her hood. It is dark, the only light comes from a lantern hanging from a beam at the far end of the stable. She and Holand are both breathing hard, as if they have been running. I wonder what he will say to her. In fact, he doesn't say anything. He kisses her and my daughter kisses him back.

They cling to each other. If I could be sure of him I would welcome this.

'What are we going to do?' she whispers.

'Joan, you are so young. I have nothing to offer you.'

'You have yourself, Thomas, that is all I care about.'

'Edward is going to marry you off to Albret.'

'He thinks he is, but I won't do it.'

'No, it is true, Salisbury himself just told me. He has today a letter from the King asking him to draw up the contract. He is to send his seneschal in Gascony to make the negotiations.'

'I have a plan, Thomas.'

This startles him; he still thinks he is holding a child. He has not seen the things I have seen. She was ready for this, prepared. She is more than a match for you, young man. 'What do you mean?'

'There is only one man I will ever marry.'

The rain falls harder. They can hear it now on the leaves, dripping from the eaves of the stable. A horse snorts and shakes its great head in one of the stalls.

'Do you mean that?'

'Do you want that?' she whispers.

How can he want this, how can she?

How can my daughter be so certain when she hardly knows this man? But then I suppose my marriage to her mother made no sense either.

'When?'

'Now. Tonight, if we could.'

He shakes his head. 'But if we were to do it ... we will need witnesses,' he says to her.

'Katherine van Artevelde has already told me she will do it.'

'Lady van Artevelde? Why would she do such a thing?'

'I don't know but she has given me her word. But we must do it soon.'

'The queen's birthing,' he says.

'Thomas?'

'Who will be paying attention to us when the whole household is in a riot over a new royal child? We could do it then, but the van Arteveldes must be apprised of our plans.'

'I will take care of it.'

'We will have little warning to arrange things.'

'What is there to arrange? If I can get away unnoticed then we simply have to say the words in front of them and it is done.'

'You are sure they will do this?'

She nods her head.

'There will be dire consequences.'

'As dire as living as the wife of some spoiled French brat and breed a nest of squabbling ugly children while I stare out of the window dreaming of the one man I loved, thinking about what might have been? Worse than that?'

Oh, Joan, despite my misgivings, I am proud of you. You do not know the trouble you are about to bring down on your head, yet I am so proud. She waits now for Thomas Holand to tell her he loves her. It is all that needs to be said to make this moment perfect for her.

'Once it is done, we will have to be circumspect,' he tells her.

'I trust you in this.'

Say it, say it to her.

'We can tell no one straight away. If we are discreet then the king may pretend he knew of it and was persuaded to agree, but if others learn about it he will have to act against us just to save his pride.'

'But you will tell your family?'

A moment's hesitation. 'Of course.'

'How long would we need to keep it secret?'

'I will go to the king as soon as he returns from England.'

'You think he may be persuaded?'

'I have friends at court. I will take care of things.'

'I love you, Thomas,' she says and wraps her arms tightly around his neck.

'You are sure the van Arteveldes will help us?'

I cannot hear how she answers, her words are muffled; her face is buried in his shoulder.

'Ask Lady van Artevelde if I may talk to her husband, then. We will wait for the right moment.'

'I cannot bear to be parted from you any longer.'

'It will be alright, I promise you.'

She kisses him again. 'I must go,' she says and puts up her hood. She lifts up her skirts and runs back to the cloister through the puddles.

Holand stands there for a long time, his hands by his sides, hardly moving. I wonder what he is thinking. If it were me I would be overwhelmed by the enormity of what I had just committed myself to; I would be thinking that I was about to leap a great chasm, and on the far side there was either an Eden or I was about to fall into a black and endless chasm and be lost forever.

I know he will jump, that is the nature of the man. What I want to know; does he do it for Eden or does he do it for Eve?

13.

Jacob van Artevelde fidgets on the cushioned bench. A servant brings a flask of wine and fills two fine Venetian goblets and then withdraws. Van Artevelde and Thomas Holand sip the wine. Holand waits patiently while the merchant examines the rafters for cobwebs.

The silence drags.

Holand looks very fine today, a fine grey tunic emblazoned with Edward's new device, English lions quartered with a French *fleur de lys*. The king has at last formally declared himself King of France, though the French still do not agree with him.

Finally, van Artevelde says: 'Are you quite mad?'

'My lord?'

'I asked if you had taken leave of your senses.'

'Quite possibly.'

'The king is your paymaster. Did no one ever tell you that it is unwise to betray the man who puts bread on your table?'

That word again. Betray. It is not deliberate, he knows nothing of Holand's family history. But a muscle ripples in the young man's jaw and the blood drains from his cheeks. He takes a moment to recover. 'Hardly betrayal. Such marriages have been made before. Edward will come around.'

'You seem very confident. But I know your king, he wants to use Joan to help him with his alliance against France. This crusade of his consumes him and you are about to queer his plans.' He leans forward and asks the question I have been asking myself. 'Is this about Joan or is it about you?'

Holand hesitates. What on earth is he thinking? I should love to know. 'I love her,' he says and the words fall into the room like a dropped cup.

'I am telling you, Sir Thomas, the king will not forgive you.'

'He may be angry at first ...'

'Angry? He will be beside himself with rage.'

'The king is about to go to war, he needs knights with boldness and ambition and initiative.'

'So this is why you are doing this? To show him your military resolve? And what about her family?' A pause. 'Do they know of your intentions towards Joan?'

'There is a problem.'

'Another problem? You have quite enough. The king alone is ten problems.'

'Her family despise me.'

Van Artevelde sighs and reaches for the wine. 'Continue.'

'It goes back to my father, their resentment is towards him not me. But I carry his sins on my shoulders.'

'Sins? What did he do?'

'Her family are from the house of Lancaster and my father was a good friend to them for many years. More than a friend, you could say he was the Earl of Lancaster's favourite. The Earl led a rebellion against the former king and my father … proved inconstant.'

'How so?'

'He failed to appear with his troops on the day of the battle. His absence was decisive. The Earl of Lancaster was taken prisoner and executed.'

'How long ago did this happen?'

'Twenty years. An eternity.'

'For hate, that is yesterday.' Van Artevelde shakes his head. 'So you wish to thwart a king's ambition and thumb your nose at Joan's family, all in one fell swoop.'

'Six years ago, a knight called Stafford carried off a maid called Margaret Audley. She was high-born, and he believed her family would not accept him, so he abducted her. The king was angry, granted, but he accepted it finally, when it was done. He even awarded him a third of her Gloucester estates, in time.'

'Is that what this is about? Money?'

'My point is that if I can persuade the king, I can persuade her family. Whatever my father did or did not do means nothing besides the king's opinion in the matter.'

'This Margaret Audley may have been high-born, but I wager the king did not see her as a valuable resource in his campaign for the French throne.'

'I love Joan.'

'The world will say that such protestations of love are very convenient for a man in your position.' He finishes his wine and pours a second cup. He does not offer any to Holand.

'If you feel this way, may I ask why you're thinking of helping us?'

'My wife wants to do this for Joan. She has become quite fond of her, she sees her as another daughter, I think.'

'We could not do this without you.'

'No, you couldn't. And if it were not for my wife I would not involve myself in such a scheme at all.'

'Will Edward not blame you as well when he discovers you have stood as witness for our betrothal?'

'Edward needs me.' He leans forward and lowers his voice. 'Even though I am just a shopkeeper.' He laughs. So, he knows what Edward calls him in private. I wonder if that is what spurs him. It is an elegant tit-for-tat, if that is the case. 'When do you plan to do this?'

'The Queen is about to go into confinement and she will want all her ladies around her. Lady Saint Omer and Lady Salisbury will be preoccupied with the birthing, no one will pay attention to Joan.'

Van Artevelde thinks this through then says the words that I would rather not hear. 'You are not thinking of consummating the marriage?'

'Of course not.'

'She is far too young.'

Holand nods. Yet he must know what every scullery maid in the Abbey already knows; that Joan's body is not *that* young. But just because she is fertile does not mean she is ready, intercourse and birthing are both far too dangerous for girls of her age.

I wish I could be sure about this: pray, ask him again, shopkeeper.

'I have your word?' van Artevelde says.

'What kind of man do you think I am?'

He leans across the low table. 'I think you are a man of opportunity, Sir Thomas. But then so am I, so do not feel slighted.' He finishes his wine. Two glasses, drained so quickly. He must be more apprehensive about this than he appears. 'I cannot dissuade you from this? You are making your life very difficult, young man. And hers, even more so.'

'This is what we want.'

'Very well.' Van Artevelde summons a servant to show the Englishman out. After he has gone he stares out of the window after him, watches him mount his horse and head back to Gravensteen at the gallop.

He smiles; there is something perverse in him that is enjoying this.

I think, yes, it is true, he likes toying with princes. Few shopkeepers ever get the chance.

Saint Bavo's Abbey

The abbey is in uproar. Maidservants dash to and from the kitchens with bowls of hot water and towels. This is women's business. The birthing chair has been brought in and though Philippa has been through this before, for her women every time is like the first. The entire household holds its breath. There is the hope and expectation of a son; there is also the terror that something may go wrong.

Bella and Jeanette hear the screams even from the nursery where they are kept busy at their needlework by one of the maidservants. Joan is not with them; the maidservant thinks she is with Ladies Salisbury and Saint Omer; they, in turn, think she is with the maidservant.

The Queen is birthing. Who has time to ask?

Servants hurry through the abbey opening all the doors, drawers, and cupboards, untying knots if they find one. Just an old wives' tale, of course, this saying about knots, but who will take chances when it comes to a queen?

Snow whips on the wind, wrapping the abbey in drifts of white. A hooded figure in a black cloak hurries into the stables and emerges leading a palfrey and rides away through the abbey gates, unchallenged. Her maidservant Anne goes with her, the only other soul in the world who can know what she is about to do.

It is but a short ride into the town to the van Artevelde manse, and when she arrives Katherine is there to greet her and hurry her inside. A servant fetches spice-warmed wine to revive her. She stands by the log fire shivering, melted snow dripping onto the flagstones at her feet. But it is not just the cold that makes her tremble so.

Not long afterwards, Holand arrives.

He comes in, shaking the snow from his cloak, and brushing it out of his long wavy locks. Their eyes meet. They stare at each other.

This is the moment.

14.

No spiced wine for Holand. Van Artevelde is straight to the matter at hand.

Katherine takes Joan's hand and leads her into a private chamber. There is another fire roaring in the hearth here also; it is a fine room, there is polished timber wainscoting, high backed chairs, an oak table, tapestries on the walls. It seems too large for its purpose for there are only the four of them to attend this little ceremony.

For once Holand seems uncertain of himself. He does not know where to stand. Katherine however keeps a firm hold of Joan's arm and leads her to the fire. Holand joins them there, facing Joan. He smiles uncertainly at her, she smiles boldly back.

Now van Artevelde stands between them, hands crossed in front of him; he knows the law. All these two have to do is say the words and the marriage is legal; all they as witnesses must do is hear them say it.

'You know the gravity of what you are to do?' he asks them.

Holand nods.

'No one must know about this outside the four of us, not until you have spoken with the king and with Joan's family.'

'Of course,' Holand says. He fumbles in his cloak and produces a plain gold ring. The ring is not necessary for this ceremony so, despite myself, I am impressed. Joan holds out her hand and he places it reverently on her finger. 'Thank you, Thomas,' she whispers.

Even Katherine looks pleased.

Joan's eyes shine with admiration, she looks up at him the way that Margaret once looked at me. She trusts and hopes for so much. By God's grace, let her not be disappointed.

Was Margaret disappointed? I fear that she was. I let my wife down, I left her a widow, I ignored her counsel and laid myself at the mercy of kings. I hope Thomas will not prove as foolhardy as me.

A log falls in the grate sending up a shower of sparks. Joan smiles; she looks to the rafters, I believe she knows I am there, somewhere.

'Say the words,' van Artevelde tells him.

Holand swallows hard. His Adam's apple bobs in his throat. 'I, Thomas Holand, solemnly vow that I will take you, Joan Plantagenet, as my wife and I will do it before a priest, as soon as I may, and I therefore pledge thee my troth.'

'Now you, Joan,' van Artevelde says.

She repeats the vow. The shopkeeper nods, satisfied, and then goes to the table and pours four glasses of brandy wine. They all stand around the fire and toast the success of the marriage.

'So,' van Artevelde says. 'It is done.'

'Not all done,' Katherine says.

Even the spirit in the room is startled at this.

'What is there else to do?' he asks her.

'The marriage is not yet consummated,' Katherine says evenly.

Van Artevelde looks at Holand. 'You gave me your word,' he says.

Holand shrugs his shoulders. I do not think he knows anything about this.

'But she is only twelve-years-old,' Van Artevelde says to his wife.

'She is a woman now and she is ready. She has told me herself. This is what she wants.'

'Is it?' Holand asks her.

Joan looks frankly into Holand's eyes and puts both hands to her left breast, above her heart. 'With all my heart,' she says.

Even Holand seems taken aback. He looks at van Artevelde who frowns at his wife and then at Joan, shaking his head. 'I have done my part, Katherine,' he says. 'I want no more to do with this.' He puts down his glass and leaves the room.

Joan has not taken her eyes from Holand.

He stares at her in shock. I wonder what is going through his mind. This was not in his calculations. But Joan is young and she is beautiful and she desires this.

If he really does love her, he will refuse.

'Are you sure?' he says.

This is just a betrothal, that is all that Jacob van Artevelde agreed to. What if Holand now gets my daughter with child? It will be dangerous for her. Besides she is not yet grown, consummation will hurt her. Neither has she been properly churched.

No, this is wrong. Can no one stop this? If he loves her he will insist that they wait, that is what an honourable man would do.

'Please Thomas,' Joan says.

'If it is what you want.'

'She knows her own mind, Sir Thomas,' Katherine says.

'But they will miss you at the abbey.'

'Not before nightfall.'

I cannot believe my daughter has said this. I should not be here listening to it but in my present circumstances there is no help for it. The look she gives him is wanton and naked, a look I should not be privy to.

Where is van Artevelde? He seems a sensible man. He should remind them all of what is right.

This is going too far.

Katherine goes to the window, points to the guesthouse at the end of the garden, snow piled against its wooden door. 'You can use the room you stayed in when you were with us,' she says to her. 'A servant has lit a brazier there and warmed the bed with hot stones. It is all ready for you. There is wine if you want it, but I have watered it down.'

Damn this woman to hell.

She takes Joan aside and whispers something to her. Holand does not hear what she says but I do; it is a reminder to take the sheet afterwards, as proof.

Holand stands by the door, smiling uncertainly. He helps Joan on with her cloak then fetches his own. I watch from over Katherine's shoulder as they make their way down the garden, leaving footprints in the snow. Holand has a hand around her shoulders.

I do not follow.

I want nothing of this. Oh Joan, what have you done? Be careful of this man.

Holand at least knows what he is about. There are ways a man may lie with a woman and not take her maidenhood and ways he may lay with her and not leave his seed. He knows this.

I do not want to know what way he chooses or how this goes for them. I cannot take you over that threshold and I am sure you understand why.

I stare at their footprints in the snow, hear the door click shut behind them. I cannot stay.

I let the cold grey wind take me; I am carried with it in stiff, chill gusts beyond the sombre walls of the abbey, past belfries and towers, over the ice on the black river. I see Edward's red and gold banners, stiff and frozen, on the walls of Saint Bavo's Abbey. I pass a shuttered window and hear screams from inside, where Philippa is still labouring in the birthing chair.

This is what love comes to, my darling; he sows the seed, you reap all the risk and the pain. I sweep restless through a grey afternoon, howling in the trees, chill as the north wind.

15.

They emerge in the late afternoon, it has stopped snowing now, but drifts are piled against walls and doors. Already the light is leeching out of the sky. Holand's squire brings his horse and he prepares to ride back to the castle in the gathering dark. Patches of snow crunch beneath his feet as his boots break the fresh crust. He puts his bare hands in his armpits to try and warm them while he waits for Joan and Holand to finish their leave-taking.

'You will tell your family?' she says to Holand.

'As soon as I may.'

'And the King?'

'I will put my, our, case to him the moment he returns from England. Until then,' and he puts a finger dramatically to her lips, 'until then not a word.'

'You think he will accede?'

'He will not be best pleased. But I am sure he will come round to it. There are precedents for this.'

Does he mean Stamford? Dear God, man, do not put all your hopes on that affair. But Joan nods her head, trusting him. Forgive me, but I hope his horse stumbles in the ice and crushes him.

'I will never forget this afternoon,' she whispers.

'There will be many more to remind you of it.'

'When will I see you again?'

'Soon. But we must be discreet for now.'

'Now we are finally together I do not think I can bear to be apart from you.' She kisses him on the lips, wraps her arms around his neck, and holds him as if she never wants to let him go. It is Holand who disentangles himself first. 'I promise you we will be together soon,' he tells her again.

He puts on his gauntlets and strides towards his horse. He mounts with practised ease and turns his mare's head. A wave and he is gone. His squire follows.

She stands in the cold and watches until the horses are out of sight, then she goes back inside the house and when she re-emerges she is still tucking something inside her cloak. The bed sheet, of course.

She goes back to the Manse and shares some quick words with Lady van Artevelde, assurances that all is well. Her maidservant is waiting in an anteroom. Anne looks thoroughly miserable, as well she might, for Joan has told her repeatedly what is at stake for her if any word of this gets out. She has her mother's ruthlessness about her and I suppose I should thank Margaret for that.

She arrives back at the abbey just on dusk, no one sees her arrival and the sounds of the horses' hooves on the cobbles are muffled by the snow. She hurries inside and heads to the nursery where her absence is not even remarked on. Everyone assumes she has been with the queen.

A servant rushes in with the news; her grace the queen has been delivered of a healthy baby boy. Both are well. There is a general air of celebration and Joan smiles and plays her part. No one sees the high colour in her cheeks, or her wistful smile.

The children are excited by the comings and goings and leap and dance around the room. My Joan, not long out of childhood herself, just watches them with a forbearing smile. After tonight, she is not a child anymore.

As she climbs into bed that night I imagine she congratulates herself on the success of her subterfuge.

But then Bella rolls over and whispers: 'Where did you go this afternoon?'

Her eyes blink open. 'I was here, in the Abbey.'

Bella smiles. 'It's all right,' she says, 'your secret is safe with me.' And then she rolls back and in a little while she is asleep.

Joan just lies there, staring into the dark.

16.

I do not know if I admire him or hate him to my bones. He takes huge risks here; marrying the king's cousin, without his monarch's knowledge or permission, while she is under his protection and he is in his pay. The shopkeeper was right when he said that men have been dismissed for less. Then what will he do?

Go to Italy and become a mercenary?

Does he know canon law? His marriage to my daughter is legal in theory, could have been construed as legal even without witnesses if there was consent 'de praesenti', as the Church likes to call it, where both made the vows willingly. But Joan is of an age where it can and will be argued that she did not know what she was doing.

For me, it is not just a point of law: *did she know what she was doing?*

Look at him, he seems so calm for a man who has just betrayed his lord. But then it runs in the family, doesn't it? And only twelve years since his father was murdered on the road by Lancaster supporters.

His father's faithlessness has not been forgotten in the north and it will not be forgotten in Holand's lifetime, unless, that is, he can manage a fine marriage. My Joan is his path to riches and to respect if he can carry it off.

He and his brother Otto have drunk too many ales in the tavern and now they help each other stagger back through the streets to the castle. Otto stops to retch over the side of the bridge and then sinks onto his haunches on the cobblestones to rest.

Otto is Thomas Holand's younger brother; he has sibling's looks but not his bearing and so appears slighter and less handsome though really they are much the same. He also has none of Holand's burning ambition, or shame, or anger.

'You are mad,' Otto groans.

'Every man needs a little madness.'

'Not like this. Nothing good can come of this, Thomas. What were you thinking?'

'She says she loves me.'

'Well that makes everything alright then.'

'What would you have done?'

'I would have gone to the king, as the king expects.'

'He would have said no.'

Exactly.

Otto is right, most men would have given up but Thomas Holand, I will concede, is not like most men. He is gambling that the king needs men like him right now and faced with the deed done, he will relent. If he can get the king's approval, he will not need my wife's. But he needs to keep this secret from her and the rest of her family for when she finds this out, she will move heaven and earth to see the king oppose it.

'Will you never be content with all you have?'

'Content? My father was once one of the richest men in the north. Now look at us! Of course I am not content. I shall never be content until the wrong is made right.'

'And when will that be?'

'When I am an earl!'

'An earl?' Otto laughs but he sees by his brother's face that he is serious. 'What happened to us is just fate, Thomas.'

'A man makes his own fate.'

'The king will sever your commission.'

'Not when there's a war with France in the offing. He needs good soldiers.'

'Not as much as he needs an alliance with Gascony.'

'I think that what I have done will appeal to his chivalrous nature.'

Otto is muddled with drink. He cannot follow his brother's reasoning. For that matter, neither can I. Yes, the king would like to have a chivalrous nature, all men would, but that does not mean he has one.

'It is like these stories of Helen and Paris and Troy that he is so fond of,' Holand says, making his point. 'I am Paris. I will tell him the story that way.'

'A story from a minstrel is one thing, an alliance with Lord Albret is another.' Otto groans and rests his aching head on the parapet. 'What will our mother say when she hears this?'

'I don't know. This is just between us for now.'

'You have not told her?'

'I will find the right moment.'

'When will that be? The day the Pope proclaims Mohammed as his prophet and prays to the east??'

'You are the only one that knows of this. I trust you with my secret, promise me you will tell no one.'

'I have drunk so much ale by the morning I will not even remember it. You think the Flemish will ever learn to make good ale?'

Holand helps his brother to his feet. Gravensteen looms against a moonless sky. 'Tell me one thing,' Otto says.

'What is that?'

'Do you love her?'

'Joan is very beautiful.'

'But do you love her?'

'Does it matter?'

'I am just curious is all.'

'Of course I love her,' Holand says. But it is the little laugh at the end that gives him away.

Oh Joan, what have you done?

PART 2

17.

Holand finds the Earl of Salisbury in the great hall at Gravensteen. The castle is abuzz, the king has just returned from England and the court has emerged from its torpor. The earl is standing by the massive fireplace, deep in conversation with Lord Derby and some of his acolytes. Holand waits patiently for the Earl to conclude his business, studies the heraldic devices on the overmantle, relics from when the castle belonged to the Count of Nevers. No one had thought to chisel them off. Well, he supposes they will not be in residence here long enough for it to matter.

A milky light suffuses the mullioned windows high above them. There is a fire raging but it cannot take the chill from this draughty hall.

At last Derby and his clerks scuttle away and the Earl turns to Holand. 'Sir Thomas, how do I find you this good morning? You look troubled. Not another one of your amours, I hope?'

'I need to see the king, my lord.'

'The king? Why?'

'It is a private matter.'

The Earl frowns. 'If you have a dispensation to ask of him I have to tell you, it is not a good time. He is in an ill humour. The Parliament did not grant him all of the money he wishes for the conduct of this war and he is still in debt to Brabant and van Artevelde.' He lowers his voice, as if hatching a conspiracy, but there is no secret about it, everyone knows the king's financial difficulties. 'He cannot even afford his daily living expenses.'

'It is a scandal.'

'That these brewers and wool traders do not think the King of England is good for the money or that he chose to keep two of the King's nobles as hostages in case he did not return? If I had my way I would rather make war on the Count of Brabant.'

Holand is barely listening, he has a faraway look in his eye. What does he care about politics at this moment, or the king's enemies?

'I hope it's not money you want?'

Holand shakes his head. He is at a disadvantage, for he cannot tell the Earl of Salisbury what it is he does want. This must stay a secret between himself and Joan until it is done. That the van Arteveldes themselves are involved only makes this even more delicate.

'The king's mind is focused on the forthcoming campaigns. I can ask for an audience if you want but if it were me I would find it politic to wait for a month or two and make my request then. You might find him in a better mood after a good summer's campaigning.'

Holand hesitates, weighing what he has been just told. Salisbury knows the king and his moods better than anyone. Wait another two months? How can he? Yet if he rushes now and the king refuses, what will he do then? The king must acquiesce, or his career could be in ruins, just as Otto has said.

The King does not even have to banish him; if he informs her family what has happened, they will claim she is too young to marry and she will be sent back to England, and even his witnesses and the betrothal will mean nothing then.

'Thank you for your good counsel,' Holand says and does not press his demands. He wanders off through the halls to think about this. The Earl is correct, he decides, why not wait a single season? When a man is playing for such high stakes timing and patience is crucial.

I would admire his restraint, were I not Joan's father. As it is I would like to see him dead in a ditch, but that is beyond my power now.

Saint Bavo's Abbey

Anne hands Joan a note. It is from Thomas Holand and it says simply: *Meet me in the garden at dawn, under the arbour.* He has taken care not to sign it, but though she does not know his handwriting she does not need to ask the author of it.

After she has read it, she warns Anne to silence with a steely glare. There is no need: the girl is shaking. She is so culpable in these intrigues now that she hardly sleeps. I imagine she has calculated that her only chance of saving herself is through her silence. It is already too late to tell anyone what she knows. She has been complicit in Joan's scheming for far too long now.

Joan wakes early and steals out of the nursery and down some private steps into the garden. She lifts her hem and hurries along the paths. A mist clings, everything drips with morning dew. It is silent out here save for the rustling of her skirts.

She sees a grey shadow under the trees, and once there she falls into his arms. They cling to each other. She searches his face for news, she is so frightened of what he may tell her she thinks she will choke up her heart.

'Did you speak to him?'

He tries to hold her tighter, but she takes a step back.

'Thomas, tell me, what is wrong?'

'We will have to wait.'

'Wait? What can you mean?'

'The king is ill disposed. It is not the time.'

'But you promised!'

'You must trust me with this. I will know when it is the right time.'

'You said you would take care of everything.'

'We must have his good approval. A victorious campaign in France this summer and everything will be different. It is just a few more months.'

'A few more months might as well be forever.'

'A season.'

'And what if it is a bad campaign?'

He ignores this. 'I will take care of everything, as I said I would. I just need a little more time.'

The castle is waking. Joan looks up at the windows, afraid that they will be seen. The mist is already clearing, the sun burning it away.

'I must go,' she says. 'When will I see you again?'

'Soon.'

'But when?'

'I am at the king's command. We may leave any day.'

'So I may not see you until after the summer?'

'I do not know.'

'I cannot wait until then!'

'We must. Trust me, my sweet.' *My sweet.* It is the first time he has used such an endearment and I see the effect it has on her. She is so hungry for his affection, God pity her.

She clings to him again, as if she can draw his essence into her own bones, enough to carry her through the warm days ahead when she will feel so chill inside. I want to do murder, as I never did in life. He has led her to this.

'I have to go,' he says, He turns and hurries away; then he returns, to hug her to him a last time. They share a look and finally he goes, perhaps for good.

19.

Sluys, on the mouth of River Zwyn,
24 June, 1340.

I was never much of a military man, and even now I am no great lover of wars. Many have forgotten Sluys, but I can tell you now it was like standing alone against a stampede, bumped and buffeted by the dead fleeing the carnage.

It was Edward's moment, his boldness was decisive, no doubt he felt he had suffered indignities enough and it was his chance to avenge himself on those who doubted his resolve. Well, he did that.

I watched him board a French galley, and I cannot tell you what I wished for most, his survival or his bloody end. Yet I could not help but admire his courage. Unless you have been a knight, held a bloody axe in your hand, staggered under the weight of your body armour, you cannot know the terror of stepping into such a melee.

So, to that afternoon; there is the stink of burning tar and smoke, the reek of fear-sweat. The planking is slippery with blood, there are bodies everywhere, that alone makes it a dangerous place to be for a man has to lose his balance just once and another man is on him, chopping and slashing. Even hardened veterans dislike fighting on a ship.

They call it chivalry when these knights ride through the towns on their caparisoned warhorses with their royal *jupons* and bright-coloured banners, but that is not what it is like when the battle starts. These young men were raised for war, but nothing really readies a man for cutting another near in half with a battle axe and having his warm blood spray on you. It is butchery, pure and simple, and fear drives them, those that survive do so through the constant drilling from their sergeants at arms from a child, and sheer, blind luck.

I watch Holand battle his way across deck, his brother knights and men-at-arms behind him, he trips on a body and for a moment loses his balance and goes down on one knee. A Frenchman raises his battle axe and he is unable to raise his shield in time and for a moment time stops.

What is it I wish for? If Holand dies, Joan's oath will count for nothing and she goes to Gascony; if he lives, then what? If I could have seen the future right then, I wonder what I would have chosen.

But I am not Fate. It is not up to me to decide.

Holand's brother Otto is quick to see the danger and steps in, takes the blow on his own shield and drives the point of his sword beneath it, into the Frenchman's unguarded groin. An unholy scream and the man drops to the deck writhing, and a few moments later he passes me on his way to whatever lies beyond this nether place.

The two brothers barely pause to consider what has just happened, there is no time. The battle continues, they battle on; it is the dance they have all learned as boys; they slash, they weave, they advance. Is it hours, is it moments? As twilight descends over the estuary it is finally over. The tide is red with blood and corpses, the French fleet utterly destroyed.

I look for Holand. He is still alive, his armour patterned with blood, it is so thick on his mailed glove that he cannot prise it from the axe handle. Joan will never know how close he came to a much different fate.

That night, in the town, Thomas Holand and his brother find a tavern and drink for two days until they are insensible. Already some of the soldiers are learning to make a joke of it. He hears one of his men say that the French knights are braver than the English ones.

'How can that be?' another fellow asks.

'Because ours do not dare to jump into the sea in full armour,' he says and they all laugh uproariously.

He and Otto fall into drunken stupor and when they wake up they drink again. Afterwards they both go to a priest who absolves them of their sins.

That night while his brother snores in his coat Holand sits by the candle and tries to write to his mother and tell her about the battle, and then confess to her about his betrothal to Joan, but his pen hovers over the scrap of parchment and he just cannot do it.

I stand at his shoulder and urge him to start but he cannot even manage the salutation. Is he numb from the battle or is it something else? I do not know. I would rather he wrote to Joan but it seems he cannot do that either.

* * *

Meanwhile my daughter is alone with her secret, with her prayer books and her needlework. She sits quiet in her circle with her young cousins, so serene you would think the worst she has ever done in her life is climb a tree. Bella prattles on about the battle at Sluys, the girl eavesdrops every conversation and repeats everything she hears. She would be an impressive spy but for her utter inability to keep secrets.

Joan just smiles; her smile is like the king's armour, no one has ever quite penetrated it and it looks so pretty, doesn't it? That night, after vespers, she kneels alone at her prayers, just a single candle to light her darkness. 'Papa help me. Show me a way out of this. Speak for me to the angels. Why did you leave me here, alone? I need you now. Help me.'

But there are no angels at hand so that I might press on them her supplication. There is only Joan and I in the chapel. Does she think I would not pledge my soul to the devil himself if there was some spirit, light or dark, that could help her?

Why, oh why, did I go to Parliament that day? But even that was not my first sin; the mistake I made was taking the bait that Mortimer dangled in front of me, my fault was in trying to help my former king, my brother. What had he ever done in his life for me? My loyalty should have been to my family, not him.

Far too late to understand this now. It seems that my daughter has learned the lesson without ever being instructed in it.

I am anxious that Joan is not with child. She is far too young for sex, for childbirth, for heartache. What was this Holand thinking, to lie with her just because she asked it? Now he has left her to kneel alone in a cold chapel, alone.

And where is he tonight? Well I will tell you. He is in a tavern in Sluys, with a serving wench pinned against the wall.

It hardly seems fair and just, does it?

20.

Wars have seasons, like life, like loves. Edward campaigns through the summer and with the turning of the leaves returns to Ghent. It has not gone well for him. In April, Salisbury was captured at Lille and it has cost the Crown a considerable sum to get him back with his head on his shoulders. More debt.

Edward sits sullen by the fire, for it is cold here already. He should never have come here, I think he realises this now. Most men think wars are about glory and courage and tactics, but they are wrong. Wars are about money. Bankers love wars. It is how they get rich and how kings and the people who toil under them repeat their endless cycles of starvation and banner-waving and grief.

Edward has spent money he does not have losing a war he cannot win.

'We shall have to agree to a truce,' the Earl of Suffolk ventures.

The king says nothing. He looks at Salisbury who shrugs and nods. He knows Suffolk is right but cannot bring himself to say the words. It is the only recourse now. Valois has outlasted him.

It is his mother's curse, this war. Isabella's father was Phillip the Fair and she had promised Edward from the very cradle that one day he would have the French crown as well the English throne. It is your destiny, she had whispered to him. He can as much give it up as cut out his own heart with a trencher knife.

'It is not over,' he tells Salisbury. 'I will not give this up. I am the rightful king and heir of France.'

Salisbury says nothing. He knows what the king thinks, what his pleasure is in this. But the hard truth is this: they have to stop this now. If this continues, the king will end up a beggar on the steps of the cathedral.

The king sends his council from the room so he might brood alone. Salisbury turns to leave also and remembers one final matter. 'I have a petition from Sir Thomas Holand.'

The king stares at the floor. Has he heard him?

'He has asked to join the Pope's crusade against the Tartars in Prussia.'

'He is one of our best knights.'

'It seems we shall have no further need of him for a while.'

A movement of the hand indicates assent. The earl turns to leave again but this also is just a tactic, as if his next gambit is an afterthought. Matters raised on the way out of the door, when Edward's guard is down, are those most likely to meet with success, it is an old courtier's trick. 'One further thing. What should we do about my Lord Albret?'

'We shall discontinue negotiations for now. I do not trust him entirely, we shall wait and see how the wind blows before we move further with such an alliance.'

Salisbury sees his chance. 'If I may be bold, your Grace?'

The king nods, gloomily.

'I thought to suggest my son, William, as a match for Joan. They played together as children. I would seek your blessing on such a marriage if the proposed arrangement with Gascony no longer pleases you.'

'William?'

The Earl of Salisbury is his greatest ally and friend. Where would he be without him? His thoughts are plainly read: *oh why not, if that is what he wants.*

He nods his head in silent assent.

The Earl tries to hide his delight. He has never mentioned this private ambition to anyone until now. See how life rewards a patient man.

The king returns to his own gloomy thoughts; they are all about money and how much he owes because of men like Albret.

Salisbury, on the other hand, has a bounce in his step, he is one step closer to royalty.

* * *

The nursery is empty. The infant Lionel is with his mother, Bella will be off somewhere listening to the scullery maids' gossip, Jeanette trailing along behind her like a puppy. Joan seems relieved to finally find herself alone. She goes to the canopied bed she shares with Bella, reaches beneath it and pulls out the oak chest she brought with her from England. The key to it is in a locket that she wears around her neck. She unlocks it and the lid creaks open.

Inside there are only old dresses, mostly velvets and brocades. She rummages through and finds what she is looking for at the very bottom. It is a man's tunic; I recognize it immediately for it once belonged to me. She holds it to her face to breathe in the scent and then she curls on the bed, her knees drawn up to her chest, and clutches it to her with both hands.

I listen to the gentle sound of her breathing.

'Oh papa,' she murmurs, 'why did you have to die?'

I am startled to hear her say it, of course. But that is the truth of grief, isn't it, it is not just loss, it is anger as well, yet it seems so unreasonable to get angry with the dead. And how can I answer her?

I could not help it, precious. But I am still here now, can't you feel it?

'I hate them,' she whispers. 'Perhaps not Bella, though I wish she wouldn't talk so. And I am sure the queen is gentle, though she is much preoccupied. But they're not my family, not really, are they? Why did Mother send me away like this, why hasn't she asked for me to come home?'

It is cold in here. The servants have let the fire go out, and they will not light another until evening now. I want to throw a cloak or a blanket over her to keep her warm.

'What shall I do about Thomas?' she says.

Thomas Holand. If I were alive, what would I tell you to do? I do not trust him, my sweet. I would counsel you to forget about him. No one can hold you to this marriage. But you will not do that, will you? Are you in love with Holand for himself, or in love with the idea of love itself?

Or was it just that you were afraid of being married to Gascony?

She sucks her thumb as she did as a child. I think she is about to fall asleep there on the coverlet but then she hears Bella and Jeanette clattering up the stairs and by the time they come running into the nursery the tunic is back in its chest and Joan sits demure on the edge of the bed, smiling as she always does, composed as she always is.

21.

Saint Bavo's Abbey

Joan is again alone and at her prayers. That she is allowed to roam with just an ancient Flemish nurse to chaperone her is unforgiveable, even if it is only the chapel. But this is a state of affairs we find ourselves in the royal court in Ghent, with the king so preoccupied. The queen has a new infant and her own children to worry for and the Countess of Salisbury has a new lover. Lady Saint Omer is too busy ingratiating herself with the Queen.

And Joan, because she is sweet in temperament and agreeable, they all think she will not cause trouble. Well, she is not causing trouble; she is merely in love but that is the same thing for a young woman of royal blood.

She hears the soft opening and closing of the heavy oak door. She knows it is him and she smiles. There is the creak of his leather boots and jerkin as he kneels down beside her.

Her eyes fly open. 'Thomas!'

He puts a finger to her lips. Her maid sleeps by the door, she is ancient, half blind and half mad.

I see hunger in Joan's eyes, calculation in his. She puts her hand on his hand; it is small and cold. She does not have time to ask the question, he already knows what it is she wants to know, and he shakes his head.

'The time is not right,' he says, and she takes her hand away.

'You said you would approach the king after the summer!'

'If the campaign went well. It went badly, and he is in a dire mood.'

'So when can we be done with this charade?'

'When I come back from Prussia.'

'... What? Prussia?'

Again, he puts a finger to her lips, looking over his shoulder at the old lady. 'The Pope has called for soldiers to assist his German knights in the holy crusade against the pagans in the east. I have received dispensation from the king for six months. It will raise my standing with the king immeasurably and when I return I know he will be better disposed towards our petition. Timing is everything.'

Her thin shoulders sag. Love is like a broadsword, Thomas Holand; you should never take it from its sheath unless you intend to use it.

'Six months,' she murmurs.

The ancient maidservant snorts and shudders in her sleep. Holand is startled, thinking she is about to wake. He kisses her cheek. She turns her face towards him for a proper kiss but he is already on his feet, ready to leave. 'Have courage,' he says. 'Soon we will be together.'

Her knuckles are white around the *prie-dieu*. He steps away, then turns and comes back. This time he kisses her hard on the lips and they cling to each other, two ardent souls drowning in their circumstance. For a while they hold each other, on their knees, desperate. But then he pushes her away again, and hurries out; he is off to glory, to wars, to choices.

My daughter will just be here.

I hope the heathen rip him limb from limb and eat his liver, raw.

* * *

And so Edward's adventure in the Low Countries comes to nothing. The bankers are happy, at least. Edward is enormously in debt, and now he has to pay Salisbury's ransom as well. He secured his release with promises and assurances, which are the only currencies that do not require monthly interest.

He returns to England with his royal house and his knights and leaves the common soldier to do what he can.

Rich kings may show gratitude; poor ones make it your fault.

22.

Westminster

Joan enters Margaret's royal apartments hoping for a splendid homecoming but fearing the worst. We always get what we are afraid of. Her mother stands with her hands before her, like a dancing teacher watching for a misstep.

Is this the woman I married? This person cannot be her, so stiff and formal. Meg, this is our little girl! Are you not excited to see her home at last?

John runs across the mats and embraces his sister with enthusiasm, shouting her name. Now this is more like a homecoming. Margaret merely pats her on the back as they embrace; she hardly bends at the waist, it is as if there is a broadsword down the back of her dress restricting her spine and making her afraid to move because of the sharp edges.

Joan is shown to her rooms by a maidservant called Beatrice, she was her nurse as a child and she hovers and grins and is so glad to see her returned she is almost hopping from one foot to the other. She chatters on about all that has happened since she has been gone, and Joan must wonder where her mother is, and why she is not there doing the hopping and chatting.

And where is she? I will tell you where she is. Joan is no sooner settled back in than Margaret is back at her ledgers and correspondence, locked away with her clerks and her attorneys.

John becomes Joan's shadow and follows her everywhere. My daughter has a family and a home once more. But it seems to me that somehow she has not only lost a father, she has lost her mother as well.

Near Balga, Prussia

The buzzing of flies. Holand rides through what remains of a village, bodies or what is left of bodies lying among the burned ruins. It is filled with the stink of smoke and two-day-old corpses. You would think he would be accustomed to this by now but by the look on his face I can see that he is not.

The Pope has called this a Crusade, but he has not found much that he thinks God would be pleased with. He climbs down from his *destrier* and kicks among the still warm ashes, turns over a black and blistered timber with the heel of his boot. He sees something glinting among the ashes and bends down to pick it up. It is still warm, he can feel the heat through his gloves. It is a crucifix; the metal has melted in the fire but its shape is still recognizable.

He hears riders, the ground shakes under the thunder of hooves. He sees them approach, they are wearing the red cross surcoats of fellow crusaders. His own men watch them approach, leave their swords in their scabbards.

The commander reins in his horse in front of him. He wears expensive armour, and his standard and shield is a gold lion on a blue shield, a French noble house.

'Your work?' Holand says to him, indicating the corpses and smouldering ruins.

He shakes his head. 'Our German friends,' he says.

'My name is Sir Thomas Holand. I am a knight of Edward, King of England and France.'

The Frenchman smiles. 'Well of England perhaps. I am Raoul de Brienne, my father is the Count of Eu and the Constable of France.' He looks around, at the dead women and children and the black pools of dry blood. 'This is not the Crusade I had imagined.'

'Nor I.'

'These Germans. They wear the cross but they are the most godless bastards I ever met.'

'Our presence here is a sham and a disgrace.'

'If that is what you think also, then we shall get along well. I have wine. Would you like to drink some with me? This war makes me thirsty.'

'I never say no to a man with wine.'

'My camp is just a mile over there. You and your men might rest there for the night.'

'I would like that very much.'

'Good. Follow me then.' He wrinkles his nose. 'What a stink. You are a man of honour, Thomas?'

'I have always liked to think so.'

'Good. There are not many left east of Paris.'

Holand gets back on his horse and follows the Comte d'Eu into his camp. They drink and talk through the night and fall asleep drunk, snoring like stable hands, just before dawn. A casual observer coming upon them in the morning might not think them quite the fine gentlemen they purport to be.

They share a breakfast of bread and stale cheese and Holand thanks the count for his hospitality and rides away, to continue his skirmish into the wasteland beyond the Balga fort.

He does not realise then that this chance encounter has just changed the course of his life forever.

23.

'I have wonderful news,' Margaret tells Joan one night after supper. Joan is wearing the face she has adopted since she was first sent to France; it requires the imitation of a smile set in an expression of benign amity. She looks like a portrait of herself. Her expression is always pleasant but appears to me as if it has been painted on.

'What is the news?'

'I have arranged a match for you. William, the Earl of Salisbury's boy. You remember him? You played together often when you were children.'

The silence drags. It is painful to watch them sitting like this.

Finally Margaret speaks. 'The Earl is one of the most powerful and wealthy men in England, and William is his heir. You will be the next Countess of Salisbury!'

Joan peers through the cracks in the shuttered window, she can tell that it has started to snow. A servant thinks she is disapproving and hurries to fasten the latch tighter, but the wood has swollen with damp and refuses to shut properly.

It seems there is an insubordinate grain running through it.

'Are you pleased?'

'I cannot marry William.'

They just stare at each other. The tension in the room makes even a ghost feel uncomfortable. Who will speak first?

'You cannot? But it is a wonderful match.'

'Yes, it is, but I will not. I cannot.'

Margaret breaks. She leaps to her feet, her hands bunched in fists at her sides. She has never heard the like of this. I believe this last ten years of being alone, bearing the burdens, have wearied her and embittered her more than anyone knows. Everything she has done, she has done for her children, that they might know the security she never has. They will not be widowed and left poor as she was; they will not be betrayed by their king; they will not be arrested and held prisoner in their own homes.

'I did not ask what you wanted! I told you what has been arranged. The contract is ready to be signed.' When Joan does not respond she repeats it again: 'It is a wonderful match.'

Joan leaves her hands folded in her lap, like gloves, and says nothing. Her passivity is unbearable to my wife.

'You will marry William, as I say!'

'I will not,' Joan says again, so softly Margaret can scarce hear her over the rushing of the wind outside the walls.

She stands over her. 'You do not have a choice in this. Do you understand?'

Joan stares into the fire. 'I cannot.'

'Cannot? What do you mean, cannot?'

'I am already married.'

This declaration is so unexpected, Margaret laughs. She waits for Joan to clarify. Joan is not inclined to do so and so Margaret must wrest it out of her.

Inch by inch, yard by unbearable yard, she draws out the truth of it; she tells her she is wed to Sir Thomas Holand, a knight in service of the king and second son of Sir John Holand, and that they have pledged their troth to each other in front of witnesses.

Margaret sits down hard. She looks ghastly, all the blood has drained from her face. I think she might faint and my wife is not a woman taken to weakness. I never saw her even cry during our marriage, swooning was not in her nature, or her family's.

She sits in stunned silence for even longer than I can bear. I urge one of them to say something. Finally, of course, it is Margaret who does so: 'I don't believe you.'

'It is true.'

'You have invented this.'

'The marriage has been consummated.'

This appalling admission removes the broadsword from my wife's back. She cries out as if it has instead entered her spine between the shoulders.

Joan has always been so placid, so compliant, and so, like many others, Margaret has misjudged our Joan completely, mistaken her gentle smile and quiet manners for docility, instead of the iron will it conceals. They did not see what I have seen all these past years spent in her private company; Joan is not cruel or ambitious; she merely knows what she wants when it appears.

'I have the bed sheet with me to prove it,' Joan adds. Margaret stands, sits, stands again. She does not know what to do with herself. Still little Joan sits there, unmoving, delivering her news with startling equanimity.

'How could you do such a thing? We are your family.'

'I love him.'

'You are thirteen years old! What has love to do with anything?'

'Perhaps you should ask papa.'

'Your father is dead.'

'But not forgotten, surely?'

'How dare you!'

'He married for love. Didn't you?'

I would very much like to hear the answer to this, but Margaret finds it convenient not to answer. 'That is not the point here,' she says. 'If this gentleman loves you as you say, why did he marry you in secret? Could he not court you openly and beg my permission for this first?'

'He is a Lancaster. Would you have even considered him?'

Margaret wants to ask the questions, she does not want to answer them. 'That is the reason you go behind my back?'

'Say it. You would never have agreed, would you?'

'No.'

'Because he's a Holand!'

'Because he's a fortune hunter.'

'He loves me!'

'Do you not understand? May God bless us, but if anything should happen to your brother, then you will be one of the wealthiest heiresses in all England. Do you think he doesn't know that?'

'Is that all you can think about? Is that what you were thinking when you married father?'

Well, who would have thought Joan possessed such a sharp tongue, and a sharper wit. Not my wife, certainly. She is rendered speechless for the moment by what her daughter has dared say. I am less surprised for I have seen her secret looks and heard her private prayers these ten years and I know the Joan that the world does not see.

Margaret feels a strange shiver down her spine. It is me, trying to get her attention, remind her to heal this, not make it worse. But she does not know how.

If I were alive I am sure I would have been more sympathetic. You should remember that Margaret was once the Thomas Holand in our marriage; she had no money, her family were not particularly high-born or influential and she was four years older than me. Perhaps this guilty knowledge is what drives her.

Because Holand, if it were not for his father's traitor stink, is not an impossible union.

'I don't understand how this could have happened,' Margaret is saying. 'Where were Lady Salisbury and Lady Saint Omer when this was happening?'

Joan does not answer which only infuriates my Margaret more.

'This man may be a knight but he does not behave like one. He has his father's blood it seems.'

Joan's cheeks flush bronze at this insult but still she keeps her eyes on the floor. But not from shame, if that is what you are thinking. If you look closely at her lips and her eyes they will tell you she is furious.

'How did he arrange this?'

'I helped him do it.'

'How could you have helped him, you are thirteen years old!'

'I am not stupid.'

'No, you are naïve and headstrong! Do you realise what you have done? The king will be furious, he will see it that you have betrayed your country and disregarded your duty.'

Joan sits like stone.

'You will marry William of Salisbury,' Margaret repeats. 'The king has given his blessing to the union, he would never agree to any other match now.'

'He would not give his blessing to this betrothal if he knew I was already married.'

'But you are not already married!'

'In front of witnesses!'

Margaret, breathing hard now, trying to restrain herself. 'This so-called husband. Has he told you where you might live as his wife?'

Joan seems confused by the question. Margaret is right; she has not thought this through. She is, as my wife has pointed out, still a child.

'As a knight bachelor he would never be home. Do you know why? Because he does not have a home. He is a second son, with no estates, no manor house, no legacy. Where is he now?'

'Prussia.'

'Do you even know where Prussia is?'

'He is fighting a Crusade for the Pope!'

'He does it for a reason, Joan. Would he fight for the Pope if he had lands to tend to at home, a manor house with a fire burning in the hearth?'

Joan has no answer for her.

'If you were married, where would you go?'

'I would go with him.'

'On crusade? And where do you think you would sleep? In the barrack room? In a tent in a field? And what about children? Would you take them with you as he trails through some foreign countryside ravaged by war?'

Joan is silent now. All reason is gone; all that is left is defiance. Which one of these two will back down when there is no one to conciliate between them?

'Joan, he wants your dowry and your bloodline. He saw a young and impressionable girl, improperly chaperoned, and seized his opportunity. He thinks if he can make the king agree to this he can bully our family into helping him re-establish his family's fortunes.'

'We are wed in the sight of God.'

'You are the king's cousin, Joan, You were not free to marry at a whim, never mind how ridiculous the choice you made. You cannot forsake your birthright and that is an end to it. You will marry William of Salisbury and be done with this nonsense.'

Joan shakes her head. 'I cannot, I am already married.'

Margaret draws back her hand and slaps our daughter hard across the face. 'You will never ever speak those words again. Do you understand?' She walks out.

Joan stares into the fire, the imprint of her mother's hand emblazoned her cheek, as clear as if it had been branded there. She does not cry. Her face is set, like stone. 'I will not give up Thomas,' she tells the fire. The fire will understand; it burns, burns so bright and white hot.

And some fires will never be put out.

24.

But Joan is neither stone nor fire, not when she is alone. It is Ned who discovers the truth of it when he finds her, curled in a window seat in a quiet nook of the palace, crying. He hears a mewing and thinks it is a cat, injured or trapped. He is astonished to find that it is Joan, for he has never seen her weep before, did not even think she was capable of it. She wipes her face with the back of her hand when she sees him and turns away, to hide her smudged tears. 'Go away.'

'What's wrong?'

'Nothing, go away.'

Ned is ten years old now, no longer a boy, but still young enough to be awkward. Yet he is a prince, and Joan is the only person in his life who has ever told him to go away. 'Are you crying?'

Well of course she is, her eyes are swollen and red. But it is Ned I feel sorry for. Oh Joan, I know you are hurting but do not be so harsh. Look at this young man's face, can't you see how infatuated he is, how smitten? He cares for you is all. He does not mean to embarrass you.

'Go away!' she shouts at him.

She runs off. In her haste she drops the scarf she is holding, it has the white hart emblem that once was mine. It is the very scarf she has kept under her pillow all these years. Edward picks it up, holds it to his face, there is a trace of her on it. He tucks it into his tunic.

Then he makes his way through the palace gardens to the practice yard where he takes out his pain of this humiliation on the young squires. Having battered all of them to their knees he hurls the wooden sword into a corner of the yard where it clatters against a wall. Now he is not only hurt and bewildered, he is also ashamed of himself.

A good day for all.

25.

Bourne, Lincolnshire

'Thomas will know what to do.'

How many times did I hear my wife say that? She refers not to our man Holand but to Thomas Wake, her brother. She relies on him too much, if you want my opinion, treats him like some sort of oracle when he is just a man like any other. Only much less so.

What he has is a happy talent for setting his opinions to the prevailing breeze, like a good sea captain. He was once a favoured son-in-law of the Earl of Lancaster, the one that Holand's father so grievously betrayed, and then his sister married me.

I have delayed telling you this; I was one of the judges that ordered Lancaster executed after Boroughbridge. My brother the king thought he should keep my loyalties better if I had a hand in Lancaster's death and let me tell you now: he was right.

So Wake had to overlook this when his sister took me into their family. It was more convenient for the Holands to shoulder the entire blame. Looking deeper into the affair would have been inconvenient.

He had also found it helpful to distance himself from his father-in-law's rebellion against my brother the king, supported Isabella while she was popular, and then saw the wind change and got himself to France after my execution.

You see, right and wrong, it is not set in stone. It is like clay and can be moulded to the present moment.

Thomas will know what to do.

I heard her say this a score of times and I think she always said it to irritate me. Where was his infallible judgment when he supported the Parliamentary council in defying Edward's demands for money while he was in the Low Countries? If you wonder why he looks so pale and thin this evening, it is because he has just been released from the Tower. It is fortunate the king did not take his head as well, like his father would have done. Perhaps he will think twice before going up against the Crown a second time.

He sits here now, savours his wine, and consults his resources of inner wisdom. It does not take long. Then he says that my daughter must do as she is told.

'I have told her that,' Margaret says. 'She refuses to listen.'

'It does not matter if she chooses not to listen.' He has a servant pour him more wine. 'Do you think her story is true?'

'Oh yes, it's true.'

'How can you be so sure?'

She does not want to tell him about the bed sheet, which she has now seen with her own eyes. She took it from her and burned it, two of her servants held Joan down while she did it. Margaret has a scratch on the back of her hand and another on her cheek for her pains. It looks like she has been clawed by a cellar cat.

'I am just sure. Take my word for it, brother.'

'The marriage to Salisbury must go ahead.'

'Do we tell the earl about Holand?'

Wake is not so dense that he would try and hide such a thing from the Earl of Salisbury. 'If we don't, Joan will. But why would she make such a marriage in the first place?'

'She says she is in love with him.'

'She is thirteen years old, what does she know of love? We cannot be held to ransom by some foolish girl's infatuation. It is clear to me that Holand coerced her. He didn't ...?'

Here we are, back to the matter of the sheet again. Another terse nod from Margaret.

'But she is just a child! What was he thinking?'

'We know what he was thinking! However, though she is young she is no longer a child.'

Wake shakes his head in astonishment. Joan must have seemed to them once a tractable daughter and niece. Who could have foreseen this?

'We should inform the earl immediately then.'

'He is not going to like it.'

'I do not care for it much myself.'

The wine flagon is empty, and Wake tells the servant to fetch more. I sympathise with him in this at least. Where would we all be without wine in the living years? I think sometimes that it was only good brandy wine that made the whole experience bearable.

26.

Bisham.

The earl is settled by the fire with a goblet of brandy wine, listens as Margaret tells her story, halting now and then for a sobbing breath. The earl is in his element here, a strong and calming presence while Wake is as twitchy as a sparrow in the garden.

When she has finished he says nothing; instead consults the burning logs in the hearth for long minutes. Finally, he pronounces judgment: 'We will of course have to revise the contract.'

Wake and my wife look at each other. There is relief, mixed with trepidation. What he means, of course, is that he now intends to take advantage of his better bargaining position, but he does not intend to cancel the contract altogether.

'There is greater risk to us now,' he explains, 'so you will need to increase her dowry substantially.'

'What was the king doing while this was happening?' Margaret says. 'I had hoped my daughter would have been better watched.'

Not the most politic thing to say as the Earl's wife was supposed to be one of the watchers. 'I imagine the war must have occupied the king's mind some of the time,' the earl answers with a wry smile at Wake, who feels obliged to smile back. 'It is not always easy, in a foreign place, when the court is constantly on the move, to see to a young lady's welfare.'

'I had expected better.'

'I sympathise with your predicament but what is done is done.'

Edward has let our family down once more and this is the only apology that my wife will ever get. Yes, the king did sign your husband's death warrant; yes, he did allow your daughter to marry into a family you utterly despise.

But what is done is done.

'But this marriage she has made with Thomas Holand is preposterous,' Wake says. 'Can we not apply to the ecclesiastical courts to have it annulled?'

'Will your daughter repudiate the marriage?' the earl asks Margaret.

Margaret looks at the floor and shakes her head.

'Then there is little chance of success.'

'If God smiles on us,' Wake says, 'he will meet a suitable end on this miserable crusade he has joined.'

The earl stiffens at this. 'I have fought alongside Sir Thomas Holand on the Scots border and in France. He is a good man and a true one. I would not have any ill befall him and besides, a crusade in service of the Church is never miserable.'

Rebuked, Wake lapses into a sullen silence. Though dead, I still enjoy moments like this.

'What shall we do?' Margaret says.

'I know Thomas well. Let me talk to him. I will resolve the matter with him amicably.'

'But we don't know when he will be back from Prussia.'

'He has applied to the king for a further six months leave of absence, but he will be back in England by the summer, at the very latest, I assure you both. He is ambitious and he will not forego the chance to join the king's next campaign.'

'Edward is going to continue the war against the French?' Wake asks.

'Was there ever a chance that he would not? As for the marriage, we shall proceed once the contract has been redrawn. William and Joan are too young to consummate the marriage so there is no harm in this delay.'

I am relieved to hear someone talking sense at last. Though royal marriages are sometimes contracted from the time children are infants, it is generally recognised that marital intimacy should be deferred until a girl is at least fifteen years old. There are dangers enough to intercourse and pregnancy for even a grown woman.

Still, I notice that Margaret is careful not to meet the earl's eyes. She has not told him about the bed sheet; she has told no one but her brother about that.

'Leave it to me,' the earl assures them, confident that he knows Thomas Holand and he knows the value of money. 'I will take care of everything.'

27.

Westminster

There are few men who sit like this with the king, in private audience. The earl is considered his greatest friend. The truth of it is, he gambled all for Edward once. It happened six months after I met my dismal end at the hands of a murderous night soil collector - yes, still bitter about that - when the present earl was merely William of Montacute. At great personal risk he found his way inside Nottingham Castle with a handful of other conspirators and there met with the young king. With his leave they then found that black-bearded bastard Mortimer and after a short brawl took him prisoner.

If he had failed it would have led William to the gallows or worse; instead, it won Edward the throne from his mother and had Mortimer on the gallows instead. William came out of the affair with the king's undying gratitude. Fifteen years ago, the man born as William of Montacute was not even a knight and now he is an earl with the king's ear.

He and Edward are cloistered with brandy wine and a roaring log fire, the king's dogs snoring on the rugs, candles throwing long shadows on the tapestries. They discuss the proposed summer campaign against France and the payment of the earl's ransom, which was agreed on as part of the truce Edward signed at Espléchin in September. The figure is exorbitant and includes a separate clause forbidding Salisbury to ever take up arms in France again. At the time Edward had no choice but to agree.

The talk moves on to the progress of the Pope's crusade against the Tartars in the east but finally even Edward tires of talking about politics.

'So, when is your son's marriage?' he asks Salisbury.

'The contract has been prepared. We shall have the betrothal on the Feast of Saint Agnes and the wedding the following Sunday.'

'It is a good match. It will be a joyous occasion.'

A tight smile from the earl.

'There is something amiss?' the king asks him.

'Your Grace, the lady Joan is amiss'

'Joan?'

'May I enquire how closely she was chaperoned in Flanders, your grace?'

'You should ask your lady wife. She and Lady Saint Omer were charged with her comforts and her safety.'

'My wife swears to me she applied herself to the task diligently, but I fear she may not have always given her duties her full attention.'

Edward leans in, perturbed. 'What has happened?'

'Joan claims that while she was in Ghent she secretly married one of your knights, Sir Thomas Holand.'

'This is true?'

'Joan says it is. When Sir Thomas returns from Prussia we shall have to find out more.'

'But why would he do such a thing?'

It is not a question that requires an answer. It is obvious to both of them, surely.

'What will you do?' Edward asks.

'Her marriage to my son, William, will go ahead as planned. I will come to a mutually beneficial arrangement with Sir Thomas upon his return. But I thought you should know of this ... indiscretion.'

Edward strokes his beard. He even smiles a little. 'The rogue! However did he manage such a thing?'

'He is young and ambitious. He has always shown exceptional boldness and resource on the battlefield.'

'Not only on the battlefield, it seems.'

'If he comes back from the Crusade, you should promote him. Such aggression and initiative begs a position of command.'

'I will consider it. I shall have to show him my displeasure first, it is expected.'

The earl's turn to smile. 'Of course.'

They pour more wine. The talk drifts back to politics and taking the French throne.

With Edward it always does.

*   *   *

My Joan has lost weight. I fear a draught under the door would blow her over. Her skin is so pale she appears almost translucent. Does she ever eat? Margaret, pay attention to our daughter and less to young John. John is healthy and plump and each of his buttocks could survive a long, hard winter without further sustenance.

My former wife regards our daughter with steely gaze. 'The betrothal will take place Sunday.'

Joan does not answer.

'Did you hear me?'

'But I am already married.'

'You were coerced!'

'I love Sir Thomas and gave him my troth willingly.'

'Enough of this nonsense, you will do as I say. If you do not there are other oaths you can take. I can arrange it with the abbess at Godstow.'

'You would not!'

A look passes between them. Once she would not; these days I believe that Margaret is capable of anything.

I never saw this in Margaret in life. Something must have happened to her when they took my head; it is as if she lost hers.

'You will do as I say,' Margaret repeats.

What else can Joan do? I put a hand on her shoulder and she shivers. There is no one to stand for her and she is alone. I am the only one who cares, and I am not here in these living years.

And so to a cold day in February, the feast day of Saint Agnes, the good Christian girl who was beheaded by the Romans. The Wakes and what is left of my little family gather at the Great Hall in Bisham for the betrothal. There is a gaggle of Salisbury girls, a number of fine lords and their wives, and in the midst of this melee my Joan, in a silk gown of ivory and pale blue, holding the hand of a bewildered-looking boy. Poor William was one of Joan's playmates when they were children and does not recognise this rather worldly and remote young girl they have told him will be his wife.

The canon signals for them to step forward and William pledges his troth to her in a shaking, reedy voice. When it is Joan's turn she does the same, or we all think so, I see her lips move and perhaps William and the canon hear what she says but no one else does. All I can hear is a dog barking a mile away in the distance.

When it is done Will embraces her and she just stands there, stiff as a statue. The congregation think she is either frightened or shy, but that is not the reason. Really, William might have received a warmer response if he had put his arms around the marble statue of the virgin in her shrine.

28.

Warmia

What a place. A wasteland, even in the summer. The ground under the horses' hooves is spongy and wet. Otto rides into the camp through the smudge of Crusader fires; even their German allies look like cutthroats, men with black eyes and brown teeth, but the red crosses on their surcoats somehow make their rapes and murders holy. Otto is heartily sick of this campaign.

He leads his horse past wagons laden with hardbread and salted beef. He sees the Holand standard next to a pavilion with walls of sailcloth. He steps inside.

Our Holand is just returned from a three-day skirmish into the plain. He and his brother have not seen each other for weeks and they embrace. Holand has his boy fetch Otto wine while his squire continues the job of removing his armour. There is a gash in his scalp some days old and it has been left untended and is crusted with dried blood. Otto regards him with a younger brother's admiration. 'Do you have to be at the front of every fight?'

He is afraid for him though I could have told him: it is not his time. How much easier it would go on Joan if it were. But there is no shadow following him, and I am well practised in seeing these anomalies now.

'I came here to further my career. I will not do that sitting in a tent.' Another squire is soon at hand with a bowl and wet cloth and starts to soak the wound. His hair is matted with blood.

"You think to make yourself the bravest soldier in the king's army.'

'What other choice do I have?'

'You will need the barber to cut off that hair and stitch the wound closed.'

Holand pours more wine from a flask into a mazer and hands it to his brother. He takes a deep draught of it himself and wipes his beard with the back of a grimy hand.

'There are men with deeper wounds than this. I shall wait until the man is less busy.'

The squire unties the fastenings on Holand's mail shirt, helps him drag off the boiled leather jerkin underneath. Holand winces and stretches his aching back.

'This is not a crusade,' Otto says. 'It is butchery.'

'The Pope says it is holy.'

'You know what I think of the Pope.'

'I do, so keep your voice down. But you did not ride all the way out here to talk about the crusade. You have bad news, it is written all over your face.' He shoves his squire away, irritated with his fussing and his clumsy fingers.

'It is Joan.'

'Joan? She is well?'

'She is well, yes. But she is also married.'

Holand stares at his brother. For a long time, he does not speak.

'I did not want to be the one to tell you this, but better you heard it from me than in an alehouse.'

'This is not possible. She is married to me.'

Otto says nothing. They both know the marriage is only valid if Joan says it is, and even then it must be proved.

'Who is it? Not the Gascon?'

'Salisbury's son.'

'He's a child.'

'So is she.'

Holand drains the mazer, refills it, drains it a second time. 'When?'

'These two months past.'

I watch Holand's face, as he imagines the possibilities. 'She raised no objections?'

'I know none of the details of the matter.'

'How did you discover this?'

'Two knights just out from England, John Cheever and Henry Falconer. They told it as they would tell any news. They did not think it was remarkable and I questioned them only as far as I could without raising their suspicions.'

Holand lowers his head. He looks stricken.

'What will you do?'

'I am sworn to service here till the end of summer. Then I will return to England and see what may be done.'

'Just give it up, Thomas. There is no harm done.'

The look on Holand's face lets his brother know what he thinks of that. He reaches for the wine flask. ''I think we should get drunk tonight, little brother.'

Little brother: Otto is the size of a barn. He grins and holds out his own mazer for wine. It is something the Holand boys do passingly well, drink.

Holand proposes a toast. 'To Joan. To not giving up.'

Otto does not join in the toast, but he drinks anyway. The wind whips the flaps of the tent, the coals glow in the brazier, a wolf howls somewhere on the plain. England, and Joan, seem so very far away.

29.

And so to Westminster Abbey and the towering splendour of Saint Stephen's chapel. Everyone is here, the entire court of England has gathered for the ceremony. It is a dull day, there is little to recommend these glorious stained-glass windows above us when the sun refuses to appear. Jewels glitter in the glow of candles and torches, silks rustle on the cold flags, the chapel is dense with incense from the silver thuribles.

Joan's hair cascades down her shoulders for the last time; from tomorrow she must wear it in the coif of a married woman. Her wedding dress is satin and gold with a tightly fitting upper bodice and buttoned sleeves from which hung long decorative pieces; it has a low waist and a flowing skirt after the prevailing fashion. There are pearls and amethysts in her hair. She looks glorious, and utterly miserable.

The Earl's brother, the Bishop of Ely, performs the ceremony.

See how it is done.

See the little girl who once clung to me with her hot wet tears on my neck stand at the altar of this great chapel, shivering with humiliation.

See the woman I loved so in life standing there with her brother and the Earl of Salisbury offering her no comfort.

See the boy, William, grinning at everyone in happiness and confusion. And why not? Life is given him on a trencher with lashings of all that he wants.

See the king watching on, lending his approval to this travesty.

But see here at the back, almost obscured by a pillar, a dark-haired prince, his expression unreadable. What goes on behind those big black eyes?

Then it is over. The guests bear down on the heir of Salisbury and his new wife, and she is lost among them, swept up in their royal enthusiasms. Even I cannot find a way among them.

PART 3

30.

August 1341

A good crossing, an easy crossing; it is late summer, and Thomas Holand has been gone from England these four years, since that day he set out with the King's army, bound for Gravensteen. He and Otto have had enough of crusades. They regard the white chalk cliffs of Sussex in the distance as their cog churns through these grey swells, even on blue days the English sea makes the guts heave. 'What will you do when you get back?' Otto asks him.

'I shall claim my wife.'

'Still that madness?'

'It is not madness, you will see. I will press my claim with the king and he must surely listen. I am resolved to it.'

'She is married now, Thomas.'

'Yes, she is. To me.'

'What will I tell our mother when I see her?'

'Tell her nothing. I will tell her myself, when the time is right.'

And so the next day Otto rides out of Dover bound for Broughton Hall while our Holand heads for London and rents a room at an inn in the shadow of the great spire of Saint Paul's. No one knows him here and he needs to drink some good English ale to recover his spirits. Even the stink of this city is better than the stench of blood and smoke and corpse fires. He makes his round of the taverns and listens to the gossip; the Queen is with child again, the Earl of Salisbury is back in France trying to settle his ransom, when he asks they tell him the negotiations have dragged on now for over a year.

He gets heartily drunk and has his fill of beef pies and ribaldry. Finally, he thinks he is ready to return to Windsor to announce himself and resume life as a knight in the king's service.

But first he has one more thing to do. He must ride to Bourne and claim his wife.

31.

Bourne, Lincolnshire

'**I** wish to see my wife.'

There he stands, proud and determined, wearing the king's velvet, one hand on his sword. Margaret has told her servants she will attend him in the great hall but has kept two men at arms standing by as precaution. 'I did not know you had a wife, Sir Thomas.'

'I have come to claim Joan. She has told you what took place between us, that we pledged our troth?'

'I am not sure what you mean.'

'Your daughter and I exchanged vows in Ghent in April last year.'

'She has said nothing of this to us. I can only imagine this is either a bald lie or she has been coerced. She is still only fourteen years old.'

For a moment I see the doubt on his face. But only for a moment; something in my wife's manner persuades him that Joan has told her of the marriage. 'I have to see my wife!'

The two guards step in front of the door. As if that would stop him! A seasoned soldier like Holand would carve these two up and serve them as delicacies for supper.

But Holand must control his temper, he knows this. 'I have to see my wife,' he repeats.

'You do not have a wife.'

He strides past her towards the two guards, though he leaves his sword in its scabbard. Even so, her soldiers look alarmed. They are only boys.

He calls up the stairs. 'Joan!'

'Sir Thomas, this is my home! I ask you to desist.'

He seems distraught. Perhaps we were wrong about him, Margaret, let him see her, for just a moment, if only for her sake.

The guards reach for their weapons. This will not do. They hesitate, their swords halfway out of their scabbards.

There is a moment when I think - when Margaret thinks - that he will reach for his own sword, cut down the guards and leap up the stairs to find her. Thankfully, he does not do it, does not want their blood on his hands and so he takes a step back, looks furiously at Margaret. 'I will not relinquish my claim.'

'You have no claim.'

'We shall see what the courts say about that.'

With one last stern look he turns and strides out.

His squire waits in the yard with his horse. But as Holand mounts his palfrey he hears a cry and turns and looks up at the high windows. It is Joan. She shouts something to him but then two of Margaret's ladies pull her back inside and draw the shutters.

For a moment he is torn. He has stormed bigger castles than this, and against worse odds. But what can he do? Slaughtering the bride's household would not sit well with the king or bode well for future amicable relations with the family.

There is nothing to do but set the jaw and ride away.

* * *

'What are we to do?' Margaret says.

Wake shakes his head. 'If only the earl were here.'

'He said he would deal with this. Where is he?'

'He is in France, finalising the negotiations on his ransom. He may be away for months yet. What did you say to Holand?'

'I told him his marriage is not recognized.'

'And what did he say to that?'

'I thought he would do violence.'

'To you?'

'To anyone who stood in his way. He vowed he will pursue his claim in the ecclesiastical courts.'

'Empty words! Courts and lawyers cost money, he cannot afford it. What about Joan?'

'After he had left, I went to her rooms to try and talk to her. She screamed at me, said she will never allow her marriage to William to be consummated, that she would rather spend the rest of her days in a nunnery.'

'A nunnery! After we have spent three thousand pounds on her dowry?'

'Let her scream all she wants. That part of it is two years away at least. She will have forgotten about this Thomas Holand by then.'

'When the earl returns from France he will settle this, don't worry. All Holand wants is the money. Everything will be all right.'

Yes, but what about Joan? I shout at them.

It is all very fine for you and your brother, this bargaining. Fine for the earl. Perhaps even fine for Thomas Holand.

But will it be all right for Joan?

* * *

Margaret frets to her brother that word of Joan's secret betrothal to Sir Thomas Holand will somehow get out, but if people do whisper behind their hands for a time it is soon forgotten, a juicy titbit that has now grown stale. Wake's assessment of Holand's position is correct; he does not have the money to pursue the matter in the courts and neither does his family. He returns home to Bourne and says nothing to his mother of the affair, perhaps because he is too ashamed of it. I cannot read his mind in this and he says nothing to anyone, not even his brother these days.

He soon returns overseas in the king's pay, guarding the king's borders at Bayonne in Brittany; Joan returns to court. Now that Holand is once again safely out of the way she is delivered again to the tender mercies of the Duchess of Salisbury and the company of the young princesses, Bella and Jeanette.

But my Joan is changed. She rarely speaks and only smiles when she is addressed directly. She appears pleasant, mild and pained. Only Bella persists with her, but then Bella does not mind that Joan does not talk, she regards that activity as her own sovereign province.

Joan now has two shadows, one thrown by the summer sun and the other a slip of a dark boy. When he is not at the tilt yards or with the sergeant at arms, he trails her through the gardens or stares with pained longing up at her window. Joan is no more aware of him than the clouds.

He fights for her in every combat, wielding his wooden sword to defend her honour; when he finds the target at the butts he imagines she watches and applauds. I could bleed for him. He is infatuated with a twice married woman.

How hopeless can a boy's dreams be?

32.

Windsor

She sits in a chair facing the garden, in the dark, huddled inside a velvet cloak. The logs are cold in the hearth. A servant edges open the door, she has come to relight the fire, for the summer is passing swiftly away. Joan hears the door creak open and she whips around and tosses the closest thing to hand, a heavy leather-bound book, her Arthurian romances. It batters against the door, which quickly closes again. The servant flees.

What has happened to my gentle Joan? She just sits like this for hours at a time, a look of utter grief on her face.

I do not understand how my wife can do this.

The next day she finally tries to intervene. The door creaks open again and Joan looks around for another missile. Her fingers close around her Book of Hours. Surely you will not hurl a holy book, Joan?

But then she sees it is Margaret.

Joan is not yet to the point where she will hurl the contents of her library at her own mother. 'Aren't you cold?' Margaret asks her.

'Cold?'

The room is like a tomb. Margaret approaches her with some caution, as she would a wild beast.

'What do you care if I am cold?'

'Everything I do is for your benefit, you will see that someday.'

'I hate you.' This is said so softly my wife barely hears her. Margaret turns pale. Even her lips are bloodless.

'Why do you persist with this?' Margaret says.

'If you can ask such a question you will never understand the answer.'

'You are married to William of Salisbury now. You must forget Thomas Holand. If anyone ever asks you about this pledge you made, you will say that you were coerced.'

'I was not coerced, and I will not give him up. I love him.'

'He has gone back to France.'

Nothing.

'Did you hear me? He has gone back to France to rejoin the king on his campaign. You will never see him again, I will not allow it. You must forget this foolishness now.'

Margaret stands over her, Joan just sits, looking the other way; the unbreakable will and the immovable heart. Six months now this has been going on. Who will prevail?

Margaret turns and slams out. Joan still does not move. A single tear tracks down her cheek. Oh, my little girl, you are not alone, I am here. Can you hear me, can you feel me?

Can you?

* * *

Ned takes the hood off the peregrine falcon on his arm, lets it fly. It soars high on the currents, circling, while the hounds below flush out their prey. A heron flaps panicked from the rushes and the falcon drops its wings and dives. There is an explosion of feathers as it strikes and the dogs bay and plunge into the shallows for the kill. Ned raises his arm and the falcon glides back to him.

'A beautiful kill,' Edward says, spurring his horse alongside his son.

Ned shrugs and says nothing.

'What is it Ned?'

Another shrug.

'Come on, out with it. Not like you to keep things to yourself.'

'Why could I not have married Joan?'

'Marry Joan?' Edward laughs in surprise. His son never fails to amaze. 'But you are meant for a foreign princess. You have a duty to your country, I have told you this countless times.'

'So why William? Weren't you going to marry Joan to a Frenchman?'

'His father is my friend. Why would I stand in his way if that is what he wants?'

'I heard she married Thomas Holand.'

Edward puts a hand on the prince's arm. 'How did you hear that?'

'Is it true?'

'No. Well, something happened in Flanders, but there is no validity to it.'

'Is that why you sent him away?'

'I did not send him away. He is a soldier, it is his career.'

'What about Joan?'

'What about her?'

'Does she not mind?'

'She's a woman.'

'So is mother.'

'Your mother is also dutiful wife. She did not have such fanciful notions when she was Joan's age.'

'What will happen to Sir Thomas? What will you do with him when he gets back from France?'

'I am not bound to do anything. Besides he is not coming back from France, he is going to join the Earl of Salisbury on crusade in Granada.'

'He is going to fight the Moors in Spain?'

'Of course. Why would a man refuse such an opportunity, to fight for God and gild his own reputation at the same time?'

Edward takes the hood from his own gyrfalcon and she leaps from his gauntlet and flaps away into the sky. A bird of prey above, wet grass below. Ned's horse shakes its head, fighting the reins. The bird dips its wings and plummets towards its prey. The king applauds.

When Edward looks around again his son is riding away from him. The king has two of his knights follow him. I can read his thoughts by the look on his face: *that boy*. He is thinking that Ned will one day be king of England so why would he want to marry Joan? He believes he is just a boy with fanciful notions and that he will grow out of it. There will be plenty of time to fall in love with women, he thinks, a man doesn't need a marriage for that.

But what he refuses to admit is that fanciful notions stay with us, in other forms, for life. Edward's fanciful notion, instilled in him by his mother as a child, was that he would one day be King of France. It is a notion that will plunge my country into a war for the next hundred years.

Beware the child with a fanciful notion, I say. Take it from the dead, we know a lot about life.

33.

Woodstock Palace

There is sunlight in the garden this morning, daffodils squeeze from new bulbs to butt their heads through the frozen brown earth; ice drips steadily from the eaves as the snow melts. A servant makes his way across the court to the buttery in a threadbare cloak, coughing against the morning chill.

The prince waits, he watches. He spends most of his days at the butts, in the yards. Finally, on his way back to the Great Hall, sweaty and dirty after sword practice with Meistre Henri, he sees her walking in the gardens, her maidservant following a dozen paces behind.

And then she sees him and stops and goes back to the Hall. Not yet fourteen years old, Ned knows how to dismiss a royal servant with a nod of the head and a scowl. To the manner born.

But Anne does not flee entirely, just remains out of sight, watching. Joan turns around and sees Ned following but keeps walking, hands clasped in front of her, bare fingers blue with cold. Frost crunches on the grass underfoot.

'Why so melancholy?' he asks her trotting behind.

'Go away, Ned. You are too young to understand.'

'Cousin, I have not seen you smile since you returned from France.'

'What is there to smile about?'

'Spring is coming. We are young. We are not dead.'

'Sometimes I wish I were dead.'

'But you are a bride, you are married to one of the wealthiest heirs in all England. What is there to be melancholy about?'

'You see? I told you that you were too young to understand.'

'Not so young I cannot hear whispers.'

Joan stops and rounds on him. That famous temper of hers; well, famous to me. Ned, though, is shocked by the fury in gentle Joan's eyes.

'What have you heard?'

'That you are privately wed to Sir Thomas Holand without the King's permission.'

'Who told you this?'

'So, it's true?'

'Who *told* you?'

'I heard my mother and father talking.'

'You were spying on them?'

'I have sharp hearing.'

She steps closer. 'You will not breathe a word of this to anyone.'

'That was brave of you. I would not have thought you bold enough to do such a thing.'

Ned, be careful. Do not taunt her, she will kick you in the shins, I saw her do it to her little brother once and he limped around the house afterwards for days.

'Who else have you told?'

Ned will one day grow tall like his father but as yet he is still a head shorter than her. Even so, he steps right up to her and glares back. 'As if I would ever, ever, do anything to harm you or your reputation!'

Her bottom lip quivers. She turns away.

'Joan?'

'Just go,' she says miserably.

'Has he tried to see you?'

'They will not allow him near.'

'If it were me, a thousand Moors would not keep me away.'

'It is a brave declaration but easier spoken than done. They have declared a truce in France, he will be back soon.'

'Joan, he has already left for Spain.'

'What?'

'The Earl of Derby is leading an expedition to support the King of Castile against the Moors and Salisbury went with him. Thomas was one of the knights who volunteered to join them.'

'But ... but why would he do such a thing?'

'He is a soldier. How else is he to make a living?'

'He should be here,' she says.

Ned watches her walk away and this time he does try to follow her. That my little Joan should inspire such passion in men.

But she is right. Where is Thomas Holand?

Why is he not here?

* * *

Thomas Holand cannot be here because he is at present in a whore house in Toledo. Well I suppose he is just a man, and a man has needs, but I cannot applaud him for it. After several hours enjoying the locals' hospitality, he emerges arm in arm with his brother Otto, who is also drunk. He has found another war, another bed, for what else can he do? Is it unreasonable that I expect more of him?

He reeks of sex and sweat and stale wine. But as he sets off he hears something in the piss-stinking alley behind him, and he turns and peers into the shadows. He thinks there is someone there. There is, he is right. It is me.

But he cannot see me and so he staggers on.

'What am I going to do, Otto? They won't settle, and they won't let me see her.'

'If it were me, I should give up, get myself another wife.'

'I cannot afford a wife, I need a wife who can afford me.'

He stops and leans with his back against a wall. A mist of rain leaves fine droplets in his beard.

'If only the king had not already taken himself to England that day I was wed.'

'The answer would have been just the same. Forget about it, Thomas, there is nothing to be done about it.'

'I cannot forget about it,' Holand says. 'I will never forget about it.'

Is that the truth? If it is, who will win this awful struggle? No one will budge; not Joan, not Margaret, not Holand, not the king.

The two brothers stagger off into a grey and mournful morning. I wish I could love Holand more. By the yard he is a knight; but by the inch he is just a man.

* * *

Back in England I wander the streets, just a gust of wind blowing down a long alley where beggars sleep, their feet protruding from the doorways, sores on their ankles. I am a flurry of fallen leaves that rustle around a dry fountain; I am the shadow that sets the dogs barking.

They have all abandoned my Joan. No one speaks for her anymore; not her mother, not her uncle, certainly not the king. But then the king is popular with his nobles because he makes popular decisions; the Earl of Salisbury is his trusted friend. To spurn him would be an unpopular act.

Thomas Holand plays no part in the King's ambitions so he will be promoted, rewarded, perhaps even praised, but he cannot and will not ever be given precedence over the man who brought down Mortimer.

It is as simple as that.

34.

Granada

Andalusia in high summer and the heat squeezes all the juice from the bones. Salisbury pushes aside the flap of the pavilion where they have brought the wounded after their latest skirmish with the Moors. Men lie screaming for their mothers on rough cots or on the ground, flies crawling over their bloodied bandages. Dear Holy God it stinks in here.

I thank God I never experienced this. I do not know how a man ever stands this.

I follow the earl inside anyway. Holand lies silent on a cot, his head swathed in filthy bandages. I wonder what Salisbury is thinking. When the herald brought him news that Sir Thomas and his men had been ambushed did he think: well that's a problem less? Somehow, I think not. The Earl of Salisbury is an honourable man and he would rather solve this problem his own way and not have God intervene on his behalf.

His worries would be halved if Holand's wound had been mortal, but he does not appear at all bitter as he lays a hand on his man's shoulder. 'How are you, Thomas?'

Holand's Adam's apple bobs in his throat. It must be a struggle even to breathe in this miasma of filth and heat, but he has to bear great pain as well. 'How bad it is, my lord?'

'The surgeon has not told you? The blow took your left eye.'

Holand tries to talk but he has no spit left to moisten his mouth. The earl holds out his hand for the water skin and dribbles a little between Holand's parched lips. 'So shall I be as ugly as you now?' Holand says to him.

A gruff laugh from the earl. Sometimes, seeing them together like this, I imagine that Salisbury would have married one of his own daughters to him if only the Holands had money. They like each other and are also much alike. After all, it was just fifteen years ago the earl was a yeoman, a lesser rank than Holand is now. They both know much about war and luck and naked ambition.

'I always thought the eye patch made me look handsome,' the earl says.

'Whoever told you that? I should have him flogged.'

Salisbury leans closer. He nods to his lieutenant, indicates he should leave. The earl has not planned this moment, but I know how he thinks, he is always strategic and can think on his feet.

He likes Holand, but now he must be practical. He has him at a disadvantage; Holand is in great pain and he cannot see. Salisbury remembers the pain of his own wound when he received it, and perhaps this figures in his calculation. Also, he knows the surgeon has given him laudanum.

There has never been a better time. 'We should talk, Thomas.'

'I had wondered why we have not spoken before. Is my wound that bad?'

'If it was, we should not need to talk at all.'

'I am heartened to hear you put it so baldly.'

'It is about Joan.'

'You mean my wife. You know that Joan of Woodstock and I are legally wed.'

The earl sighs, which could mean anything. Holand cannot see his expression because of all the bloody bandages.

'I am sorry about your plans for your son. But my claim is legitimate, and I intend to pursue it.' Holand's hands are clenched into fists at his sides, it pains him to talk. I understate it; in truth, he is panting in agony.

'Lawyers are expensive, Thomas. Do you have that sort of money?'

'I will find the money somehow.'

'Surely we can make some better accommodation? I am a wealthy man.'

Holand says nothing for a long time. I believe the earl is encouraged by his silence.

Finally: 'I love her.'

'Love? Come, Thomas, you are just bargaining on your price now, surely?'

Another silence, accompanied by the groaning of dying men.

'What do you suggest?'

Salisbury grips his shoulder like a true comrade in arms. 'How much does love cost, Thomas?' He brushes a fly from the bandages.

'It costs a very great deal.'

'Give me a figure.'

Holand gives him a figure and it is, indeed, a very great deal. They haggle. Holand exhausts himself in the negotiation but by the time Salisbury leaves, they are both satisfied. He promised my wife he would arrange things, and he has.

I hover over Holand all that day and night, wishing him dead. But he doesn't die. He is as tough as boiled leather, this one, especially now he has his price.

I knew it, I knew it all along.

35.

Joan sits in the garden. A fine summer pastime but this is winter and today it is snowing. She will freeze out here for all they care. Snow settles on the hood of her thick, fox-fur cape.

What is she doing out here on her own? She watches the snow settle on the grass, listens to the boatmen call on the river, their voices echoing from the walls of the palace. There is ice on the holly berries, they are bright red, like virgin blood.

It seems to me her virgin blood is the only part of her anyone cares about. No one cares about the rest of her; not her mother, not her uncle, not her king, not the boy she is to marry.

No, wait, this one cares, the dark-haired lad watching from the high castle window. I believe if he could save her, he would. She is his Guineverre, his *donna di scalotta*. But he is just a boy and she has crossed the ford to womanhood and is for now beyond his reach.

She always will be, but try telling the prince that.

The snow falls in gentle whorls, under the lowering sky, the indifference of heaven.

* * *

The king sends heralds to France, to Brabant, to Flanders, to Burgundy, to Hainault and to Scotland to announce a tournament at Windsor. It is to celebrate the establishment of a round table of knights, as there was in the time of Arthur. He is offering safe conduct to the elite of Europe's knights to attend.

It is just politics, of course. The French king cannot rival such a display of pageantry and Edward is hoping to attract more allies to his cause by hosting it. While Edward's father had to be dragged to war, he has to be dragged away from it.

He waits until Salisbury is returned from his crusades against the Moors and his embassy to the King Alfonso of Castile. But once he is safe home, preparations proceed apace. As Marshal of England, Salisbury will play a prominent role in the affair.

When the day arrives, all of England is present for it; the king, the queen, the royal princesses, they have even let the king's mother Isabella out of retirement to attend. The cream of England is here; barons, knights and noblemen, London's foremost citizenry, even some of French Phillip's leading knights have risked his displeasure by accepting Edward's invitation. And for every knight there are six men-at-arms, a dozen pie-sellers and two dozen whores, all of them camped outside the walls.

Bright-coloured pavilions crowd the upper and lower wards of the castle, where a small city has sprung up almost overnight. The air is dense with the smell of cook fires, there is a din of trumpets and shouting and drums.

On the Sunday there is a feast in the Great Hall, which is transformed into a splendour of silks and jewels. The stone walls are covered with hunting tapestries, all vivid greens and browns and blues.

The royal party enter through massive oak-and-bronze doors. Joan is seated on the high table with her mother and the Countess of Salisbury. She loses her customary composure for just a moment when she catches a brief glimpse of Holand as he escorts his mother to her place at one of the lower tables. She even puts a hand to her mouth when she sees the patch he wears over one eye. It should be disfiguring but it only makes him look more dashing, romantic and tough; there is nothing like a war wound, bravely borne, to make a woman melt.

She hopes he will look her way, but he takes care not to glance even once towards the dais. And then he is gone.

36.

A chink of light shines through the shutters. It is not yet dawn. Joan tiptoes out of bed and peers through the window into the court below and hears a familiar voice. She sees a knight in the king's livery come out of the kitchen with a hunk of bread and a mazer of watery ale, an early breakfast.

She gathers a cloak around her shoulders and tiptoes out. She steps over the noblemen and servants sleeping on pallets in the great hall, slips past the guard snoring at the door. It is bitterly cold out and it takes her breath away for the moment. The only light comes from the torches on the iron sconces around the walls.

The wind is thrumming in the banners overhead; a dog stands shivering in the middle of the yard.

'Thomas.'

He turns startled. 'Joan. What are you doing here? Someone will see you, you must go back inside.'

She rushes up to him and throws her arms around his neck and kisses him on the lips. He tries to disentangle himself. It is no use.

'Please,' he whispers.

'What happened?' she says and tries to remove the patch over his eye.

He takes her hand and stops her. 'It is not something you would want to look at.'

'You were wounded!'

'No, the eye patch is just for you. Do I not look handsome in it?'

Is this an attempt at jesting? If it is, it is in poor taste. She tries once again to take away the eye patch, but he catches her wrist. 'No,' he says, serious now. 'It is not pretty.'

'How did this happen?'

'In a war, in a battle. The details of it are not important.'

'They are to me.'

'I do not want to talk of it now. When we have more time.'

'Thomas, I have missed you so. Why have you not tried to see me?'

'You are guarded better than the king.' This is a lie. But it will do, I suppose he thinks, at least for now.

'You did not even try to send word? When I heard you had gone to Spain I thought I should die. Thomas, you are my husband!'

He seems confused by her ardour. Really. 'I tried to get word. I sent a letter. Did you not receive it?'

Another lie. They slip so easily from his lips. The man should have been an ambassador or a priest.

'Thomas, what are we going to do?'

He puts a hand to her lips, glances nervously around. 'You must go back inside, we will talk later.'

'When?'

'When it is safe.'

Is he not going to tell her, this man who would board a French galley bristling with armed men, this man who will ride to Crusades in icy wastelands and boiling Andalusian plains; is he too afraid to tell my Joan what he has done?

She kisses him again, presses herself against him as if she would like to melt into him. He takes her by the shoulders and holds her away from him. 'Not here,' he says.

'Promise me you will not leave Windsor without seeing me.'

'I promise,' he says. By now you will know what I think of his promises. He kisses her back with accomplished ease. 'I promise,' he repeats and sends her scurrying back inside.

He lets out a breath and sags against the wall. Is it because he is afraid of discovery or does his conscience trouble him? I should like to be charitable and think it is his conscience.

The castle is beginning to stir now, smoke drifts from cook fires outside the walls, a squire shuffles towards the stables wrapped in a threadbare cloak, a servant with a chicken fussing under one arm bends his knee to Holand and hurries on to the kitchens.

Oh Joan, these men in your life. None of them deserve you.

* * *

The field is ablaze with pennants and banners, heraldic shields are displayed outside each pavilion to announce the family crest of the owner. Some tents are silk, and the size of a small castle; others are no bigger than a scullery and have rents in the poor cloth. Holand knows his own tent would have looked much like this, if he had been competing, but the injury to his eye has not yet healed and he has not recovered his balance enough for jousting.

The Earl of Salisbury, of course, has one of the finest pavilions on view, it is pure silk and the size of a small village. When Holand announces his presence outside, Salisbury is busy preparing for the lists, he has an army of squires fussing around him, some fastening his breastplate, others kneeling to buckle his greaves. The earl drinks from a jewelled goblet of brandy wine. His face is unnaturally flushed.

'How is the eye?' he says when he sees Holand.

'It is slow to heal. But the pain is bearable.'

'I shall lend you my physician. He has a poultice I apply whenever mine troubles me. I recommend him.'

'I cannot afford a physician.'

'A favour,' the earl says and offers him a goblet of brandy wine. Holand declines. He is serving on the king's guard today.

'You came to wish me luck?'

'I wished to ... the matter we discussed in Spain ...'

'You have not given thought to changing your mind?'

Holand says nothing.

Salisbury pushes his squires aside and puts an arm around Holand's shoulder. 'I should not be pleased if you were to reconsider now.'

'I think I do love her.'

'When the tournament is over I will arrange to pay you what you asked. However, should there be any difficulty, your life in England will become untenable. Do you understand?'

For one mad moment I think Holand might defy him and restore my faith in other men. Of course, it would have meant the end for his love affair with Joan, for the earl does not make threats he does not mean. Holand would have found himself in exile, hawking his military skills on the continent to the highest bidder and Joan would still be married to Salisbury's son just the same.

But what a glorious thing it would be to see it.

'I am going to make you a rich man, Thomas. I don't have to, but I will do it because I believe it is the honourable thing. You must do the honourable thing also. Your king expects it of you and so do I. Are we understood?'

Holand nods his head.

Salisbury holds out his arms so that his squire can finish attaching the breast plate. He smiles and drinks more of the wine. There, finally it is settled. Holand bows and takes his leave.

There is nothing more to be done.

37.

Joan rides to the tourney with Margaret and the Countess of Salisbury in a curtained litter. On the fields beyond the castle a hundred pavilions have been raised and thousands of commoners have flocked there to watch the jousting. Stands and barriers have been built for the royal and noble families and as she steps out of the litter and takes her place in the viewing gallery she appears dazzled by the splendour of it all; the bright caparisoned chargers, the packed crowds in the common enclosures, the banners with the heraldic emblems of a hundred royal houses snapping in the wind.

The jousting field is directly in front of the viewing stand and down the middle of it is a wooden barrier known as the tilt.

The aim of the joust is for the knights to strike each other with the lance while riding towards each other at high speed, if possible breaking the lance on the opponent's shield or armour or better, unhorsing him. Such combats are not meant to be lethal and the loser is expected to yield honourably to the dominant fighter. To inflict serious injury is in fact considered dishonourable, but accidents can happen, of course. You cannot ride a horse pell-mell at an armed rider and presume that you might still be fit to dance the galliard at the feast that night.

Joan took her seat to watch the entertainments, but I can see her mind is on other things. The jousting goes on all day, the hooves of the great war horses pounding down the lists until the field has been transformed into a bog of churned and half-frozen mud. Time after time the crowd cheers and screams as the knights crash together, and wooden lances explode into splinters.

"It's all right,' Lady Salisbury tells my daughter. 'These are just tourney lances. They are made to splinter on impact, so no one gets hurt."

As I have said, this is not strictly true, but it seems to be the day for telling my daughter lies. At that moment the Earl himself appears in the lists, he is drawn to fight some young knight from the provinces, and it is reckoned that he will win easily. But something indeed goes wrong, perhaps his warhorse loses its footing in the quagmire that previous fights have created in front of the viewing stand, and Salisbury is unhorsed so violently that he flies backward off his *destrier*, and his head hits the frozen ground with an audible crack that makes the crowd gasp. Lady Salisbury is out of her seat in an instant, her hands to her mouth.

Even the king is on his feet.

The earl lies motionless on his back while his horse gallops riderless to the end of the list and must be retrieved by one of his squires. Other squires in Salisbury livery rush out with a great shield to attend him and eventually lift him onto it and carry him away.

The viewing stand empties. It is not unusual for a knight to fall badly in a tourney. But this is the Marshal of England; this is the Earl of Salisbury.

A boy runs onto the field and shovels dirt over the spot where he has fallen. He is covering up a rather large puddle of blood. This cannot be good.

Salisbury is carried to the surgeon's tent where he is put on a wooden trestle and covered with furs to keep him warm. He is unconscious, and his breathing can be heard from a hundred paces away. There is blood dribbling from his left ear.

The King and the Countess gather around and talk to him and tell him that all will be well. I doubt that he can hear them. In fact, the Earl of Salisbury does not hear anything ever again. He does not wake up and less than a fortnight later he is dead.

39.

'**S**tupid. At his age.' Wake helps himself to brandy wine and sits down hard. He is furious at Salisbury. How dare he die! He has ruined everything, the inconsiderate bastard. 'He said he had come to an arrangement with Thomas.'

'Well that is of no use to us now, with nothing written down,' Margaret says. 'As for William, he is only sixteen years old, still two years from inheriting the Salisbury money. He cannot make good on anything the earl promised.'

'God's teeth!'

'Do you think ... that we might?'

Wake gives my wife a look of contempt, something he does passing well. Give good Lancaster money to a Holand? Besides, there is not enough of it. Margaret and Wake have royal blood, not dirty money.

'The king might have settled this,' Wake says.

It is true; I find it curious that he hasn't. Young William is now his ward, Joan is his cousin, and Thomas Holand one of his household knights; he is hardly uninvolved. Instead, he makes one of the earl's executors, Sir John Wingfield, young William's guardian in his stead, and grants William an annual income of three hundred pounds, not nearly enough to buy Holand off. I wonder if he sympathises with Joan's predicament - or his wife does - but does not want to offend the Salisburys or my wife by openly taking sides.

So like him to sit on the fence.

'What are we going to do? Margaret asks her brother.

'You must make sure Joan understands her duty.'

'What of William? Can we hold him to the marriage without his father's influence?'

'As I understand it, he still wants to proceed. Besides, he is too young to withdraw. He made the contract when he was above fifteen years old. Under canon law he cannot withdraw.'

'Joan still insists she will not go through with it.'

'Joan must be made to understand.' He looks hard at Margaret. Clearly the onus for the family's future now falls squarely on her own increasingly hunched shoulders.

'What about Holand?'

'If we continue to deny this marriage and refuse him leave to see her what can he do?' He slams down his wine cup, imagining that this makes him look forceful. 'Damn him! Why did he have to die?'

'Why do any of us?' Margaret says and for a moment I wonder if she is thinking of me. She talks of me seldom enough, I have noticed.

But though his death could not have come at a worse time for them, it was inconvenient for the Earl of Salisbury also. I am sure he is also irritated by the turn of events. So many wars and he meets his end during a tournament celebrating chivalry! God must have his little jokes.

You ride out in the morning to take part in an entertainment, you think you will be back for supper; you ride to Winchester for Parliament, you think the worst that will happen is that you will be put to sleep by the pomposity and the politics.

Your daughter's tears are still damp on your cheeks when the devil calls.

That is the way of it. Mortality is inconvenient, at best; at worst it leaves you haunting the halls at night, unable to find a moment's peace, never mind an eternity of it.

Death. You simply never know when that ne'er-do-well will call.

Westminster

Only Philippa speaks out for Joan now. She is closeted with her husband in the solar, away from the noise and smells and bustle of the Great Hall. How can he let this continue? she asks him. It is his prerogative, his responsibility, to intercede.

'She married without coming to me first to ask my permission and my blessing and now it is my fault?'

'She loves Thomas.'

'Love!'

It is the wrong thing to say. Yes, they themselves married for his mother's political ends, and yes, they made a good marriage despite, not because of, this prosaic beginning. But whatever the origins of their betrothal, a man derides love in the face of his wife at his own peril. He may be a king and unlike other men, but he is also a husband and in this at least he is very like every other man. There is a cold silence and Edward feels obliged to give ground.

'What would you have me do?'

'Make a decision. Save the poor girl from her abandonment.'

'She is the Countess of Salisbury. No one knows about this other wedding. How can I rule in favour of it? We do not even know if it is legal!'

'You cannot let this continue!'

'I have no choice but to let it continue! Joan will relent. She must. She knows her duty.'

Philippa points to a tapestry on the wall above their bed. It shows Paris stealing Helen and taking her back to Troy. 'He did no worse than that. You and everyone here at court think that what Paris did in the days of Hercules was an act of great valour and boldness. You love to hear the minstrels sing about it.'

Edward does not have a ready answer for this.

'The siege of Troy lasted nine years. Expect Joan to resist at least as long.' Philippa sweeps from the room.

For once her counsel goes unheeded. The king, it pleases me to say, is troubled much by his conscience these days. As he should be.

He deserves to writhe like this. He keeps telling himself that circumstances are beyond his control and some days he even believes it. But if what overtakes his subjects is not his fault, then why is he the king?

* * *

In despair I return to my wife, though I hardly know her now. Life changes so quickly and when we are gone the world moves on without us. Take my word. If you think yourself important take a bucket of water out of a lake and then observe how much the lake has changed; that is the difference your passing will make, no matter how integral you think yourself while you yet breathe.

In life I too thought myself an important man, I was son of a king and brother-in-law to a queen. For a few moments of time my death was a matter of some outrage and general mourning. Who even remembers me now?

Where did I go and did anyone notice?

Joan is all I care for on the earth now. The politics and power I once thought so vital now seems so futile. The king will die one day: there will be another king. Does it matter who it is?

But I cannot bear to see my daughter suffer. This is the one thing that truly disturbs.

I whisper to my wife in her vivid dreams, and she wakes with a start in the middle of the night and says my name. But come the morning she dismisses her encounter with my restless spirit as the fancy of an overburdened mind.

123

She is so determined to be proved right now, even if she is wrong.

Very well, then. If you will not hear me in your dreams, there is always the Queen. She sleeps light these days, and she still has fond memories of her uncle, Edmund.

40.

Joan hears her mother striding in her boots down the long halls of Windsor Castle. Her pale white shoulders stiffen. She turns towards the door.

'This has to stop,' Margaret says, throwing open the door. 'Now.'

Who is this virago, this unnatural force of nature concerned now only with getting her own way? She is the raging flood; gentle Joan is the rock that turns her aside. 'I love him.'

'Stop it! Stop saying that! It's not important. What is important is that you are destroying our family's hopes.'

Joan shakes her head.

'Where is your loyalty?'

'To my husband.'

'William is your husband!'

Joan says nothing; she is a pale, fragile and unassailable wall. My wife is equally determined to prevail, yet still Joan holds out, a garrison of one, heroic, magnificent and apparently invincible.

Margaret looks set to leave the room but pauses at the door. A curious smile appears on her face. 'Your witnesses? The van Arteveldes?'

A sharp intake of breath as Joan looks up. 'What of them?'

'He was beaten to death by a mob in Ghent a few nights ago. It seems not even the Flemish will trust a shopkeeper to rule them for very long.'

'What of his wife?'

Margaret does not answer directly. 'You see how it is all falling down around you?' she says.

Joan lowers her eyes again.

She slams the door behind her.

Margaret will not break the siege and Joan will not sue for truce. I cannot bear to watch this, but I cannot turn away. Margaret is right, Joan scarce knows this man Holand, this is unreasonable of her, yet what of her mother?

Is she kind?

It is so long that I have wandered here among the living, and I should very much like to go to my own peace now. But I cannot leave my Joan, even though she does not know I am here. I cannot leave until we have seen this through together.

I still feel her arms tight around my neck. I still hear her shrieking my name.

This time I will not ride away.

41.

Six years.

Six years my Joan has endured this; six years a clandestine bride, five of them married to two men. Her life slips past her; she spends the long seasons at her needlepoint. Spring finds her staring out of windows at daffodils pushing up through frost hard earth; an eternity later there are forget-me-nots and roses blooming in these same gardens, now green and scented; another lifetime goes by until autumn and the leaves fall and rot under the yews in damp and earth-rich drifts; then comes the smell of chestnuts roasting over hot fires and another endless winter crouched beside the hearth while bitter snows pile against the castle walls.

And then, again, the daffodils.

Season after slow season she grows from a girl into the Countess of Salisbury. She listens to the endless chatter of women, the rustle of gowns, the gossip of maids. She is one of the most beautiful women in all England, yet she spends her days without the consolation of a husband's kiss or the promise of any family other than her own, which now consists of a mother and uncle who despise her and a brother who does as he is told.

I follow her as she goes to pray in the royal chapel. It is hung with bright tapestries, vivid painted statues of the Redeemer and the blessed saints. There is a pure white alabaster figure of Mary and Joan kneels before it. She whispers first to the Madonna and then to me, tells us she has decided to abandon her resistance. She whispers that she does not have the strength for it any longer.

They have broken her spirit, finally. The damage they all have done. It would have been better if she had surrendered from the first.

What will be left of her now? The wax drips from a candle and pools on the stone flags. Christ shivers on his cross. Saint Jude, patron saint of lost causes, looks the other way.

* * *

But then Holand returns.

Joan is walking in the garden and suddenly he is there. She throws herself at him, almost knocks her brave soldier off his feet. He laughs and tries to shush her, but she will not be stilled. Her mouth is on his, her arms squeeze his neck. My passionate, lovely daughter, she does not care even if her chaperone sees, but in fact her constant maidservant is not there. She has been given instructions to be absent by the queen herself.

In fact, I was present when Phillipa arranged this meeting; her king may not wish to take sides, but the queen has no such qualms.

Holand wants to talk but she will not let him. She holds his face in her hands, kissing him near to suffocation. That any man should be loved like this! Finally, he holds her at arm's length.

'We do not have long, we must talk.'

'But I have missed you so, I simply cannot live another day without you! Tell me you have a plan!'

'There will be many more days for us yet, I promise.'

She clings to him. I can read his thoughts: he is amazed at her constancy. When he married her, he did not expect this. How can she still love him after so long? He cannot comprehend how he has inspired such passion and constancy, after all it has been four years now and they have spent just one night together. Why has she not renounced him?

Her affections are so starved that she is wanton with him. I have seen this Thomas Holand take whores and other men's wives standing up against a wall and I pray he will not dishonour her the same way now, here in the arbour. She is so ardent and so rapturous in her relief at seeing him again that she might allow it. They kiss for an inordinately long time.

Finally, she breaks away: 'What are we going to do?'

'I will find a way.'

'How? They are all against us.'

'Trust me,' he says. Trust me. If the Earl of Salisbury were still alive he would have taken his cash and renounced her. You could argue, I suppose, that it would have been the reasonable thing to do. How could he know that Joan still longed for him like this? How could he know she would be loyal?

It is Joan who is unreasonable. Love like this simply does not make sense.

But trust him? How can she?

'It will be alright,' he says.

'How?' she says.

He has no answer for her, just this endless empty reassurance. Yes how? It is the refrain of every soldier gone to war.

It will be alright.

How can it ever be alright?

'I will think of something,' he says. 'You are the wife of my heart and I will move heaven and earth to make you my own before King and before God.'

After so long apart they have an afternoon in a rose arbour and that only through the impudent grace of Edward's queen. They exchange endless kisses and he makes her endless promises. But is anything of substance said or done?

No. Of course not.

* * *

Holand has been asked to be godfather to Thomas FitzRoger, and he rides to Merston, in Sussex, to attend the christening at St Bartholomew's church. His mother Maud is there also and they both stay at Fitzroger's manor house that night. They have seen each other seldom over the years and Maud is eager to hear her son's news.

Maud does not spend time at court, and so is spared much of the politicking and gossiping that goes on there, but whispers of what her son has done have reached her, even in her country retreat.

So that afternoon they settle by the fire at Fitzroger's manor and she asks him how his fortunes are progressing. She tells him about the unkind rumours she has heard and asks him if they have any substance.

He takes his time about it, prevaricates as only a man with a guilty conscience can, but finally confesses to her what he has done.

Maud is a formidable woman. Thanks to her husband, she has had to endure much, and she now regards her second son with something between bemusement and exasperation.

'So, let me see if I understand you, Thomas. You married Joan of Woodstock in secret ... when?'

'On the last day of March, four years ago.'

'Four years ago.' An eyebrow is raised. That is all. Really. Such composure. She reminds me of Joan; Margaret would be hurling books and psalters. 'You did not think to tell your mother?'

'There was a need to be discreet.'

'You think me indiscreet?'

'I mean there was seldom opportunity. I have been much in the king's service.'

'We have seen each other but seldom these last five or six years, I allow. But on those occasions when you have been home one thinks the matter might have been raised in private conversation.'

'I hoped the situation might be resolved privately long before now.'

'Because you are embarrassed by your own behaviour. Am I correct?'

Holand chews on a lip. This commanding knight with an eye patch and patchwork of scars perches on the edge of a chair, enduring this scolding like a little boy.

'Four years,' she says, tapping a long finger on the arm of her chair. 'And the Countess of Salisbury has maintained her affections for you for this long?'

'It would appear so.'

'She could so very easily have said she had been duped. It would have gone much easier with her.'

'It seems she chooses not to.'

'Yet if the Earl of Salisbury had not fallen off his horse in such spectacular fashion you would have taken his money and forgotten all about her?'

'Her fidelity is ... unexpected.'

'I would have said astonishing, but we shall not quibble over the phrasing of it. We are not lawyers. I thought you a charming boy, but I thought I was biased as you are my son. And I have always been proud of you. But with this affair it seems to me you have both outshone your brightest moment and at the same time fallen to the depths of greatest shame.'

She shakes her head in bewilderment.

'What is your advice?'

'My advice would be not to wait so long to tell me next time.'

'I assure you there will not be a next time, Mother.'

She laughs heartily at this. I should have liked to have met Lady Maud in life, I like a woman who can appreciate a man's absurdities. 'It is indeed a blessing to hear you say so.'

He waits, penitent, for further instruction.

'This is your chance, isn't it?'

He feigns confusion.

'Come Thomas, don't make that face with me. You have this calculated by the yard and the pound, I know you. You are not Otto. Thanks to your fool of a father, may God bless and keep him, you are penniless and landless. Joan however is royal and well connected. It would be a master stroke if you can pull this off. Do you love her at all?'

This last spoken casually. Such a consideration is usually irrelevant to such matters, but Joan's glittering resolve makes the question pertinent. Lady Maud holds her breath. I have no breath to hold.

'At first I gave it no thought. I ... lusted for her ... and saw opportunity there ... though it seemed too outrageous to believe it might actually happen. But her passion for me has ... yes, I love her. I think.'

'A pity, because as I see it, the situation is hopeless.'

He nods, agreeing with her.

'You have no money to pursue the claim through the courts and the law is your only hope. I know Joan's mother, she will not relent.'

Holand leans forward, his elbows on his knees. 'Neither will I.'

Lady Maud sighs. 'It is not what I would advise.'

'I leave for France soon,' he says.

'Make sure you come back.'

'I am glad you hope so. Many wouldn't.'

'Well I am your mother, I have to think that.' And she laughs again.

I love her. *I think.*

What did he mean by that?

42.

Will looks miserable. He still mourns his father, and his countess and bride insists on saying she is married to a landless knight. Why has this happened? Until now he has been accustomed to a life of ease and unquestioned serendipity. His way was always strewn with rose petals.

He is not even inured to mild irritation, so tragedy has left him bewildered and defenceless. He sleepwalks through his duties each day, distracted by a simmering rage at God and at life for thwarting him in this manner. He is an earl; he considers himself above disappointment.

He has spent the afternoon at practice with his squires but has spent most of the time leaning on his sword and staring at the clouds, as if the answer to his problems might somehow be transcribed on the heavens. Ned trails him back to the armoury, there is a fountain in the yard outside and they take off swords and scabbards and then strip off their mail, their leathers, their sweat-soaked woollens. William is so tired his fingers fumble with the fastenings, he can barely get them undone.

He and Ned gulp water bare-chested from the fountain and slump to the ground side by side. William hangs his head between his knees, Ned puts a hand on his shoulder.

'What am I to do with her, Ned.'

'With who?'

'With Joan. Why is she so intractable? I've known her since we were all children, I care for her, she must know that. I can give her a life of ease and luxury. Why couldn't we make a good marriage?'

Ned had thought William was still grieving his father, he had not realised that this was the reason his friend looked so stricken.

'She is making everyone miserable,' William mutters.

'Herself most of all. I am sure it is not deliberate.'

'You defend her?'

'I think I understand her.'

William grips his wrist. 'Then talk to her for me! You're her cousin, she will listen to you! Just one word from her is all that it will take to end this and we can all get on with our lives. Will you do it? Please?'

'I will try,' Ned says because he feels it is his duty to his friend to do so.

But of course, it does no good. Joan remains steadfast, as he knew she would. I watch Ned's face as he tries, half-heartedly, to persuade her to reason. He is so transparent, anyone but Joan would see the longing in his eyes. He is prince of England, he has the world at his feet, and yet at that moment he wishes to be a landless knight with one eye called Holand.

Ned knows there is no hope for his own desire. If she does not marry Thomas Holand, then she must marry William.

'You are resolved on this course then?' he asks her after he has pleaded William's case without success.

'I love Thomas.'

Ned, now fourteen, does not flinch. 'I will help you all I can then,' he says, and I think he means it.

'What can you do, Ned? Can you persuade your father to intercede, can you make my mother relent?'

She strokes his face. There is tenderness but no passion in the gesture, his aunt sometimes touches him the same way. Look at the hurt in his eyes, he would rather she had not touched him at all.

'Sweet Ned,' she says.

Later that day he batters two young squires all around the practice yard; they wilt in the face of their young prince, wonder at the reason for the rage in his blazing, black eyes.

43.

Caen

Here is what war really looks like; it is not gentlemen in polished armour riding through cheering crowds followed by heralds in pretty hats blowing trumpets. It is this: a desolate and flattened land, smoke drifting from blackened villages and corpse fires; empty-eyed soldiers with scarves tied round their faces, their eyes red and streaming from the foul and acrid air. It is the stink of death in every gasping inward breath and bodies rotting everywhere you look.

I never cared for it much in my life and I am glad I shall never have to take part in a war again.

Ned has camped in the shadow of the priory of Fontenay-le-Pesnel. A long trestle table of rough-hewn pine has been set out under an elm tree and covered with a torn scarlet cloth. The prince is there with his commanders and advisers, his crimson-and-gold standard with three lions rampant hanging limp in this putrid summer afternoon.

His army has arrived outside the walls of Caen and is preparing to attack the old town. Two fortified abbeys have already fallen. Ned has sensibly wasted no time on siege preparations for the simple reason that he has no siege engines.

I look over his shoulder at the torn and filthy map laid out in front of him. Caen is broken into three parts, either side of the banks of the river Orne, and further split by a branch of the river into the old city and the new. The ancient citadel has a curtain wall and a strongly fortified castle, but the wall has crumbled in places and here it is vulnerable to attack. One of the prince's commanders is pointing these weaknesses to him, punching the map with one stubby finger.

The newer part of the city is a wealthy burgh of merchants and landowners who live on the island formed by a tributary of the Orne. This district is more easily defended, as the river forms a natural perimeter and the only way across it is by three fortified bridges.

Ned makes his plans. But what he does not know yet is that although the French had originally planned to set their defence inside the castle, pressure from the wealthy citizens of Caen have forced them to shift the defence to the island. They seem more worried about losing their money than losing their lives.

When heralds bring Ned this news, he can hardly believe his good fortune. He sends a small force to blockade the handful of soldiers still inside the castle and he and his chief knights pull together a new strategy for an assault on the island.

But events continue to overtake him. As he moves his troops into position for a co-ordinated assault, a band of his English archers and men-at-arms, eager to get at the loot, decide to rush one of the bridges. The Earls of Warwick and Northampton try to pull them back but they are pissing in the wind, as we used to say when I was with the king's army.

Ned sees this debacle unfold and sends messengers down to order an immediate retreat, but the situation is even beyond his control now.

As he watches, hands on his hips and swearing like an infantryman, scores more English longbowmen and Welsh lancers wade into the shrunken river while others find boats the French have not had time to scuttle or hide, and they push them into the stream and pole their way over to the other side. Suddenly the French are overwhelmed, the defenders are hard-pressed just to maintain the bridges, and now they are being attacked from the rear as well.

The English battle tactics are brilliant, if entirely accidental.

Ned turns and grins at his high command. 'Well, it seems our decisions have been made for us,' he says and calls for his horse. 'If we win, I shall take the credit. If we don't, then we hang any soldier that survives! Gentlemen, let us take Caen!'

A war horn sounds, a deep mournful note that chills the blood. Squires help their knights into the saddles of snorting coursers while men-at-arms buckle on their sword belts and run to keep up.

And here is Holand and his brother, struggling to their horses, they cannot let the prince leave them in his wake, honour and glory are at stake here. Holand's *destrier* is a formidable coal-black warhorse, as eager to be at it as any of them. It is not easy to mount one of these beasts in full armour, but finally Holand is settled, and his squire hands him up his battered helm, and then his shield, a massive slab of ironwood banded with iron, and finally his battle axe.

The young prince has already put his spurs to his horse and is thundering towards the river. Holand goes after him. He has Otto, on his left, to cover his blind side. He does not know it, but this is to be the most important day in his life, the day that all the sacrifice, the endless years of campaigning in France and Scotland and Andalusia and Prussia pay off.

A man needs courage and ambition in this world. He also needs luck, and today it will smile on him and throw him her token and even blow him a kiss.

* * *

Holand's courses splashes into the water. There is a melee on the far bank and the French line breaks in several places. He holds tight to the reins. Come off here and the weight of his armour will sink him into the mud and he will never be able to rise. There are English men-at-arms on either side of him in their boiled leather jerkins and pot helms wading over beside him, eager for their part of the spoils. One of them goes down with an arrow in his throat. His fellows do not even break stride.

A hissing fills the air; more arrows arc down from the left, where French archers have retreated almost to the base of the stone tower guarding the bridge. He lifts his shield and one arrow thuds into the ironwood, another clatters off his helm. He is well protected. I hold no fears for him yet.

As his *destrier* thunders up the far bank he looks for his prince but does not see him. All is confusion. There are shouts, the whicker of horses, the clash of steel. In such situations the battle shrinks to the few feet of ground around your horse and this is indeed all that Holand can make out in that moment.

He charges in to what remains of the French line. A man-at-arms wearing the *fleur-de-lys* of France thrusts at him with his spear and Holand strikes out with his axe, knocking it aside. The man retreats and aims again but Holand spurs his horse forward and rides straight over the top of him.

He looks for Otto, sees him surrounded by three French foot soldiers. Otto smashes a lance point with his axe and rakes the hook of the blade across the man's throat on the backswing. Holand uses his charger to trample the other two. Really, this is carnage. They may as well be in a butcher's shop.

Holand sees a thrown spear coming at him and raises his shield and it lodges there. He charges at his assailant, the man screams and raises his shield above his head to protect himself. Holand circles him, raining axe blows on the man's shield, and chips of oak fly through the air as he batters him to his knees. He does not have time to finish the job. The man disappears under the hooves of another war horse.

The French are either screaming or running, they are overwhelmed on three sides and these foot soldiers are helpless against the warhorses. The French captain throws his sword aside, finds a horse, and gallops past Holand for the safety of the tower.

Suddenly it is over. Holand circles, looking for danger, but by now the only ones left on the battlefield are the dying or hideously wounded. Ravens are already gathering, looking for carrion.

The battle had moved on to the base of the tower, which is besieged now by those English soldiers who have battled their way across the bridge and the rag-tag of English and Welsh irregulars who ambushed them from the river.

Holand looks around for his brother; Otto is still there, guarding his left flank. They ride towards the tower where the foot soldiers are already trying to batter down one of the heavy oak-and-iron doors using a timber they have dragged up from the muddy river bank. A white flag flutters from the battlements. Holand shouts at the men to stand to, though he has to batter some of them with the flat blade of his axe before they will listen to him. He circles on his warhorse, he can hear the battle is still going on at the other bridges. But here, for the moment, there is an uneasy calm.

Three French knights emerge from the tower holding a ceremonial sword. They walk up to Holand and offer it to him. The *Comte d'Eu* delivers his sword to Sir Thomas Holand, they say. He wishes you to accept his surrender.

Holand steps down from his courser and rattles through the mud. It is deadly difficult to walk more than a few paces in battle armour but now it seems he must also climb the tower steps. By the time he reaches the archer's nest he is exhausted.

The *Comte d'Eu* is waiting for him. He has taken off his helm and is escorted by two of his knights as well as several foot soldiers.

The count grins when he sees Holand. 'It is good to see a familiar face on such a black day,' he says.

'How did you know it was me?'

'I recognized your colours.' He nods at the eye patch. 'I hope it was not a Frenchman did that.'

'A Moor.'

'Then I hope you will accept my surrender. I know you as an honourable man, Sir Thomas. I ask that I and those that remain of my men are treated with mercy.'

'You will be under my protection. You have my word.'

And so the Count is taken hostage. It is the way it was for Salisbury, the way of it for all noblemen who go to war, for such men are worth more to their captors alive than dead. Only the common foot soldier is skewered or trampled underfoot in these affairs. You can always make another pikeman; breeding someone with a title takes work. The *Comte d'Eu* has rightly calculated that it will be better to surrender to an Englishman of his acquaintance, and live to fight another day, than risk slaughter in a lost cause.

Holand is perhaps thinking he is worth a few hundred pounds. He has not counted on Fate and a mercurial king.

* * *

The burghers should have relied on the count's military counsel instead of worrying for their homes and possessions in the new city. The English loot and burn the town and murder half the population. I wonder what the *comte* is thinking when he looks over his shoulder and sees the smoke rising over the town and hears the dreadful clamour? I am sure he and his men must congratulate themselves on a good decision. Fighting to the death is all very well in its place but glory is fleeting, and death lasts a very long time, I assure you.

44.

Caen is not the pinnacle of Edward's campaign in France, just the high point of Holand's. A month later he faces Philip, at Crecy. The French have a much larger army, perhaps twice the number of men and knights that he has. But the English longbowmen prove more than a match for Phillip's Genoese crossbows and French cavalry and he wins an overwhelming victory. Phillip himself barely escapes alive from the battlefield.

The French losses are enormous and include the flower of the French nobility as well as King John of Bohemia and the King of Majorca. Holand fights in the vanguard of the prince's division, newly elevated to a position of command alongside the earls of Warwick and Northampton. Militarily, at least, he has eclipsed William Salisbury, and my own son John, who is serving alongside the king and thankfully sees no action at all.

By now Edward is in fine spirits indeed. He is so buoyed by his recent successes that he summons the queen to join him at the wars: he insists she must bring all the royal ladies for company. They will celebrate Christmas in the new town he has built for her in France. From there she can watch him invest Calais.

Is he mad? He would bring the ladies of his court to a siege camp in a land riven by war? In the winter?

What is he thinking?

But Philippa is as always eager to obey her husband and king. Wherever she goes then her royal ladies must attend her and of course Joan is eager to accompany her. It is her chance to see Thomas Holand again.

Where might all this have led if not for Caen and the Comte d'Eu? I confess I do not know. Would she have defied her mother to the grave? I have asked myself this question many times.

Just how long *does* love last?

The royal women prepare to leave. It is an adventure to them, none of them know what war is like, they have only the vaguest notion of what it is to join a siege, even in the great comfort that Edward has promised them. They pack ermine cloaks and gowns and boots and jewels and thick gloves and glass goblets and embroidered cushions. They will certainly need the warm cloaks and fur- lined gloves.

And don't forget posies for the nose.

These ladies have no idea just how bad a war can smell.

45.

Villeneuve le Hardi - the brave new town. Look at the size of it. It straddles the causeway leading to Flanders, signal of Edward's intent to stay where he is until Calais submits. As they arrive Joan peers through the curtains of the litter expecting to see tents and pavilions but instead there are wattle-and-daub houses and shops and even hospitals.

That is not all she sees; before Lady Salisbury forces her to draw shut the curtain, Joan sees a pair of hairy buttocks ramming a camp follower against a wall, a man with no nose and no legs begging in the mud and a sergeant at arms pissing in the street.

Welcome to the siege, ladies.

Edward has prepared an elaborate welcome for them. The great hall in his erstwhile palace is hung with tapestries. There are carved screens to keep out the worst of the draughts and a polished oak table is laden with Italian glass and pewter plates, all of it looted from the French. The king is effusive in his welcome for the Queen and his two daughters.

Meanwhile Joan hangs back, looks around the hall hoping for a glimpse of Holand.

'He's not here,' a voice says.

It is William. She looks shocked at his appearance; indeed, so am I. He appears haunted; the fair and scraggly beard he has grown does not hide the dark hollows in his cheeks. He has grown tall since the last time she saw him, but he is still all bone and awkwardness. This campaign has shown him that he does not have his father's belly for war; this one would never have taken on Mortimer for Edward. A man can pass on his blood but not his balls.

'You are looking for Holand.'

'Is he here?'

'Somewhere.'

The look in his eyes scares her; I have seen this happen to men in battle. Their eyes fix on some far spot, as if they are seeing things no one else can; angels perhaps, or the dead walking. 'How are you, Will?'

'I did not think war would be like this. Can you smell that? Do you know what it is?'

She shakes her head.

But he does not tell her what it is she can smell, though that will become obvious soon enough. 'Is that Ned?' she asks him.

The prince has changed much. He has a full beard and has acquired the confidence and bearing that only royalty and the killing of so many men at Caen can lend a young man. Sixteen years old now, long-limbed and darkly handsome, all the ladies in the queen's entourage crane their necks for a better look.

'He is in his element here.' William says. 'He was meant for this life. You should have seen him at Crecy.'

'I heard we won a great victory. You must be proud.'

'The longbows did all the work,' he tells her. 'It was just slaughter.'

'You are unharmed?'

'Would it matter to you if I wasn't?'

'Of course, it would matter. We have been friends since we were children.'

An odd smile. 'And soon we will be husband and wife.'

She smiles back and does not answer.

'I am a man now, Joan, this nonsense must stop. You are my wife, you are Lady Salisbury.'

'This is not the time to discuss this,' she tells him.

'When?'

'The day after Nevermas,' she says, and it takes him a moment to understand her wit.

The King calls her forward, but William takes her arm and will not let it go. 'When this is over you will come and live with me as my wife,' he tells her.

'Oh Will, you know that could never happen,' she says, gently. She pulls away from him and steps forward to pay her respects to the king and queen.

William stalks from the hall.

* * *

Ned watches him go. What is he thinking? I think he feels sorry for him. It is not an unkind look, for after all, he must understand how he feels.

After she has been welcomed by the king, Ned strides up to her and enfolds her in an embrace. He is a head taller than her now. 'Cousin! I rejoice to see you again.'

She throws her arms around him and hugs him back, she tells him how happy she is to see him safe and in the next breath she asks news of Holand.

His smile flickers but does not falter. He tells her of Holand's success in capturing the count of Eu. Joan does not understand what this means, not yet. She just bites her lip and says that she wishes to see him.

She must see him. She must.

Ned looks from her to Lady Salisbury, who is watching them as a gaoler might look at two prisoners she has seen passing messages. She is still in mourning for her husband, still in her widow's weeds and it is almost three years. Perhaps she just wants to keep new suitors away. She has lands, estates, money - why spoil it with a husband who wants to tell her what to do with it?

'It is good to see you again,' Ned says to Joan and gives her a last, lingering look and hurries on. The young prince is much in demand these days, by the king, by his knights, by chambermaids and ladies-in-waiting. By all except Joan, in fact.

He looks back once over his shoulder hoping to see her staring after him. But of course, she isn't, she is still looking round the Hall for Thomas Holand. Lady Salisbury takes her by the arm and chaperones her promptly out of the Hall to the chambers that have been set aside for her.

46.

This place is not Woodstock or Westminster. The apartments are draughty, there is not a single glazed window and the shutters warp in the damp and will not close properly. The women are crowded in together and cannot leave their brave new town without an escort, for they would be in danger not only from the French but from their own soldiers, a motley lot, as most of the king's armies are. By now some of them are missing hands or feet or eyes and crouch in doorways begging alms from their former comrades.

In short, it is not a place for women. Edward must have quite lost his mind or at least Bella thinks so. Now she has grown she is not the chatterbox she once was, but she is still a girl who knows what she thinks and is not afraid to speak her opinions aloud. She complains endlessly to her mother and indeed, to anyone who will listen, about their privations. Her little sister is of a milder temperament and seems not to mind as much as her sister does. I know which one of them I think will make a better marriage.

Lady Salisbury is determined not to fail in her commission a second time and follows Joan everywhere; my daughter cannot go to the privy without her waiting outside the door. But she cannot steer her away from Holand forever and finally they come upon him in the great hall, deep in conversation with the king. Joan hears Lady Salisbury draw a sharp breath. You would think she had stumbled upon Beelzebub himself.

Holand gives her an uncertain smile. I can see that she would like to run up and throw her arms about him but that would not be wise, would it?

'Ah Lady Joan! Lady Salisbury.' The king laughs. Is he nervous or is he enjoying himself? I cannot tell which. 'I believe you know Sir Thomas. He has brought me the latest reports. He has acquitted himself admirably on this campaign, haven't you, Thomas? He took a valuable prisoner at Caen and served beside the young prince himself in the vanguard at Crecy and held the line. He has proved himself to be one of my best knights.'

Lady Salisbury mutters something under her breath but Joan does not hear it. It is as well, they are not pleasant words or even proper for a lady of her standing.

'He will be a rich man by the time the campaign is finished,' the king goes on, perhaps for Joan's benefit. 'I believe the French king will pay a tidy sum to have the *Comte d'Eu* returned.'

Does Joan finally understand? I don't think she does, I don't think even Lady Salisbury can possibly anticipate the largesse that the king intends to bestow on Sir Thomas Holand. Joan has always believed that her love would prevail through justice and determination, but these are poor fellows indeed next to money.

She also no doubt believes that now she and Thomas Holand are in the same encampment then they will surely find a few moments alone but if that is what she thinks then she has underestimated Lady Salisbury and her son. In the weeks that follow, there is not a single moment that she is alone. Besides, Holand is often at the walls, commanding operations with Ned and when he returns to the encampment Lady Salisbury is at Joan's heels more often than her shadow. Lady Salisbury is diligent in her duty to her son. If only she had been as dedicated six years ago.

It is Bella who breaks the impasse. Lady Salisbury leaves them closeted in their rooms, sees no harm, but as soon as she is gone the young princess produces a letter from her cloak and hands it to Joan.

Joan's hands shake as she rips open the seal. It is from Holand, of course; she holds it so close that even I cannot see all that he has written. But it is clearly a love letter, and he finishes it by telling her that the king has promised him a goodly reward for the capture of the *Comte d'Eu*, and that he plans to use this money to pursue his claim in the ecclesiastical courts in Avignon.

We will be together soon, he finishes. *The reward that I shall claim for the count will change everything for us. I have received his dispensation to return to England to organize my affairs. My mother will help me in this, as she has some knowledge of legal procedure.*

You are the wife of my heart and my dreams. Soon you will be my wife before the whole world.

Thomas.

Joan hugs Bella. It is the first time I have ever seen her cry in front of anyone else. She thinks it will soon be over.

She thinks it is almost done.

Of course, it isn't.

* * *

Edward has a viewing gallery constructed so that he and his commanders and their wives can view the siege. He thinks the ladies will be impressed. He is wrong;

145

few of them can stand it, the smell is sickening, and the landscape is one of utter desolation. It is only at night that the view has anything to recommend it; the English camp fires look like fireflies.

Lady Salisbury tells Joan that the king wishes to see her and leads her up to the gallery. But it is a ruse; as soon as they are there, William appears out of the shadows.

'My son would like to speak with you,' Lady Salisbury says and hurries away.

William wears the light leather-and-mail of an outrider, has just come from the fortifications at the siege line. Joan puts her nosegay to her face. She supposes he has grown accustomed to his own stench, but it still turns her stomach, it has permeated everything, even the leather hauberk he wears and the silk jupon with Edward's quartered device.

They stand facing each other quietly in the dark. William's face is shadowed by the torches that light the gallery. 'The siege will soon be over,' he says.

'To which siege do you refer?'

'You are not under siege, Joan. You can end this at any time.'

'So can they,' she says and nods towards Calais.

'It is hardly the same thing. I do not understand you, we have known each other from children. Do I repulse you so that you would go to such lengths to avoid our marriage?'

'William, it has nothing to do with you.'

'I care for you a great deal. I would be a kind and generous husband and you would want for nothing. I am not a brute, or a drunkard. What is it that would make you resist our lawful marriage for so long?'

'It is not lawful, William.'

'With a word, you could make it so.'

'I love him.'

'You do not know him! My father had made an agreement with him to end this before he died. He was going to buy him off!'

'So you say.'

'It is true.'

'Yet he is still here, fighting for me.'

'He has no choice! He cannot marry without money or lands, and he fights for Edward because he has to.'

'I will not forsake him.'

'You are in love with the romance of it. He is not Lancelot and you are not Guineverre. A marriage is not like that.'

'You are sixteen years old. How would you know any more than me what it is or what it is not?'

William sighs. He can see that haranguing her will get him nowhere. I could have told him that. 'Will you not just let this be, Joan?' he says with a weary sigh. 'We might be happy you and me. You have no need to suffer this exclusion any longer.'

Joan places a hand on his arm. 'My mind is made up, William. It is no reflection on you. You are going to be a fine man and a valorous knight one day. Now I think I should go inside now, the night is chill.'

She leaves him there, confounded, staring towards Calais. It seems good Englishmen are meeting stubborn resistance everywhere. But Calais will only endure its own suffering for eleven months.

They are burning the bodies inside the walls again tonight. From where I am, I watch as thousands of shadows rise from the wretched city, leaving their emaciated bodies behind them in the street. They pass me on the way from life, but they do not speak. They barely notice me.

I am not ready yet to follow them and they have no wish, it seems, to linger.

But I, I cannot leave my daughter just yet.

47.

It is almost a year before the starved burghers of Calais emerge from the gates with the keys to the city. With the siege over, the king and his army return to England and Edward celebrates his successes with a round of tournaments in Bury, Eltham and Windsor, Canterbury, Lichfield and Lincoln.

Edward agrees to pay Holand eighty thousand florins for the *Comte d'Eu*, to be paid in instalments over the next three years, each yearly instalment to be made in equal payments at Michaelmas and Easter. Overnight Sir Thomas Holand is rich beyond his dreams.

How might I explain this to an outsider with no understanding of warfare? Eighty thousand florins is a vast amount, unthinkable; such outlandish ransoms are reserved only for crowned heads of state. By comparison, the *Comte de Tancarville*, who was captured at Caen along with the *Comte d'Eu*, was ransomed for just over six hundred pounds - twenty times less than what Holand is to receive. It seems that finally the king has decided to intervene in the affair, while still pretending to remain aloof. At a stroke he has given Holand the means to pay for the legal steps required to regain Joan as his wife, if that is what he wishes.

I had never expected this. The victories in France have quite gone to his head.

Holand and his mother waste no time. They do not bother with the English courts, presuming quite rightly that they will not get a fair hearing there. Instead they submit a petition to the Pope, requesting that Joan's marriage to William of Salisbury be annulled on the grounds of her own prior betrothal.

The cat, as they say, has been thrown into the dovecote. Now let us see the birds fly.

Bisley.

'He has done what?' William stares at his mother aghast. He cannot believe that Thomas Holand would dare such a thing. This is beyond all honour. 'How will I ever show my face at court? I am humiliated.'

Up to this point, both parties have kept Joan's marriage to Thomas Holand secret, or as secret as anything can be inside the royal court of England. Oh, there have been whispers, of course, hints of scandal, but gossip thrives on novelty and Joan's situation has gone on too long to still excite interest. Since the earl's death my daughter has been referred to publicly as the Countess of Salisbury but this will change everything.

'This is the king's fault,' Lady Salisbury says. 'He has set an outrageous sum for the count's ransom. And you still say he is impartial? He has enriched Holand deliberately so that he might pursue his claim against us. Your father was his greatest friend! He would not have ever become king without him. This is the thanks we all get, witness the gratitude of kings!'

There are two other women present at this gathering; one is Will's grandmother, Elizabeth, and the other, I am sad to say, is my wife. It seems she has rather become a Salisbury in this last six years.

Elizabeth raises a calming hand against her daughter's outburst. She takes a sharper view. 'The fault lies with Joan, not with the king! That vain and indecent woman!'

William rushes to her defence. He is a good man, William, and as he rightly claimed that night on the king's siege gallery, he would have made Joan a fine husband, in my opinion. He reminds his grandmother that Joan is not only his wife, but his friend from childhood and he does not think her either vain or indecent. It is a fine speech; I wish Margaret would have made it.

But Elizabeth is unmoved. 'Then why has she done this to you?'

'Holand has undue influence over her. She is infatuated.'

'Infatuation does not last six years and account for months and years of absence.'

William has no answer to this. He drains his brandy wine, pours another from the flask on the table and stares gloomily into the fire.

His mother is relentless. 'You cannot let this continue. You must do something.'

'What would you have me do?'

Lady Salisbury and her mother exchange a look. As it happens, they have already thought of this.

They tell him what they have in mind. He looks horrified and turns to Margaret, hoping for her support against their scheming but she simply looks away, she has already given them tacit approval. I can scarce credit this. I make a log jump in the grate and they all start with fright. It is the most protest I can make.

Margaret, I want to shout at her, she is our daughter, our little Joan. Where is your conscience in this?

Is this the chivalry Edward is so enamoured of?

Is this what it means to be a true knight in England?

48.

Bourne, Lincolnshire

I see him coming before anyone, of course, riding with his squires and men at arms along the avenue of beech that leads to the castle; the hooves of their coursers thunder on the wooden drawbridge and clatter on the cobblestones in the court below. Ostlers rush from the stables to attend them. William jumps down, pulls off his heavy leather gauntlets and tosses them to his squire. He is brusque about his business, will not give himself time to think about what he is doing. He just needs to get this done.

Joan is with her ladies, at needlework, they all leap to their feet when they hear the young earl stamping into the hall, she is the only one that remains on her stool for the moment.

William is shouting her name. Finally, she obediently lays aside her work and glides down the stair to meet him. 'My lord. What brings you here so unexpected?'

He cannot meet her eyes. 'You are to come with me.'

'Come with you where?'

'I am taking you to castle Donyatt. You are my wife, that's where you should be.'

'Donyatt? Why was I not told of this?'

My wife appears through a curtain, watches all this over William's shoulder.

'William?' Joan says. 'William, tell me what is happening.'

'Do not delay. Your wardrobe will follow in a few days. Fetch your nurse and two women, tell them to be ready to ride in an hour.'

He turns and stamps back outside. Joan looks at her mother.

'You knew about this?'

'You have brought this on yourself,' Margaret says and goes out after him.

'No, I will not go,' she says to her retreating back. She turns and runs towards the door that leads to the garden. Where will you run to, Joan? Where can you hide at

Bourne? But I never discover what she has in mind for one of William's men-at-arms is guarding the door and she runs right into him. She dashes to the other door but as she pulls it open she finds another strongarm blocking the way. This is shameful.

Joan knows it is also, but there are no hysterics from her. Knowing she is beaten she finds her ladies and tells them to prepare. They know what to do, Margaret has already advised them.

Joan sits back down on her stool and picks up her needlework and works with fierce concentration until the horses are ready and they come to escort her out of her own home. She looks back once. Her mother is not there to farewell her, just her favourite servants.

So this is how it will be. She lifts her skirts and walks with some dignity down the steps to her exile.

Let us hope it is a brief one.

49.

'This is outrageous!' Ned shouts. 'Have you heard what he has done?'

The king shifts uncomfortably. How much trouble can one woman cause? This was not his idea and not his doing, why must he be called to account for it?

What does his son want of him?

'She is his wife, he can do as he wishes.'

'He has her in solitary confinement with guards at her door day and night.'

Edward wonders why his son is so exercised about this. He knows the young prince was once enamoured of her but that was a while ago surely and besides, this is really none of his business. He is pacing and raving as if it is his own wife that has been kidnapped.

The truth of it is, Edward is so taken up with the latest affairs in France he cannot see what is under his own nose. I know what ails the young prince and it alarms me. But at least here is someone who actually cares about her. Not that it will do the young sir any good, or Joan for that matter.

'How long will he keep Joan a prisoner?'

'As long as he wishes. We will have to wait for the papal courts to decide this.'

'The papal courts will still be in session come the Day of Judgment. God himself could not argue with a canonical lawyer.'

'The Pope has appointed his nephew, Cardinal Adhemar Robert himself, to hear the case. Holand has used the money from the ransom to retain Magister Robert Siglesthorne Beverley.'

'Beverley, doesn't he act for Mother? Did she recommend him?'

'Your mother is not exactly indifferent to Joan's plight, or Sir Thomas's. Beverley has some experience of the Avignon courts.'

'You should do something.'

'William is my ward and Joan is my niece. I cannot be seen to show either of them favour. Besides, William is still under age, he does not have access to his inheritance as yet, Holand can outspend him. What else would you have me do?'

'Yet you have awarded him some of that inheritance, ahead of time. Is that not showing your favour?'

'After the ransom I have allowed for the *Comte d'Eu*? You forget, it is within my power to award William his entire inheritance and then God alone knows how long we would be waiting for this to end. Give a lawyer a gold coin and he will argue with himself. I have to give the Salisburys some chance to fight back, William's father was one of my greatest friends.'

'His son is not worthy of him if this is how he behaves.'

'You say that because you do not know his father! This is precisely what he would have done. He would not have just sat idly by.'

It is the very point William's mother makes to him the next day. But she makes it more forcefully. 'You should take her,' she tells him. 'That will settle matters.'

'She refuses.'

'I didn't say ask, I said take.'

A sudden chill in the room makes the women draw their shawls tighter about their shoulders. It is me. Margaret is sitting there listening to all this, will she silently accede to the brutalization of her own daughter? Because that is what this wicked crone is suggesting.

William squares his shoulders. 'I won't do it.'

'Do you want her as your wife or not?'

He looks at his mother. Lady Salisbury looks back.

'It would be dishonourable,' he says.

'It is what a powerful lord would do.'

William does not even have a beard, just a scraggly down on his chin and already he is urged to rapine by his own mother. Is this where the nobility is headed? At feasts William and the flower of English knighthood listen to minstrels sing of King Arthur and his gallant knights, yet in private even their matriarchs consider young girls no more than chattels to be traded and violated as necessity demands.

You damned hypocrites. Stand your ground, William. Joan may be stubborn and difficult but there are parts of her that are yet fragile. Do not break my little girl, do not become as monstrous as they are.

William shakes his head. 'I won't do it,' he repeats and walks out.

The three women stare sullen into the fire. The wind howls around the castle walls.

No one is prepared to step in and stop this, no one will help Joan; not her mother, not her uncle, not her brother.

So we must leave it to the Pope and his lawyers now. If we must leave it to men of the cloth and men of law to do what's right, then God help us all.

Donyatt, Somerset

It is a pretty prison, all hung with tapestries and there are benches with bright cushions and an embrasure that looks out over the gardens. There is a bedchamber separate, with bed hangings and two small pallets for her maidservants. But it can be reached only by one set of narrow stone steps and the two manservants look more like guards to me. On Lady Salisbury's orders my daughter is not allowed to leave her rooms and is allowed no visitors. Really, she might as well be in the Tower.

But a wife is, after all, the property of her husband and William can do as he wishes, though he is hardly ever here. This is his mother and grandmother conspiring in this. I imagine they think it is the last chance to break Joan's will, and I think they are right. This is as desperate as it is shameful.

And my wife has had a part in it.

Meanwhile William tours his other properties, pretending to busy himself with affairs of management, but he stays away from court, too humiliated to show his face there.

Joan celebrates the Yule in her lonely eyrie, Lady Salisbury is magnanimous and says she may join them in the Hall for the feast. I imagine Joan would rather dine in Hell with Beelzebub but instead of saying so she just smiles and politely declines, as if she has an unfortunate prior engagement elsewhere.

She listens to the merrymaking downstairs and peers at the falling rain through the arrow slits, for even the weather is too dreary for snow.

Late in the evening she hears footsteps on the stairs. It is William.

He has the grace, at least, to look ashamed. Joan looks around when he walks in, then pointedly turns her back and returns her attention to the garden. She has a shutter open halfway, so it is cold in the room, though the fire is well stacked with logs. Joan is huddled inside an ermine cloak.

Her whole youth has been spent waiting. Even I would like to see her give this up now, for her own sake, though I do not want them to have the satisfaction of seeing her break. I would very much like to see her win and perhaps this is what this is about for her now.

'Will you not join us for the feast?' William asks her.

'I am not sure my gaoler will allow it.'

'You are not in gaol.'

'Then you will provide me with a horse and an escort and let me share the holy day with my mother at Westminster?'

'You know I cannot allow that.'

'That they will not allow it, you mean.'

'Joan, why are you doing this? What is the point of it? Is not one man like any other?'

'I am married to Sir Thomas Holand, I gave him my troth. That is why I cannot marry you.' It is the same litany she has repeated all these years. She will not budge from it.

'I thought once that it was just a strategy, so you should not have to marry the Duke of Albret.'

'Thirteen-year-old girls do not have strategy.'

'But thirteen-year-old girls can grow up and see sense at last!'

I can see he did not intend to lose his temper. But Joan shows not the slightest offence at him raising his voice.

He takes a deep breath and tries again. 'End this now. For all our sakes.'

'I knew from the moment I saw him that we were meant to be. I do not know why, but it is so.'

'If you go to him, how will your lot improve? He has no lands, no titles, and nowhere that he might take you that you could live and raise his sons. I can give you all of that and more.'

She looks at him coolly. 'He speaks to my soul,' she says and then returns her attention to the garden.

William is confounded. I can see that he has no idea what she is talking about. He admits defeat and leaves.

I can see his point of view, of course I can. None of this makes sense. But what in life make sense? Men were slaughtered at Crecy, they will die soon in hedgerows at Poitiers. Yet you do not hear anyone in England ask about the sense of it. Men die for their king, for their liege lord, sometimes they die for their religion; I have never heard anyone contend with them about their reasons for doing it.

Yet they want to know why we love, as if you can apply reason to love when you are not required to apply the same rigor to a man's appetite for violence.

I loved for love's sake and never regretted it, until now. Did my wife forget about that, or was it only me who experienced the especial madness of intoxication with another?

Perhaps it was. Now I think of it, from her point of view marrying me was just plain common sense.

50.

But the end is coming. Joan will not have to wait too much longer for her love to triumph.

First, she must see out a long winter in exile. Finally, the daffodils push through the bare brown earth. Spring is coming, sweet daughter. The roof drips with melted snow, the sun hangs cold and yellow in a washed blue sky.

The Pope orders the Archbishop of Canterbury and the bishops of London and Norwich to secure Joan's release. He says this must be done immediately so that she can appoint a proctor and she can provide her written evidence and thus expedite Holand's case before the papal courts.

The three witches of Donyatt have no choice but to comply.

I am there the day Joan is released from her confinement; so is William, who seems almost relieved that the responsibility for the impasse has been taken away from him. He has been pulled every which way in this affair and he looks utterly sick of it. I think if it was not for his mother and grandmother - and my wife - he would have walked away from this whole sorry affair long ago.

He does not have his father's drive, which makes him both a better man and worse, depending on what you expect from him. He arrives at Donyatt with an armed escort and asks Joan to accompany him across the bailie to the waiting horses. He will take her himself to Windsor, from this point on she will stay with the princesses under the king's watch rather than with her mother at Bourne.

He talks amiably on the journey as if none of this has happened, as if her release from confinement is due to his own magnanimity and not the Pope's express command. Perhaps he hopes to win her with amity now he has been defeated in law. Oh William, can't you see? She likes you well enough, she always will, but not that way.

Joan asks him about Thomas Holand on three separate occasions and he pretends not to know. He will not give up on this. Not just yet.

* * *

Soon after Joan arrives at Windsor, Edward inaugurates a new chivalric order, the Order of the Garter, and both Thomas Holand and William of Salisbury are among the twenty-four knights chosen. The king and the young prince are of course the primary members, the others have been chosen for their military prowess rather than their money and their status; the Earls of Lancaster and Warwick are to be invested along with ordinary knights such as Sir John Chandos and Sir James Audley, who both fought valorously alongside Ned at Crécy.

The king holds a tournament, a finale to the round of celebratory tournaments begun on his return from Calais the previous autumn. Joan watches from the battlements as bright-coloured pavilions blossom one by one in the lower ward. People have travelled from all over the country to attend and they are lined up as far as she can see, waiting to enter the gates, dogs and whores and tinkers and pie sellers, all the hawkers and hangers-on that such great gatherings attract.

For Joan all it means is another opportunity to see her husband. You know, not William, the husband no one wants her to have.

* * *

On the appointed day Joan is in the stands with the queen and the royal princesses as the fanfare of trumpets and tambours announce the knights of the garter on the field. They fan out behind the two royal Edwards, men and horses draped in the deep blue livery and silver-buckled garters of the new order.

The trumpets fall silent. A brisk summer wind snaps the cloaks of all twenty-six knights in the quiet. A horse snorts and jangles its harness. Then the nobility watching from the viewing stands all rise to their feet and give them thunderous applause. It is the flower of England on display, the brightest and the best, Arthur and his knights reborn.

Look at these gallants, these defenders of women, men of chivalry and honour.

If I were alive, I would spit.

* * *

There is a feast afterwards in the Great Hall. Everyone tries to forget about the great juniper fires burning in the castle yard and the reason for them. The smoke hangs so thick about the castle that it makes the eyes and throat burn. The ladies and fine gentlemen sip honeyed water for their coughs, and do not talk about the one thing that everyone else in the country is talking about.

On the day that Edward is heralding Camelot reborn, the priests are announcing the end of days.

Joan sits at the high table, with the king and the other royal women and watches the Holands, at the end of the hall. The looks that pass between her and Thomas Holand are fierce and hungry. Maud is with him for this his moment of triumph, and his two brothers. The Queen takes care to keep Joan away from them in public, but later, when the troubadours are performing their courtly love songs for the king, Joan is escorted to meet with the Lady Maud in seclusion.

It is not a pleasant walk. Everywhere around the castle men lie passed out from drink or are fornicating with serving women.

A man can have too much chivalry, after all.

Maud waits for her in one of the royal apartments, she is sipping from a crystal glass of wine, invites Joan to sit opposite her. Joan's escort retires to wait outside the door. The two women regard each other.

'So, you are Joan.'

Joan does not wilt under the close scrutiny.

'They said you were a great beauty. They did not lie.'

'Thank you, my lady.'

'Will you take some wine?'

Joan shakes her head.

'My son tells me you pledged your troth to each other in Ghent and have resisted every attempt to dissuade you of the legality of your actions. I find it astonishing that you have held out for so long. It is not only me, I think the entire court is amazed. You are a woman of very strong character.'

'I am flattered that you think so.'

'You do not think that of yourself?'

'I married your son and gave him my troth. What else was there to do?'

Maud is intrigued. She leans in. 'So all this was done because of your personal honour.'

'No, it was done because I love Thomas.'

'You hardly know him!'

'I know enough.'

'What do you know?'

Has Joan expected this, to be interrogated so fiercely this way? I warrant that she has not. But if she is shaken by it, she does not allow it to show. 'I know he is strong and valorous and honourable and that he will love me until the end of his days.'

'William of Salisbury would have done that.'

'William does not talk to my soul.'

'I do not pretend to know what that means.' She sits back again.

'Between William and your son, who would you say is the braver knight, the bolder man, who has the greater determination, who is the more intriguing for their weaknesses as well as their strengths?'

'I should have thought the answer to that was obvious,' Maud says.

'It is to me, also.'

The corners of Maud's mouth twitch into a smile.

Now it is Joan who leans in to probe with questions of her own. 'You do not approve of your son's choice?'

'I approve of it very well, very well indeed. It is yours that I am uncertain about.'

'Mine?'

'Every mother loves her son, of course, but I wonder if you know him as well as you think you do. You have spent such little time together. Your actions have already convinced me that he has found an extraordinary wife. Few men are ever as lucky. But will you have an extraordinary husband?'

'I like to think so.'

'Joan, you are right, Thomas is ambitious, headstrong and fearless. They can be great qualities for a lover and a warrior. But I wonder if they will make for a good husband.'

'I knew he would be my husband from the moment I first saw him.'

'Did you indeed? Well I am not here to change your mind, Lord knows you have had enough people trying to do that for some considerable time. I just wanted to meet you, that is all, and see for myself what kind of woman could scare a king. I have not had the chance before, for I come to court but rarely, a woman of my rank seldom has cause to be here. And I must confess, I never thought it important to meet you before now, for I never thought this marriage could ever happen. But it seems you are poised to win.'

'I have not been told of this.'

'My dear, unless something happens to Thomas on the battlefield, I expect the Pope will accede to your petition within the year.'

'I was told that this is by no means certain and that under canon law-.'

'-Canon law has nothing to do with it. As the Pope sees it, allowing this marriage will embarrass Edward, cause discord among his nobility and mean he cannot use you to barter an alliance against the French. Canon law is whatever Avignon wants it to be.'

'I will believe it when it is done.'

'A sensible attitude. You have had so few of them! But you have my blessing should you wish it. Look after my son, give him only boys and do not expect too much from him.'

Joan feels that she has been dismissed. She gets up to leave.

Lady Maud calls her back. 'What if I told you that this was only ever about the money for Thomas?'

'I should not believe you.'

Maud smiles. 'And rightly so, I'm sure. It was a great pleasure to meet you, I am sure we will see a lot of each other in the future.'

Joan lowers her head and leaves. Has Maud put doubt in her mind? None that I can see. Joan lifts her skirts and glides back through the palace to the Great Hall, escorted by two of the king's knights and resumes her place beside the Queen and the princesses to watch the fools perform for Edward.

51.

Joan knows she has to see Holand, she cannot bear to be so close to him and not talk to him. Yet Lady Salisbury has her all but under armed guard. So Joan turns to the only person who can help her: the prince.

'It is not possible,' Ned tells her. 'The king will not dare upset Lady Salisbury.'

'But the Queen might?'

'My mother? Even she will not go against the king in this.'

'Please, Ned.'

She looks up at him, her eyes liquid. And so he gives in to her, as he would give in to no one else. What does he care about Thomas Holand, or about William? Look at him, all he wants to do is please her. So, he says he will do it.

After all, he is the prince, the scourge of the French and all he has to do is intimidate a maidservant, ensure she is absent from her duties for a few minutes. Common women, noble women, maids; they would all do anything for Ned.

Poignant to watch, this. The only woman he wants he cannot get; the only woman he wants is standing in front of him now, begging him to give her a few moments alone with another man.

* * *

So what Ned does is this: he has Thomas Holand come to the castle without fanfare, as an ordinary knight, riding with Ned's own escort, the hood of his cloak pulled up over his head. It is raining hard and no one at the gate looks up anyway.

Joan is waiting for him in the cloister. Ned dismisses her maidservant with a nod. The girl has been told by the king not to allow Joan from her sight, but the king is not here and the young prince is. She hurries away and spends the next week sleepless, thinking she will be found out and called to task. But her secret is safe with us, yes?

Ned hovers, watches Joan and Thomas Holand fall into each other's arms. Holand is wet, his cloak soaked through. She does not seem to mind.

Ned holds his ground for a moment, hoping for at least some small gesture of thanks from the woman he loves, but Joan is too taken with her own passion to even remember he is still there.

He cannot bear to linger. I leave with him, I do not know what Holand and my daughter do with their few stolen moments of solitude, I do not wish to know. The rain splashes into large muddy puddles in the courtyard and the din it makes mutes all other sound.

Once out of sight, Ned slumps against a wall; the flower of English chivalry, the most eligible prince in Europe, reduced to despair by a slip of a girl. I feel for him. He knocks his forehead hard against the stone. I believe he curses himself silently for a fool. Better to be Thomas Holand, ardent and without discrimination and lucky, than be in our young prince's clothes, faithful to a lost cause.

52.

Fires of juniper wood dot the upper and lower wards, the smoke is thought to keep away the deadly vapours that accompany the pestilence, for the plague has returned to England. The church bell in the town has already rung several times this day for the dead: even while Edward celebrates his new age, an old death is ravaging England.

The king pushes on with his Garter celebrations, determined that death will not interfere with his plans. Well, I suppose we are all like that.

Down in the ward, his entourage trailing behind through the mud, Ned searches out the young Earl of Salisbury's pavilion. He pushes the tent flap aside and strides in. William has just been suited into his armour. 'William. How are you this fine morning? All ready for the sport? I see you are drawn in the lists against Sir Thomas Holand.'

William has his helm under one arm; his squires hover around him though there is nothing more to be done. He looks far too young for this. Beneath his bluff demeanour Ned appears uncomfortable; so much he would like to say but is constrained. 'Give a good account,' he says.

'I will do more than that. I will win.'

Ned changes the subject. 'The rain overnight has churned up the field, the horses are uncertain in their footing.'

'Did you hear me? I am going to win. I will show Joan which of us is the better man.'

It is plain on Ned's face: he feels sorry for William. Of all the men in the young earl's circle he alone knows the foolishness and the anguish of loving a woman. Well, you would think so. But I suspect with William it is not quite the anguish that Ned feels; it is more that his pride is hurt.

'Give this up,' Ned says to him. 'This has nothing to do with Thomas, or with you, or with the Pope. It is Joan that has decided.'

'Does she love him, do you think, or does she do this just to prove that she can?'

'Does it matter?'

William is not a big man and he looks as if he will topple over in all that shining armour plate; the gorget, the lobstered greaves, the pointed steel boots. 'I will win,' he declares a third time and clatters out. He slides in the mud and almost topples but a squire comes to his aid just in time.

* * *

Joan sits between her Aunt Blanche and the two royal princesses. Blanche is Lancaster's daughter and Wake's wife. She married beneath her, just as I did. Wake is always conscious of this, and Blanche reminds him of it often in case his memory should fail him.

Bella nudges Joan's arm as Holand enters the lists, his helm still under his arm. He looks noble; a silver dragon snarls on his blue shield and he wears his family's colours over his chain mail. I see my sister-in-law's lips twist in contempt. Even the sight of the Holand crest makes Blanche want to do unladylike things.

'Well this adds some spice to the contest,' the king says.

Indeed it does, but Joan does not allow even a flicker of consternation to show on her face. Holand puts on his helm and takes up his position in the lists. Now it is William's turn; he raises his visor for a moment, salutes Joan and the other ladies in the Berfrois. Both men couch their lances.

I watch my daughter, now the attention is no longer upon her she allows herself an unguarded moment. I see her bite her lip and her hands clench into fists in her lap.

Oh, don't worry, my sweet, Holand will be alright. It is William you should worry for.

The gallery trembles as the horses charge towards each other. William leans forward slightly in the saddle, holding his lance straight and steady, but Holand shifts slightly in his saddle just before impact and turns the point of his adversary's lance against his shield while his own finds its mark.

William's shield shatters, and he fights to stay in the saddle. A squire runs up to his horse as he pulls up at the far end of the lists and a new shield is brought.

'Sir William looks to be in some pain,' Bella says and earns a scowl from Lady Blanche.

But William is made of sterner stuff that I had supposed. He takes the new shield and jerks the reins, spurring his mount back to the lists for a second pass. Holand's lance has splintered and he has already tossed it aside and taken a new one.

They all can see that William is too eager, too angry, wants to win this contest too badly. A man needs two things in the lists, as he needs in any fight: a clear head, and experience. William has neither.

He spurs his courser too hard, wants to take Holand's head off. Holand again shifts in his saddle just before impact but this time William does the same. Both lances shatter. William drops the reins, reeling in his saddle, and goes down. There is a ragged cheer from the commons; they love to see a knight unhorsed.

Holand reaches the end of the lists, and his horse canters to a halt. He slides from the saddle and lies still on the ground. At this point Joan finally gives herself away, jumping to her feet and putting both hands to her mouth.

Bella takes her hand and pulls her back down into her seat.

Edward is more concerned about the result. 'Who do I declare the winner?' he asks Ned beside him. 'Or is it a draw?'

'I would give the purse to the first man to rise,' Ned says.

Neither man looks ready to do so. William's riderless horse walks away and starts to graze. He is attended by his squires but is yet to move. Holand's own squires run towards him, but he raises one hand to send them scurrying away again.

He raises himself and removes his helm. He rises slowly, it is not easy in such heavy armour; to his knees, first, then to one knee. There is applause from the royal pavilion.

Meanwhile William's squires place him on a broad shield and carry him off to the surgeon's tent. Holand limps across the muddy field, ignoring the wild applause from the galleries, not even a glance at my daughter, who sits on her hands and frets.

Instead he goes direct to William's tent, wishes to know what damage he has wrought. He finds his rival lying on a wooden trestle, groaning. They already have his body armour off, there is a livid purple bruise growing on his pale and hairless chest, but the barber declares that his injury is not mortal. It seems he will not be following his father to the shades in the same wasteful fashion.

He holds up his right hand when he sees Holand. He takes it.

William beckons him closer. 'Be a good husband to her,' he croaks.

Sir Thomas Holand has won in the lists and in the heart and soon it seems he will win in the courts too.

He will win everything. For some men it is like that.

53.

The next morning, while wisps of fog cling to the river in ghostly white fingers, men blunder through the half-dark, throwing saddles on horses, tramping out fires, loading wagons. Down come the poles of the great pavilions and the blue and silver pennants of the Garter knights. Trestles and benches are hauled away, trumpets echo around the walls waking those slow to rise. Horses whinny as they are led from the stables, and the sun inches over the Berkshire fields.

The great families of England prepare to go home.

But this is no ordinary leave-taking, it is more like seeing an army off to war. The plague is ravaging the entire country, and no one is sure if they will see friends or family again. Who knows who the pestilence will strike next? It is no respecter of rank or privilege.

Joan watches from one of the high stone walls as Holand finishes saddling his horses, down there in the bailey with the grooms and his two brothers, laughing as if there is nothing in the world to trouble him. He believes himself indestructible.

A drowned dog floats in the river. A rat scurries along the castle walls, keeping to the damp and the shadows.

It finds a hole and scuttles in.

* * *

Jeanette has been betrothed to Peter of Castile, the son of King Alfonso of Castile and Maria of Portugal, for some three years now. A month after the Windsor tournament she leaves England for Spain. At sixteen years of age Edward considers her old enough to consummate the union.

She is to be escorted over the channel by a hundred of his best bowmen, most of them veterans of Crecy. Edward spares no expense; her wedding dress is made with more than one hundred and fifty metres of a thick imported silk called *rakematiz*, and her trousseau requires an entire ship to transport it. He is eager to make a display of power and wealth to his Spanish allies in Castile.

The fleet consists of four English ships, they sail from Portsmouth and are received in Bordeaux by the mayor, Raymond de Bisquale. As soon as they arrive, he warns Joan's protectors that there is plague in the city but they think he is being over-cautious. They settle in the royal castle overlooking the Gironde estuary, as planned, and then watch in horror and disbelief as members of the royal entourage begin to fall sick and die all around them.

Jeanette is hurriedly moved to a small village called Loremo, outside the city, but it is too late. At midday on the first day of July she takes to her bed with a fever, by the afternoon she is raving and by sunset she is dead.

I am present there the day she leaves her hopes and cares behind. Death plays no favourites, royal or not, he does not care; there is no by your leave, your grace, not as far as he is concerned. I escort her small and scared shadow across the divide. She is my great niece and I owe this to her, at least. She trembles, even beyond the veil. Just a quiet girl who is dead before she even lived.

Don't ask me why, there are no answers over here, no one on hand to finally explain things. It hardly seems fair, even to me, but then life isn't.

Ask William. Ask Jeanette.

Ask me.

54.

Otford

O h, for the love of the Saviour, enough. Do they enjoy torturing her like this? It is no longer about persuasion, they just want to punish her now.

It is the first day of the Yule feast, Joan is free from imprisonment and living now with the King and the royal ladies. It is a different kind of exile, this, they want to keep her away from Holand as long as they can. Joan, in her heartache, does not join the royal party for the festivities, Ned is the only one who goes looking for her, a servant tells him she in her apartments, staring gloomily into a fire.

Why is she so miserable, I wonder? Is it because of her separation from Holand, or is it something else?

Because I cannot believe Margaret has allowed this to happen. If someone is ever to relent in such a situation, then it should be the parent. If it is the child, then you break their spirit; a mother or father merely learns humility in the face of fierce youth.

But her family, my family, they have all abandoned her; Blanche, her aunt; Wake, her uncle; her mother most of all. She is the one person in this barbed world who should have stood beside her, to protect her.

There is a tapping on the door. It inches open, it is the prince.

'Joan? They are about to start the feast. Won't you join us downstairs?'

'I am not hungry.'

Ned steps confidently into the room, all colour and force. 'Now that cannot be true, the servants say you have not eaten since the breakfast.'

'I am not in a festive mood, Ned.'

'Listen, can you not hear them? The revels have begun. You always loved the dancing.'

Joan shakes her head.

Ned has a hand behind his back, he is concealing something. With a flourish, he brings it out to show her, a beaker of silver with her name engraved. She is touched by the gift, it is evident by her face.

But she still does not want to join in the revels.

'There are many handsome knights to dance with, you might even choose a poor specimen like myself.' Indeed, the pleasant uproar from the Great Hall grows by the moment. It is the first day of the New Year and the Noel is celebrated anew. Will Joan sit here alone for all the fifteen days?

There is the blaring of trumpets and flutes and tambours. They are bringing out the feast; there will be wild boar, pies, cheeses, puddings, coffins filled with minced pork, eggs, fruit and spices. 'No thank you, Ned. I may join the queen later to play at cards.'

Ah, the Queen! She is still in mourning for little Jeanette, she will not be dancing or watching the masques either. Ned looks crestfallen. 'You will not come, not even for a little while?'

She gives him a sad smile and shakes her head. I imagine he was expecting such a rebuttal. But a man, even a prince, lives in hope.

'Perhaps tomorrow,' she tells him.

55.

And so to 1349, the tomorrow she speaks of. There are, in fact, very few tomorrows for many people.

The whole country is laid waste. Entire villages are abandoned and there are no labourers to harvest the crops or till the fields. In many places there is not even anyone to bury the dead, so they are left to rot in the street or in their houses. Noble blood might spare some, those living in the finer houses, but it is by no means guaranteed. Death is not so particular that it keeps itself to the hovels and the tenements.

William of Salisbury is spared, after a fashion, but he loses all his supporters and most of those he loves. First, in the spring, Lady Salisbury succumbs, hurrying from the world as quickly as a crofter's wife, when it is done she is just another shadow and I do not recognize her as she passes. At the end of May, Thomas Wake follows her.

Neither are the Holands untouched. The mother, Maud, and a sister are both claimed by the pestilence.

And then in the autumn, news is brought to Windsor from Lincolnshire that Margaret is mortally ill. I had seen this, saw a shadow attach itself to her, but there was nothing I could do to warn her, and it would have made no difference if I had.

Joan insists that she go to her. But the roads are not safe, the king tells her, there is nothing you can do, you must stay here at Windsor. But Joan insists that she go to Bourne, she believes that just one word from her mother at the end will make all the difference. So Edward, urged by the Queen, provides a fast horse and an escort of his best knights.

It is a strange and silent country now, England. The inns are closed, the windows are boarded, the roads lawless, and if it were not for her escort, who ride in armour, ready for a fight, Joan would not have made ten miles. Eyes peer out at them from shuttered windows, no one trusts travellers any more, for outsiders bring plague with them. Her knights force farmers to let them shelter in their barns or intimidate monks into letting them sleep overnight in abbeys.

But by the time Joan arrives at Bourne, Margaret is already gone. She lies shrunken in the great bed, doors and windows open wide to let out the foul humours. Her fragrant necklace of herbs proved no protection at all. Her body is covered in boils.

Joan is not allowed near her for fear of contagion. I watch her fall to her knees and weep. What is there to weep for? I wonder. The mother she wished she had, perhaps. No doubt she thought there would be a day when they would heal their wounds.

She will always have to say now: *my mother never loved me.*

Joan walks in the orchard as the body is wound in a shroud with sweet smelling herbs. They burn the bed sheets at the bottom of the garden on a huge juniper fire. Joan holds a spice ball to her nose and looks around.

The estate is in ruins. Windfall apples, pecked by birds, turn brown where they lie; hay rots in the fields beyond the stone walls and the cows low in pain, for there is no one left to milk them.

Margaret is hastily buried. Her shadow passes right through me and does not linger. I think she hardly knows me now.

I loved her to the point of distraction once. But her soul is so withered by care and by the world that she appears stained and crouched, even in death. I do not try and call her back. It would only be to admonish her and that would do no good.

Some troubles in life make our spirits stronger and brighter; with others it just withers the soul and leaves it putrid.

William has now lost all his supporters, and with their passing he loses his appetite for the struggle to keep Joan. Perhaps they were the only ones who still really wanted it anyway. He arranges to marry Elizabeth, daughter and co-heiress of John, Lord Mohun of Dunster.

Joan goes home to mourn or to wish that she could.

56.

Eltham

There is an abandoned nest in an overhang high in the tower. A murder of crows call plaintively from the bare trees and leaves skitter across the gravel path below.

Fog rises from the river. Bundled in furs, Joan stands on the battlement and watches a barge swing in to the landing. It is yet bitter cold but for my Joan the long winter is finally over.

A hooded figure steps from the barge and strides up the path to the castle. He has an escort with him, but he leaves them at the gatehouse and continues alone. He nods briefly to the frozen wretches standing guard duty inside the barbican. It is his habit, she knows from years of watching him come and go in many castles, many keeps, to stop and share a few words with some common soldier, but not today.

Joan waits for him in a high-backed chair by the fire. She is still in mourning; black velvet, some onyx beads. I thought it would be different from this if it should ever happen; I thought there would be trumpets and fanfare. But this is a plague year and besides, I think what Joan feels is just an overwhelming sense of disbelief.

She fidgets as she waits: should she stand, should she sit?

What if there has been a last-minute delay in the courts? She stares at the carved oak door and closes her eyes in silent prayer.

She hears his footsteps coming along the corridor. A servant leads the way in, leaves them cheese, ale and winter apples. They both wait until the man steps outside again and then throw themselves in each other's arms. At last, there will be no more clandestine meetings in the shade of buttery walls.

Holand whispers to her what she already knows; the Pope has confirmed his cardinal nephew's judgment, their marriage has been declared lawful by the Church and Joan is now Thomas Holand's wife before the world. Ten years have gone to waste but at last she has her choice. I know of no one else I have known in my lifetime who could have endured so much, or who would have had the will or the determination to have defied the world in this way.

She at last allows herself to cry in plain sight. He holds her, enfolds her, whispers that everything will be alright now.

I almost turn to leave, thinking he is right.

But I stop at the door and return. Why, I am not sure. Something in me is troubled and warns me that she may yet need me again.

57.

Their marriage is consecrated by the Bishop of Norwich himself, at the Pope's express command. Edward and the prince cannot be there, they have clandestine affairs of their own to settle, another foray into France it is said. The Queen and Bella attend and smile reassuringly at Joan, but the list of guests is more remarkable for who is missing than who is there.

My Joan looks glorious in a rose bodice and lavender skirt embroidered with gold thread. The nave is lit with torches and tapers as she enters. She clasps her husband's hands and whispers the words of marriage as she had promised she would on that winter's day almost ten years ago.

There. It is done.

And so tonight they are finally alone without the fear of discovery or punishment, and the journey is at an end.

Or is it?

As every wife and husband knows, even the greatest love only truly begins when the passion ends.

As soon as her hair is brushed through and the candles are dimmed and the last servant leaves, she gets into the warmed and downy bed and waits for her husband. Tonight, she believes their love will last forever. But will it always be this way, now she has what she wanted, will she always love him as she has when he was merely a dream?

We will leave now: we know what happens next. I am her father; even a ghost is discreet. I brush past him briefly as he hurries towards his prize. Be good to her, I tell him, though he cannot hear me.

Be good to her.

The heavy door closes. I drift along the cold passageways and deserted battlements the night long, worrying for her. A single candle burns behind a shuttered window. She has a husband now, her father's duty is done.

But a father's watch is never ended. You will see.

58.

A year later

A marriage is the ending of one story and the start of another. Look at Margaret and me; it was a love match once. Keeping love means taking quite a different story to its happy end.

And what is this story? Once, long ago, there was a countess whose husband was one of the wealthiest noblemen in England. She lived at court, a busy and colourful and crowded and affluent place. There were feasts and dancing and tournaments and gallants and women in beautiful gowns and handsome men in the king's colours going about their business every day.

But she was in love with a handsome but landless knight, and they proved their love against all obstacles thrown in their path.

And at the end of this story the countess has her wish and marries her true love. So she leaves the court, and she gives up nobility for being a wife, moves from palace to humble hearth, from the very heart of England to a quiet country manor where there is never a trumpet or a drum to disturb the birdsong. I concede that Broughton is no hovel: it is a perfectly fine house, it is where Holand's mother Maud lived out her days in some comfort before she, too, fell victim to the pestilence that has devastated England.

But it is not Windsor. It is not Eltham.

Holand prowls the great hall like a caged lion. Joan watches him, wondering what she might do to assuage this restlessness. She dreads the day he will leave her here in this draughty place alone.

It is like this: William of Salisbury's income was around one thousand five hundred pounds a year. Holand earns twelve pounds a year in the king's service, three times that when he is on campaign. With the income from three Northamptonshire manors he earns a little more. After Crecy he should have been awarded the rank of banneret, but a knight needs two hundred pounds a year to support such a rank and he earns nothing like that.

If he is to advance he needs money; but he needs money to advance.

'What about the ransom for the Count of Eu?' she asks him.

'Most of that went to the lawyers.'

'But that was just the first instalment,' she says. 'There were three instalments intended for you from the king.'

I can see his face: it surprises him that she takes such an interest in financial matters. Money bores him, except when he needs it.

'The king allowed him to return to France to raise the rest of the ransom money. This is a normal arrangement.'

'I know. William's father did the same.'

'Except that the Count of Eu was arrested for treason soon after he returned and was summarily executed. The French no longer feel quite as inclined to pay the rest of the money.'

She has not heard this news: now she is no longer at court, she relies on Holand to tell her what is happening in the world beyond Broughton. Once she was at the very heart of things and heard everything before it was even a whisper.

'Executed? But why?'

'Does it matter? It is convenient for the King of France, whatever the reason.'

'But the promise was from Edward, not the French.'

'Edward has no money. Now he has given me enough to pay the lawyers, he is not inclined to pay the rest.'

'What will you do?'

'It depends on the king.'

Her face says it all. 'You will go back to war,' she says.

'I am a soldier, that is what I do.'

I know what Joan wants: she wants him to stay here and help her run the manor but that is not in his nature. Besides, it is not wise. Aside from marriage, war is the only way a knight can better himself. He had likely hoped for better from the king, but Edward is not of a mind to reward him for causing him so much embarrassment and tribulation.

He has his marriage, and the king considers this all the abundance he will get from him. He has not been invited to the king's inner circle and he has not had titles heaped upon him, as he had hoped.

The king does not need more lackeys with titles; what he wants are good soldiers. All Holand has done is put him out of sorts with his family and made him look uncharitable or negligent before the world.

Why would the king love him for that?

Joan winces and rests a hand on her belly; their first child is growing and is soon to join them in the world. Holand sees a letter lying on the table, among the dried candle grease, it is unsealed, unfinished. He picks it up and peruses it quickly. The letter is for him, in case the birthing does not go well. It tells him how much she loves him and what to tell the child about her when he is a man, for she is sure that it is a boy.

He stares at the letter as if it is an affront to him personally. 'You will not be needing this,' he says.

'It is surety in case God decides otherwise.'

'I said you will not be needing this!' He takes the letter and tosses it into the fire. It flares and crumbles to ash. She sighs. Now she will have to write it again.

'I don't know what I would do without you,' he says and walks out. I have watched Holand closely for a long time, in peace and in war and this is the first time I have ever seen him frightened.

* * *

Joan is frightened also. Isn't every woman? There are pallets set up in her bedchamber for her three companions during the waiting in. When the day comes she walks the carpets supported by a midwife and one of the maidservants.

So on this day I am to become a grandfather, or I should be if life had been more kind. I pace the halls at Broughton in step with my son-in-law, every bit as anxious as he. Childbirth is a dangerous and bloody business, and with the first the dangers are greatest. It is not a business for the faint-hearted.

I am not one for the screams and so when he removes to the bottom of the garden, so do I. I wait there with him until a servant comes breathless to tell him, tell us, that he is father to a healthy baby boy.

'Joan, what about Lady Joan?' he says.

'She is safely delivered,' the man says.

Holand runs back to the house and I follow him up to her bedchamber, look over his shoulder as he holds his new pink son in his arms. Joan looks pale and damp and tired. But she is well.

They already have a name; they will call the boy Thomas. I am disappointed, a little; I had hoped he would be Edmund.

Little Thomas is laid in a wooden cradle next to Joan's bed in a shadowed corner, so that the light does not hurt his eyes. He sleeps securely bundled in sheets of Rheims linen with fur coverlets decorated with the Holand crest. There is a servant constantly at hand to rock him to sleep.

A few days later he is christened in the Broughton church and the prince himself rides up from London to attend as godfather. He brings his new godson the gift of two silver plates. Such a godfather will be an extremely valuable and influential patron for my son-in-law. Do you not think?

Ned is the hero of all England now, a knight of the garter, the scourge of the French. They say he has a child of his own now somewhere, though he has not married. When he does it will surely be decisive, for Ned's father is nothing if not tactical.

That night the prince and Thomas Holand sit by a roaring fire at Broughton with their brandy wine and discuss the war and politics and past campaigns, as old friends and old soldiers do everywhere. Inevitably, the talk turns to Holand's own future. Ned tells him there will be a new campaign in France in the summer.

'I shall stand with the king, of course,' Holand says. 'I have no choice.'

Ned is suddenly careful, sensing criticism of his father. 'On the contrary, you might do as you wish. You could stay here and enjoy your inheritance, if you choose.'

'The few estates my mother left me are not enough to support Joan in the manner to which she is accustomed. And thanks to the pestilence there are few men left to run the estates or the mills.'

'It is the same all over England.'

Holand stares into his wine. 'I was rather hoping for more from the king.'

Ned smiles and says nothing.

'Besides I am bored here.'

'With Joan?'

A sharp look. 'No, not with Joan. But after Crecy and Calais, life in Broughton is a little slow.'

'Joan will miss you if you take up the king's colours in France this summer.'

'But that is a soldier's life, it would have been no different with William. I am told Joan's brother, John, will join the army for the campaign. How is he these days?'

'John is well,' Ned says.

'I imagine there will be another christening to attend soon.'

'I have heard nothing about that,' Ned says.

Why is he cautious in how he answers? Because Holand's question may appear to be innocuous, a man asking after his new brother-in-law's health and family, but it is nothing of the sort. These two are fencing around dark subjects here. When Holand comments on the king's favour, Ned is on difficult ground. His father's action or inaction is nothing to do with him, though he might influence it if he wishes to.

And they both know very well that my son John has no aptitude for the military. He served under Henry of Lancaster in the Crecy campaign, but he was not present at the battle. He is not like the prince or like Holand. Lancaster kept him safe at the king's request.

Neither did Holand ask about the fecundity of John's marriage from fond feeling. When Wake and Margaret fell victim to the pestilence, John inherited estates in seventeen counties including forty-three manors, thirty advowsons and an income of six thousand pounds a year, an eye watering sum.

William supports the lifestyle of an earl on just *one thousand*.

So here is what both Holand and Ned know but do not say; if anything happens to my son John before he has heirs, Joan will inherit everything and Thomas Holand, as her husband, will have control of all of it.

He is a heartbeat from every glorious dream he has ever dreamed and many that he had dared not. But if John lives a long life surrounded by a brood of children - or even just one - Holand must go back to the wars and live in respectable penury the rest of his life, with nothing to pass on to his new son but an unsavoury reputation and a good military record.

But John is only twenty years old and in perfect health. He enjoys good relations with his new wife. What can ever be amiss?

'More wine?' Holand asks Ned and they let these dark matters lie and return to talking about the wars.

Later that night, after everyone is abed, the prince prowls the dark halls. Then he puts on a heavy ermine cloak and goes outside to stand in the snow, stares at the crisp cold moon. His breath freezes on the air.

I stand beside him. I hear him whisper a name.

'Joan.'

You see? Everyone harbours secret dreams they dare not voice; Holand, Joan, Ned, I wonder which of them will see their dreams fulfilled?

PART 4

59.

Time passes. Joan is plump now with another child. Holand has been at Westminster with the king but today he returns. His arrival is accompanied with shouting and commotion, as always. Joan is upstairs sitting in a chair by the window, resting.

He is breathless when he rushes in. He is still in his riding boots with the mud of the road on him. He tears off the heavy leather gauntlets to embrace her and has barely greeted her before he gets out his news.

'I have been appointed captain of Calais castle! My brother Otto is to be my deputy! It is a great responsibility, a huge honour, everything that I had hoped for. Calais is the king's bridgehead to France, a haven for our ships. Edward has said that he wants to repopulate the town with Englishmen and I am to oversee it all!'

'That is wonderful news,' Joan says, and she contrives to smile and look happy for him.

'It is what I have waited for! The king has placed great trust in me. I shall not disappoint him.'

He has not disappointed the king perhaps, but can he see how he much he has dismayed his wife with this news, how hard she tries to hide it from him? Ten years she waited for him and now he cannot wait to get away from her. Still, it will further his career and they cannot survive on what the manor estates bring in.

I believe she only wishes that he would appear less effusive about going back to the wars, that is all.

'I will miss you,' she says.

'I will be back before you know it.' His one good eye shines. He is so eager, she suspects he will not miss her at all. 'I will appoint attorneys to help you run the estates while I am gone.'

'Thank you, Thomas.'

'I will make you proud of me.'

'I am already proud of you.' And she is. He is one of the king's best commanders and all the court knows it.

He kisses her again and goes upstairs to peep on his son, who is asleep. Joan shifts uncomfortably, the new baby has been kicking her and her back feels as if it is breaking. I wonder, too, if she still remembers that day at Woodstock; one day Holand will ride away and not come home, just like her father.

* * *

Joan misses the bustle of the court, or it is what she tells her ladies, out of earshot of her husband. There, she could choose to be alone, if she wished, but it was never imposed on her; here at Broughton there is often no choice but to be solitary.

And she is anxious, the baby will arrive soon. This time her husband will not be fretting at the bottom of the garden; instead he will be in Calais, making it a happy place for Englishmen.

He leaves, but she is trapped here. She cannot leave the castle, she is too heavily pregnant; and so England instead comes to her. In quick succession, she has visits from the princess Isabella and from her brother John.

Ah, John. I have not forgotten him, but I worry about him less. I was there to watch him grow, to see how his mother cosseted him and made him think he was the only boy in the world that mattered. Still, for all that he has turned out a decent enough young man. Not much of a soldier, but at least he is kind to his sister.

John is delighted to see her, as he always is. He lives in no little comfort these days; his mother did well by him. He has money, a good marriage, and all before his twenty-third birthday. The king may have had his father's head hacked off but his son is now one of the wealthiest men in England. Margaret knew what she was about, in affairs at least.

John asks if his sister is well and happy, after so many years and so many rumours. She says that she is. His new wife Elizabeth asks about the baby. There is longing in her eyes, Joan can see how desperately she wants a child of her own. She answers diplomatically, trying not to reveal too much of her own pleasure and excitement about her growing family. She says that if it is a boy, they will name him John. Her brother is delighted.

Then he asks her if she has heard about the royal princess, Bella.

'The king arranged a marriage for her to the Duke of Albret's son.'

'Oh him,' Joan says, letting her guard slip. 'He's been hawked all over the place for years. You would have thought he was stale pie by now.'

John smiles at this, though he thinks his sister intemperate.

'I was supposed to be his wife ten years ago.'

'I remember. It was why you married Thomas, wasn't it?'

There is a long silence. This must remind her of something Margaret would say. He is sometimes too much his mother's son, my John, he has always held the family line and why not, I suppose, he did not become his mother's favourite by being difficult.

'It lent urgency to what we did,' Joan says at last. 'But I would not have waited ten years for an excuse.'

'Well the king thought him more than stale pie. He arranged the marriage and sent her off to Sandwich to take ship.'

'I heard she did not want the marriage, that she was utterly opposed to it. Really, Edward always claims that he loves her, yet he would have sent her off to Gascony against her wishes?'

'Well it didn't work out, did it?'

'You knew about this?'

'She visited me recently.

'Bella visits you often, I'm told. Was it you that put her up to this?'

'I am just her cousin.'

'Well, someone said something to her. When she arrived at Sandwich she refused to board the ship, they had to escort her back to Windsor.'

Joan smiles.

'You approve?'

'It's better than going to Castile and dying of plague, like poor little Jeanette.'

'That was just unfortunate.'

'Everything is just unfortunate if you are not the one it happens to. As for Bella, perhaps the king will consider more carefully next time before he pushes her into a marriage she does not want. It is good to hear my pretty cousin has a back bone. I thought she would never do it.'

'I knew I saw your hand in this somewhere!'

'I told you, her actions had nothing to do with me.'

'She was here just two weeks ago. What was it you said to her?'

'I wished her well with her marriage to possibly the ugliest man in Europe. Oh John, don't look at me like that.' She laughs. 'Of course I didn't.'

But he looks at her a long time before smiling back.
Yes, you did, he thinks.
Yes you did.

60.

He and Elizabeth stay for three days and then ride back to Woodstock. Joan does not know then what I already know and can scarce believe; I saw a shadow clinging to him in the days before he left.

So he and Elizabeth return to Woking manor to spend Christmas there. He is conducting business as usual, granting his manor of Ryhall in Rutland to Bartholomew de Burghers, when he is taken ill. A few days later the news is sent to Broughton; her brother is dead.

This is not how it was meant to be. Of the four of us who played out our dramatic scene at Arundel these twenty-seven years ago, now only Joan remains. They bury my son in Grey Friars church in Winchester next to my old bones.

John's soul is with me now. He did not think to see me again so soon, or I him. But that is the nature of it, some of us are given warning but there are others, like me, like my son, who are as shocked by our leaving as those we leave behind.

Joan only hears of his illness on the day he dies. She does not even think it serious enough to worry overmuch, but she could not have gone there to be with him even if it was. She has just given birth to a little boy called John.

And so the wheel of life turns; a shadow in, a shadow out.

It changes nothing here in these ethereal halls. But down there, where Joan and Holand are, it makes all the difference in the world.

61.

S ome men have fortune heaped upon them, like pumpkins on a cart, other men could not find a cow pat in a pasture. It is the way of it. Do not ask me to explain it, there is no greater wisdom on this side than there is on yours. But you would have to concede that a man like Holand had enough good fortune in his life for a regiment of others.

He hurries home from France to comfort his wife. Joan has been stalwart through ten years of exile, disapproval, loneliness and uncertainty but now, exhausted from the birthing of her new son, she learns that her own family is now all gone. John was the one certainty in her life. She doesn't care to be one of the wealthiest women in England at the cost of her only brother.

Holand rushes to Joan's side and holds her in those stout arms, whispers the words of comfort she needs to hear. I am glad of him now. He does his utmost to portray grief but he hardly knew John, and he would not be human if he was not privately the happiest man in England.

He does not know the extent of the fortune his wife has inherited but it will become clear to him in the following days; interests in twenty-three counties and forty-three manors; countless fee farms, knight's fees and advowsons as well as rents in six more counties. By terms of the inheritance Joan has a one third share in this.

In crude terms, my daughter's share of the income from all this plenty is three thousand and five hundred pounds a year, an enormous sum, three times that of young William of Salisbury.

Before today, Holand could not even support himself as a banneret, being short of the two hundred pounds per annum required for such a position. He left England's shores a journeyman knight, he has returned as one of the richest men in England.

The gamble he made when he married Joan has paid off in a way that he could not possibly have dreamt. He collects his winnings in mourning black, looks grim as the casket is interred in the church, stands firm for his wife and takes everything.

* * *

Castle Donington sits on the west side of the town, its crenulated walls dominate the river and the ferry crossing over the Trent. It has its own chapel, park and fishery and is surrounded by woodland; there is a meadow and pastures where cattle graze. It is his and Joan's new home, and she and Holand arrive there with their two young boys to start their new life.

It is, of course, no longer just the four of them. They will not rattle around in this draughty manor with just a handful of servants. As befitting their position and their wealth, they have brought an army with them; fifteen knights; a hundred squires and heralds; fifty clerks as well as chaplains, confessors, almoners, grooms, valets servants and minstrels. There are also goldsmiths to keep Joan in jewels, laundresses and chambermaids to keep her household in shape and a dozen ladies of the chamber each with their own maidservant.

But their new idyll is not without its problems. The estates have been devastated by the depredations of the pestilence, as has the rest of England. On the first day they ride into the town, down empty streets rutted with wheel and hoof. It is market day but the wooden stalls in the town square are deserted. The small neat houses of log and undressed stone are mostly boarded up. When an old man sees them, he drops the bundle he is carrying and hurries away down an alley. Two old women bend the knee, clearly terrified.

They inspect the water mill, find scum floating on the pond, loose timbers creaking and flour rotting in sacks. The cottages where the workers lived are empty, their families dead or fled to the city. The lead mill is similarly abandoned.

One of the councillors, charged with running the estate, tells Holand what needs to be done; they will have to re-establish the arable crops and the livestock to bring in food and income; new workers and leaseholders must be brought in; a proper accounting needs be made. I can see that Holand does not much like the sound of it, it appears to him like months spent poring over ledgers and supervising staff and bailiffs and seneschals, not just here, but from one end of the country to the other.

He frowns and rides away. Joan stares after him. Perhaps she harboured hopes that with such a windfall, he might choose to remain in England.

But that is not his nature.

62.

He is drinking late with his knights at the table in the Great Hall and is late to bed. He staggers going up the stairs to his private chambers and almost falls. This is not like him. Men like Holand hold their drink, they are accustomed to it. Tonight though he drank enough for a regiment of brothel-keepers and there is red wine in his beard and even stains on his tunic.

Joan is awake when he enters the bedchamber and I linger only long enough to see him collapsed still half-dressed on the bed. She makes no move to help him; instead she rolls on her side and pretends to sleep but her eyes are open and I see she is crying.

The next morning she finds him alone and talks to him about all that must be done; she has appointed a council and has charged them with collecting the overdue rents and finding new tenants for the empty holdings. But there is much more to do.

'Have you thought we might rationalise the estates,' she says.

'Rationalise?'

'Our holdings are spread all over England. It would be good husbandry to buy lands and sell others until they are concentrated together.'

'That would take time.'

'Do we not have time?'

He frowns as if the question was intended to irritate him.

'And you have not yet attended parliament. The king will expect it.'

'If the king thinks so much about me, he would make me Earl of Kent. It is my due.'

'He will in time. He cannot be seen to act too hastily.'

Another sour look. He gets up and announces that he is going hunting and calls for his falconer. Important questions are left undecided. She watches him walk away. She reminds herself that this is her Thomas; she cannot make him John as well.

* * *

The painted chamber at Westminster was built at the command of the old king, Henry, and under his order it is as imposing as his craftsmen could make it, long and narrow with a canopied state bed at one end, its four posts painted green with golden stars. The paintings that cover the walls are mostly colourful Biblical scenes with explanatory texts beneath. Above the bed itself is a large painting of Edward the Confessor.

I was never there, though my brother the former king once told me it is a draughty place and that he hated it. Gaveston hated it also and used to make unwise jokes about it.

But it is here that Edward and his queen take their ease when they are at Westminster; it is here they discuss private matters, some of them personal things between them, some of them political. Tonight, they are discussing what to do about Thomas Holand; the new, powerful and wealthy version of the man, the one whose king now needs him more than he needs the king.

Or so it would appear.

'What are you going to do?' she asks him. 'You need his men and his money.'

'Joan's money.'

'You talk like a lawyer. The truth is, he has control of it. Will you not even make him a justice of the peace? It would be outrageous not to, it will attract comment.'

'And reward him for all the humiliation he caused me? He has recompense enough for one lifetime, does he not?'

Philippa sighs with exasperation. But then, this is Edward, he can be petty like this at times. Yet it is unlike him not to put away his pride when he needs something.

'You need to encourage him somehow.'

'I do not need to do anything.'

'And how do you surmise this?'

'Thomas will not stay at his grand castle when there is a new campaign to be fought. Soldiering is in his blood. He could hate me till his bones ache, but he could no more see the army go to France without him than he could cut off his sword arm. You will see.'

Sometimes Edward astonishes me with his acuity. He is a complex man, his grace the king; clay in the hands of his mother, fawning to those he needs and ruthlessly perceptive with others.

And he is right about Holand, he does not need to do anything to bring him into line.

Except lay the bait.

The bait in this instance is command of Brittany and Poitou. Ever since the fall of Calais there has been an uneasy peace between England and France. Some of Edward's allies, even his own local commanders, have taken advantage of this uncertain situation to enrich themselves. The situation is worst in Brittany; Edward's lieutenant there, Sir John Avenel, is clearly not up to the task of controlling his rogue captains. Edward needs someone with a proven track record for tough leadership yet with enough private wealth to support such a position; someone who wants the honour and the glory of it.

Someone like Thomas Holand.

It will place him in control of one of the most volatile and strategically important regions in Edward's entire kingdom, a position of true eminence. Rather than a single garrison, he will command an entire duchy.

How could a man like Holand refuse such an opportunity?

63.

And so he must say goodbye to Joan yet again.

'I will be back before you know it,' he tells her.

He is eager to leave, he can barely contain his excitement. In a few days, in a few weeks, he will miss her again. Men like Holand, wherever they are, they always want to be somewhere else.

I watch him say goodbye to his two young sons. It is a poignant moment for me, watching the carelessness with which he does it. Was I so distracted when I left for Winchester and the butcher's block?

'Saleby and Raynford will look after everything,' he tells her as he climbs on his horse, referring to his clerks, Randolf Saleby and John Raynford, whom he has appointed as attorneys in his absence. He could have appointed Joan, but he didn't; he yet thinks of her as just a woman.

I could feel sorry for my daughter but in truth it is like this for every noble wife, they are expected to wait out the summers while their men find fame and fortune across the little sea, or else die there. Yet it is not quite the same for Joan; most wives have not had to endure what she has endured, have not waited ten years against all odds for their husbands.

I suspect that we men never really grow up. As little boys we go off to climb trees and swim in fast flowing rivers and fight other boys in the mud and expect our mothers to be there to put us in hot baths and hug us and put salves on our bruises when we return from our adventures.

When we grow into men, it is still the same.

And so after Epiphany he rides to Plymouth with sixty men-at-arms and a hundred archers and sets sail for France. It is the greatest command he has yet been given, the one he has waited a lifetime for, two French provinces under his direct control.

And where is Ned? He is somewhere in France, in a silk pavilion, studying charts on a trestle table while squires bring him wine and help him strip off his armour. He lies in a dead man's bed in a captured castle with a woman sent to please him, and he takes out a kerchief from beneath his pillow and stares at the emblem emblazoned in its corner; a white hart, from the house of Woodstock. He holds it to his nose for scent of her.

He has kept it all these years.

64.

Bella is a woman now, and still defiantly unmarried. She and Joan have remained close friends, closer since the princess defied her father and refused to cross the little sea to Gascony. She visits Joan whenever she can, sometimes staying for two or three days, the court is anyway tedious and uninspiring for her with her father and all his knights away at their wars in France.

They stand on the walls and watch the ferryman poling across the river below, a herd of plump cows grazing the pastures nearby. Slowly, the estates are returning to their former prosperity. It will take years but by the time their son is old enough to inherit, there will be plenty again.

Bella talks about her father's continuing negotiations to find her a suitable husband and her ongoing efforts to resist him. She does not know what she wants, she confesses; so why does she resist so stoutly? She says to Joan what she will not admit to anyone else; that perhaps she is wrong to be so headstrong.

She asks Joan how she thinks her life would have been if she had married William.

'It would have been easier,' Joan says, 'and I think I should have been content. Perhaps I would not have been unhappy.'

'Yes, you would,' Isabella says. 'You would have been miserable.'

Joan nods, because this is true, and adds a rueful smile. 'I don't know why I was so stubborn about it. At first it was my passion for Thomas that sustained me, but after a while it became something else. They pushed me so hard I found it natural to push back, for its own sake. It was then that I discovered a strength I never knew I had. I suppose you could say that Thomas brought out the best in me.'

'It was not his intention.'

'Yet without him I would have been just another wife.'

'Instead, you are a scandal.'

'Is that what they say about me at court?'

'Of course not; not out loud anyway.' She watches a bumble bee at work in the garden, fly here, fly there; fertilize this flower, then go to that one.

'Men are bees, women are flowers,' Joan says. 'It is just nature.'

'No one goes into a garden to look at the bees,' Bella says and laughs. 'Do you worry for him?'

'Of course. I worry that he will not come back. I would not have worried so for William.'

'That would have been better?'

'Easier. I would have spent my life at the high table, neither fearing his death nor desiring his presence. But with Thomas I either stand on the high tower beside him with the wind in my hair or wait alone in the dungeon eating stale bread, listening for the gaoler and the key.'

'You do not have to be in prison. He does not have to fight any more.'

'If he was more like William then he would not be Thomas, and I would not love him. Besides we must let God decide these things. Look at my brother John, the king kept him safe at Crecy and he stays at home and dies without warning when he is just barely a man.'

'I do not understand why God would do such a thing.'

'It is not for us to know, Bella. We must stand back and rejoice or endure, that is the way of it.'

'You cannot say you do not privately contest with God,' Bella says, laughing. 'If it were not for you, I would be living out my days in Gascony with the Lord Albret.' She looks at the two young boys playing on the lawn, stares at Joan's swelling belly. 'Still, I should like to have children of my own someday.'

'You only have to say the word.'

She shakes her head. 'When I have children, I should like to love their father, as you do. You have taught me at least this much, cousin.'

There you have it, another reason for Edward to dislike my daughter; not only has she tormented him with her disobedience for over a decade but now she has infected his one surviving daughter with her obstinate and scandalous opinions.

In life I grovelled at his feet; in death I can laugh in his face. He cannot hear me or see me, of course, but I do enjoy seeing how the wheel turns. We are seldom afforded the grand view while we are alive, but wait long enough in the veil and you can witness how justice is finally done.

Vannes, Brittany

Thomas Holand and his brother Otto sit at the long table, they spend long days now in the company of men. Wine from a hundred cup spills has stained the oak and it is chipped and pierced from a thousand trencher knives. Two of their number are snoring with their heads on the table, others are dicing before the fire. Otto draws closer to his brother.

'I heard that you are going back to England.'

Holand grunts in acknowledgment.

'So soon?'

'Orders from the king. I am entrusted with the heir to the Duchy, he wants me to bring him back here under escort.'

'Still so young!'

'He has fifteen years, he will soon be old enough.' Holand takes another draught of the thick red wine, it leaks into his beard. 'I have thought to take the opportunity to bring Joan back with me.'

'Joan? You are serious?'

'I am very serious indeed.'

'Bring your wife here? At the very least that will invite comment.'

'I think you know me well enough to understand that I have never minded what the gossipers say about me.'

'But why would you do such a thing?'

'Why not? The king takes the queen with him when he goes to war.'

'But he is the king.'

'Still, if he does it, why not I? Besides, he does not have the common concerns that I have.'

'And these are?'

Holand ensures that none of these other knights are listening. There is a roar and laughter from those who are gaming. The rest are insensible. 'I do not like to be so long away from Joan. I worry about her.'

'But she is as faithful a wife as any knight could have.'

'I do not worry about her in that way. I worry about William, I worry about our position. She is the richest woman in England and our marriage is disputed. If I am away, who knows what might happen?'

'But the Pope signed a bull declaring your marriage legal.'

'Clement is dead. Innocent is Pope now. It is my experience that a Pope is only infallible while he is alive. When he is dead his successor may discover that he makes mistakes, like everyone else. It has happened before. What if William decides to dispute the bull?'

'You think he might?'

A shrug.

'But William is married now.'

'He thought he was married before.'

Otto sighs. 'They do say a man with a castle on the frontier and a beautiful wife should always be prepared for war.'

'It is neither the castle or the beautiful wife that is under threat, Otto. Joan's inheritance stands at three thousand pounds a year. That is enough to make men question anything. It is why I have made formal application to the new pope to ratify his predecessor's ruling.'

'Then that should be the end of it.'

'Sometimes I fear I will never see the end of it.'

'But even the king ...'

'The king will forever be remembered by Joan and her family as the man who signed the papers for her father Edmund's execution.'

'But it was not his fault, he was only a boy.'

'He was old enough. Yes, he was bullied into it, but I believe he still blames himself for it and a man never likes to be reminded of his own guilty failings. That's why he doesn't like Joan. When I married her, I became the second stone in his boot, so I can never rely on him, believe me.'

'But he needs you.'

'If he thought he needed me, he would have made me Earl of Kent, as is my right. I think it is a wise precaution to bring her here, safe from all eventuality.'

'What eventuality?'

'She was abducted once, it might happen again. Or worse. Imagine if something happened to Joan, Otto, do you think the Salisbury's or the king would allow me to continue to oversee her inheritance?'

Otto raises his eyebrows. It is clear he has never thought of this, which is why Holand is the royal lieutenant In Brittany and he is not. 'But to bring her here! This is not like Windsor or even Woodstock. The men are on campaign, there is war right outside the walls. Our knights are not ... as fine with their manners as they are in England.'

'Neither is Joan as delicate as she seems. She will cope.'

I would prefer to like Thomas Holand but I do not enjoy these private conversations he has, his spirit is not as chivalrous as he would have many believe. But he did not become one of the richest men in England by being only chivalrous; a man has to have some sense of calculation as well.

And my Joan loves this man. Let us not forget that.

65.

A few weeks later, a herald brings news of his return to the castle. Joan has her ladies prepare her, and when he arrives the next day, mud-spattered, filthy and exhausted, she is waiting for him, freshly bathed, her hair brushed out, children clean and ready to be presented. She wears the new velvet gown her seamstress has made for her and a necklace of garnets and rubies.

Holand minds none of it but drags her upstairs to their private bedchamber. He is a man and he has missed her. I hover in the Great Hall with the children and the escort and the servants. They are all uneasy and they do not know why. There is a chill in the room, a draught upon the stairs.

A cat sees me and bares its claws.

I never liked cats, even when I was alive.

* * *

Joan is worried about her husband. His hair has grey in it now and it seems that every time he returns home there is a fresh scar. He has dark rings under his eyes and that night he does not sleep as soundly as he usually does. She shakes him and he comes awake, breathing hard and slick with sweat.

Later, as they lie side by side in the candlelight, he tells Joan why the king has sent him back to England and that of necessity his stay is only short. It is then that I hear him whisper: 'Come with me.'

'To France?'

'It will not be easy. You will be living among only men and the conditions there ...'

'What brings on this change of heart, Thomas Holand?'

'I miss you.'

Does she believe him? I am not sure. But knowing Joan I would guess she does not. Still, she does not press him on his motive. She asks instead about the children.

'We cannot take them there. They are too young.'

'They are too young for me to leave them.'

'Joan, I know men do not take their wives on campaign, but I cannot bear to be apart from you again.'

These are the words she has been waiting to hear. But still, she is cautious. She tells him she must think on this though she already knows her answer. I think he knows it, too. It is true that he might command her to do his bidding, but she knows he would never do this. He does not wish to face ten years of defiance from her, as her mother and the Wakes and the Salisbury's did.

Whatever his true reasons for asking her, it will make her happy to oblige him. It seems that life is working out in her favour and soon it will be safe for me to leave her. But still I linger. John, Margaret, they have all gone ahead of me; surely Joan does not need me anymore.

But I cannot bear to let go now. If you have had a daughter, you will understand. They are not always the first love, but they are the love that lasts.

Bourne Castle, Lincolnshire

'The boys are too young to travel to France,' Joan says. 'We are looking for someone to care for them while we are away, look to their education and upbringing.'

Lady Blanche offers no comment. She calls to a servant for another flask of wine. Joan does not expect great sentiment from her, she was after all married to her uncle Thomas Wake for all those years, and besides she does not seem to be a woman much accustomed to great outpourings of affection. Familial duty is what she understands, and it is what has brought them here today.

Joan watches as a servant fills her husband's cup. Blanche shakes her head when the servant offers the wine to her. 'Joan, shall we walk in the garden?' she says. Holand understands that he is excluded from this conversation and has anticipated this. That he has even been allowed into a Lancaster house will set the Wakes rolling in their graves.

Lady Blanche leads Joan out into the garden, among the lavenders and honeysuckles. She walks with a limp, complains of pains in the joints, and of being an old lady, though I suspect this is another manipulation and that I will not see her on this side for some time yet.

'You are brave to go to France. Is this what you want?'

'I do not want to say goodbye to him again.'

'A woman's place is with her children.'

'As a mother I will insure that they are always cared for by loving hands.'

Blanche laughs, something she does seldom. 'Beautifully phrased. They all underestimated you, didn't they?'

'Aunt?'

'Understand me, Joan. I am not a Wake and I did not bring Lancaster prejudices to my marriage with your uncle. But I took his part in it all because that was the right thing to do, and I will be honest with you, I did not approve of what you did. But what is done is done. Those boys are Wake boys and one day they will inherit Wake lands, this Wake house, this Wake estate. So I will love them as I do my own. If you wish me to take care of them I will.'

Joan smiles. 'Thank you.'

There is a moment. The past is being healed here, the traitor's stain will not be passed to Holand's sons. I wonder if my daughter's reputation will be healed with it.

'Many unseemly things have been said of you,' Blanche says, as if she can hear my thoughts, even over on her side.

'Yes. I have heard the talk.'

'I wonder what your father would have said.'

'I think he would have been proud of me,' she says. Now what makes her say such a thing? Oh Joan, you amazing child, of course I am proud. Have you felt me standing here through these long years cheering you on? I would like to think so.

Blanche looks back to the house.

'He is a dashing looking man, Thomas.'

'I have always thought so.'

'But it must have been more than that. You look happy. I am surprised, I always thought you would regret your decision.'

'I have no regrets.'

'Still, if it came to it a second time, I would not take your side. I would do the same again.'

'So would I.'

Blanche sighs. I think she is beginning to admire her niece, even if she does not like her yet. They go back inside where Holand has helped himself to more of the wine. He is a soldier after all, and soldiers do like their wine.

*   *   *

Joan is to be eight months gone from England, a long time to be without her young sons. Holand tries to prepare her for what she will see when she gets to

France, but she is still shocked. The castle at Vannes is just a stone shell perched on a rocky outcrop over a stream. This is not Eltham; this is not Woodstock. The countryside has been ravaged by the war, everywhere there are burned piles that once were villages and towns. Even in the truce the smell of death lingers. But the truce is but a short reprieve; it lasts only as long as it takes the French to renege on their promises to Edward. When he discovers their duplicity, the king is beside himself with rage, though few others are surprised.

And so there is to be another campaign, more warring.

Holand is barely settled in with his wife when he is recalled to England. He drags himself back across the little sea, to England, to his manor house, to his fickle lord and king.

66.

Joan is excited to be reunited with her two boys and relieved to be back in familiar surroundings for she is carrying a third child. She is also eager to review the progress her commissioners have made with their many estates, which are still dotted all over England.

My son-in-law is less enthusiastic. The news from France is that the prince has cut another bloody swathe in his *chevauchée* through the countryside. For once there is a major campaign going on in France and he is not part of it. He can scare contain himself.

Ned remains in Gascony in the winter of 1355 reasserting English control. Many of Holand's former comrades-in-arms are with him; Roger de la Warr and of course William of Salisbury, now in joint command of the rearguard with the Earl of Suffolk.

Holand finally returns to France in late Spring but is forced to serve under the Duke of Lancaster who has been ordered to take his force back into Brittany, where Holand's intimate knowledge of the terrain and the politics may prove invaluable. But at the last moment Lancaster is sent back to Normandy instead.

In September the young prince meets the French king, John the Good, and his army at Poitiers. The French have overwhelming numbers but are comprehensively routed, the English bowmen decimating the flower of the French nobility. The final humiliation is the capture of the French king himself; they say that after the battle Ned took him back to his pavilion and served him dinner with his own hand, ever the chivalrous victor.

Can we believe such stories? It sounds as if it is something the king's minstrel would have written. But who knows?

* * *

The following spring the prince and Edward return in triumphant procession with the King of France and the rest of their royal prisoners. They are escorted by the mayor and the leading citizenry of London from Kennington Palace to the Duke of Lancaster's Savoy Palace. The streets are hung with banners, ribbons of gold and silver leaf are thrown down from the rooftops, every church bell in the city is set to ringing. All the guilds and companies stand in their liveries at intersections to salute them.

Joan is there, too, for the banquets and the dances. It seems as if all of England turns out to applaud their hero, their prince, the future Edward IV.

This will be the young prince's finest moment, though he does not know it yet. When we have our laurels so young, it is hard to imagine that this is all there is, all there will ever be.

There is a feast in the Great Hall and afterwards she approaches him as the minstrels in the gallery play a galliard for the dancers. She brings him news of his godson's progress and he promises that he will visit him at his first opportunity. She tells him she now has a daughter, whom she and her husband have called Maud, after his mother and she does not forget to congratulate him discreetly on the birth of his own son, though he will of course be a bastard.

'Still so eligible and still unmarried,' she says to him.

'My father has found several suitable brides, but the Pope always seems to find a reason to withhold permission. He returns always to the law of consanguinity.'

'If that law was always kept, no one in Europe would be married. Not in a royal house anyway.'

'It is just politics, Joan. He does not want my father making too strong an alliance against his friends the French.'

'So you will never marry?'

Ned smiles. 'Oh, I have a plan to blunt the Pope's tactics. But so far none of the princesses my father has proposed have pleased me enough to suggest it to him. Besides the king has enough heirs, he no longer relies on me for such things. I shall have the crown one day, that is the important thing.'

'It seems he has had better fortune with his sons than with his daughters.'

Ned's face clouds when he thinks of Jeanette. 'Isabella is still unmarried. That was your doing, wasn't it?'

'What makes you say so?'

'You fool many people, but you have never fooled me. I saw your hand in what happened.'

'Your sister has a mind of her own, Ned.'

'So you say. Well what is done is done. Shall we step into the garden?'

Outside there is a warm summer scent of flowers and herbs. Stars wheel across a cloudless night sky and they watch them in companionable silence for a while, listening to the music and hubbub of voices coming from inside. Torches flicker around the walls.

'I often wonder what would have happened if Edward had arranged for us to be married,' Ned says without preamble.

'You and I?'

'Is it such an outrageous thought?'

'Why would he ever have done such a thing? I could not bring him Gascony or the Aquitaine.'

'Neither could the Earl of Salisbury, but he gave his permission for you and William to be wed. If you think on it, I might have been a more likely match.'

'But by then I had married Thomas.'

I think she knows what he is asking her and does not want to talk about it. This is too close to her heart right now.

'Imagine then that you had been born French. Like his mother.'

'He would not have let you marry his mother.'

'Joan, you are being obtuse.'

'I do not even know what that means, Ned,' she says smiling.

'You well know what I mean. I am asking if you think we would have made a good match.'

'You and I? Not at all. You need someone fiery to control you.'

'You think you are not?'

'I am the most placid woman in the entire court.'

'I remember once I came to you in the garden, I was only a boy, no more than ten years old. You told me to go away and the way your eyes flashed, I have never seen a more tempestuous woman.'

'I do not remember it,' she says though I would wager she does.

Ned reaches into his tunic and shows her what he has kept close to his heart all these years, the green silk kerchief she dropped that day in the garden in her anger and her haste to be away from him. She would perhaps have disavowed it, but he shows her the white hart emblem stitched into it and she bites her lip, looks quickly into his eyes and then away again.

And then she raises her eyes a second time and for a moment I think it will happen. I see her waver. Their eyes hold each other's, and Ned holds his breath thinking she is going to kiss him. Instead she rises on her tip toes and touches her lips to his cheek. 'It is late, I must to bed,' she says and sweeps from the garden. He is left only with the kerchief once again.

He returns to the great hall and his swooning admirers, the countless daughters and wives who will dance with him, and sleep with him too, if there is opportunity. He does not have to court my married daughter, but I understand why he does.

Thomas Holand, you should come home soon.

67.

Holand is with the Duke of Lancaster, who has unsuccessfully besieged Rennes. The blockade continues through the entire summer without any satisfactory result and finally Holand is sent home, arriving unannounced at Castle Donington. Joan watches him and his knights and squires dismount in the bailey. He does not have the usual bounce in his step. In fact, he looks deathly tired.

He has been at war now these twenty years; he has battled the Scots, the French, the Moors and the Tartars from one end of Europe to the other, in searing heat and numbing cold, on mountains and on barren plains; he has seen endless sieges and bitter and deadly skirmishes. His beloved profession has finally exacted its toll.

She does not go down to greet him. On this occasion, she waits for him to come to her.

'How long are you returned?' she asks him, and it is the first time I have seen her with a chill look when she is with him.

'Is it not enough that I am back for now?'

'You have not answered me. How long?'

'I will not leave you again, Joan. You have my word.'

'You have said this before.'

He sweeps her up in his arms. But instead of ardour there is something else in his eyes, something she has not seen before. It is compassion. 'I am sorry,' he tells her.

'Sorry?'

'For having left you so many times. I promise it will never happen again.'

She shakes her head. She wants to believe him but she is not sure that she can.

'I have a confession,' he says.

I watch her steel herself. Is this promise born of contrition? Has he fathered French bastards in her absence?

He says: 'I have not always loved you as I do now. There have been many times when my ambition has overruled my heart.'

'I know.'

'But this is not true now. I think I finally understand what a fortunate man I am to have a woman such as you love me. You are the truest wife any man could ever have.'

They kiss. Twenty years now since that first time and it is a kiss as ardent as any newly wedded husband would give his bride. Perhaps it is true, perhaps Sir Thomas Holand, wearied of war, and with all his ambitions won, has finally come to know what it is he truly wants. Or perhaps it is because of the grey in his beard; age teaches a man things that wealth and glory never can.

My Joan waited ten years to be with her husband; she has waited another ten for his heart. Smiling, she takes his hand and leads him to bed.

* * *

He is as good as his word. Later that year the king appoints him warden of the castle of Saint-Sauveur-le-Vicomte, a major fortress at the heart of the Harcourt inheritance in Normandy. He is entrusted with the delicate task of keeping English control against the Navarrese claim to the duchy while at the same time working with local Navarrese forces against the French. There will be diplomacy and there will surely be more fighting.

But he does not go alone. Joan accompanies him to France, and this time not because of the Pope, not because of the Salisburys, but because he wishes her there with him. They leave the children with Blanche and ride for the coast, bound for Brittany.

68.

Vannes

This Thomas Holand is a different man to the one she married, one she has yet to fathom. He thrashes about in his sleep, starts at loud noises. When she alerts him of this, he grows sullen and irritable.

He is with her, and yet he is not. He spends most nights after supper drinking in the Hall with his men and there is always the sour smell of wine on his breath. Something has shifted in him. The castle is bleak, the mood of his men sullen.

Joan misses her children; there is not much laughter here, little joy. This is exile of a different sort.

And then one day Holand's brother Otto is badly wounded in a skirmish and dies a few days later. Holand again looks for solace in the wine mazer, and Joan lies awake waiting for him, but long after the men have stopped their melancholy singing and shouted oaths, he is still not abed.

Joan puts a fox cloak around her shoulders and searches the castle looking for him. She has a maidservant with her but still it is not something an ordinary lady would think to do. But then, my daughter is no ordinary lady.

She sees a light burning in the chapel and finds him there. He is kneeling beside the bier where they have laid out the body. Otto is covered with a sheet because his wounds are too terrible to be displayed, or so she has been told. There is incense burning in the censers but still she smells the taint of death in the room.

Joan dismisses her maidservant and pads barefoot into the crypt. The stone is frigid under the pads of her feet.

Holand hears her and turns around. 'You should not be here,' he says.

She ignores his admonition and comes to kneel beside him on the stone. 'You should be asleep, Thomas. You need your rest. You have not closed your eyes for days.'

'He was my brother, he was at my side in a score of battles. I am bereft without him.'

'Your tears cannot bring him back.'

'Would that they could.'

'You won't do it, will you, Thomas? You won't die before me. Promise.'

He does not answer her straight away.

'I promise,' he says at last, but I do not like him for it. No one should make such promises, and I should know.

Because to love wholeheartedly takes such immense courage, doesn't it? We know one day the most faithful lover will leave us or we will leave them. There is a grim interloper that will one day cause the most ardent heart to stray.

So, do not make such promises to her, Thomas Holand.

She takes his hand in hers.

'But if something did happen to me,' he asks her, 'what would you do?'

'There will never be anyone for me but you. I will never marry again, as God is my witness.'

They look up at the Madonna above the bier, candles shimmer either side of her gentle and lovely face. They kneel and pray, they both look so innocent, so hopeful, and so very fragile.

Soon after they return to England and Holand vows he will never go back to France. He has done good service to the King of England and he is exhausted by the endless campaigns and wounds and slaughter.

Let the wars go on without him. Wars always will, that is the way of the world.

69.

The King makes a new treaty with the Dauphin, who rules France now in place of the French king, who is still hostage to Edward. This latest sham is known as the Treaty of Brétigny and it will require a skilled knight and ambassador to supervise its proper implementation. Edward seeks out his son for private audience and asks his advice.

They discuss candidates for the commission and Ned says: 'Why not send Thomas Holand?'

I am startled to hear him say this.

Does he know of Holand's vow to Joan? I would wager he does not. But he does know that he has said he will not return to France, that he wishes rather to be a better husband and father, so why does Ned plant this seed in the king's mind? It may be true that Holand is the best man for the job, but I suspect there is also something in Ned's temperament that moves him to suggest it, perhaps a half-formed and malnourished desire to put Sir Thomas Holand in harm's way just one more time, to see if the fates will yet change both their destinies.

Or do I read too much into this? Perhaps, perhaps he is just being practical.

'He has expressed to me the deepest desire never to set foot in France again,' Edward says.

'That was several months ago. You know Thomas, his mind changes with the season. If you offer him a rich enough plum, he will eat it. Here is one last chance to be glorious for England. Besides, he only needs to be there until Christmas. It is a short posting.'

'What if he is difficult?'

'You can persuade him. Father, tell me this. What is it he really wants?'

Edward smiles; for he knows the very thing.

* * *

After the king leaves, Ned reaches for a mazer of wine and drinks the bowl in one draught, then wipes his beard. In that moment, he looks like a man who wishes he could take back his words. Does he have a premonition of what he has just done? Is there even now a shadow of guilt?

Time always flows as it should, I can hear it and feel it around me on this side, but sometimes men make unexpected choices and then those ripples shift, which is what they do now. The King sends orders to Thomas Holand, ordering him to the Harcourt posting, almost as if defying him to disobey. A few days later, far away in Leicestershire, Holand receives the missive from the hand of a royal courier. He breaks the seal on the vellum and reads quickly though the king's command.

For days, he hesitates. Is he yet making up his mind or just waiting for the right moment to tell Joan his decision? Like Ned, I too believe the temptation will be too great for him. Soldiering is in his very marrow. If he accepts, he will be breaking his promise to his wife, but he thinks it will do no harm, he can talk her round to it:

After all, it is not a lengthy commission. It is just until the Yuletide.

Joan hears of his decision one night at the long table. But for once Thomas Holand displays cowardice. What he does is this: he announces the news of his posting to his entire household first, his family, his knights and their ladies, his entire retinue of servants and retainers, shouts it to them as if it is good news, cause for celebration. Joan cannot object in front of the whole castle without dishonouring him and she would never do that.

He will not meet her eye. She must wait until later, when he is drunk from too much wine and they are alone in their bedchamber before she can express her feelings on the matter.

He throws off his boots, ready for combat. But she says nothing.

'Joan?'

She is already in their bed, her back towards him.

'Wife!'

'Did you not think of telling me this news first?'

'To what purpose?'

'You were frightened of what I would say.'

'Sweet one, I understand why you are angry ...'

'You broke your promise. You said you would never again leave without me.'

'It is only for a few weeks, I will be back in time for the Christmas feast.'

'Take me with you.'

'For such a short time? I should look like a fool.'

'It is better to break a promise to your wife?'

'Joan, it is three months at most. And he has finally made me Earl of Kent! I at last have the one thing he has always denied me!'

'He plays you like a lute.'

'We cannot ask Blanche to look after our children yet again.'

He throws himself on the bed, puts a hand on her shoulder but she shrugs it away. Too drunk to continue with this argument, he rolls onto his back and falls asleep, in his wine-stained tunic.

* * *

In the weeks before he leaves she takes to her own chamber, the door locked and barred to him at night. He thinks she will come around. But the morning he leaves for the coast she is not there in the bailey to wish him goodbye. She watches instead from a high window, out of sight of the courtyard. He looks up, knowing she is watching him, but there is no farewell, she does not even wave him goodbye.

Ten ships are commissioned for his passage, and late in October he is officially instructed to publish the peace and supervise handover of English fortresses as agreed at the Treaty of Brétigny. He takes with him to Normandy sixty men-at-arms, ten knights and a hundred and twenty archers. It is the high point in an illustrious career. He will return at Christmas as Thomas Holand, Earl of Kent.

It is perfect. It is completion.

* * *

But that is not the way it happens.

Is it something in the water, something in the food or something in the air? It is just something. It is just God's little joke perhaps.

I am there the day his shade leaves him. He looks dazed and will not let go as he hovers between your world and this one. He cannot believe this has happened to him.

He is the Earl of Kent. How can he die?

A soldier always thinks he will die of a wound, even when he has lost so many friends from the bleeding flux or the ague. But it was a sudden and unexplained illness that brought him his fortune and it is also how he will lose it. He looks over his shoulder at me. He does not know who I am, of course, and besides, there is no comfort that I can give him now.

This life was all he ever wanted, and he has no desire to leave it. But in the end even a man like Holand can overreach himself. He had filled his basket to the brim yet still it was not enough, and in reaching for the very last plum on the tree, he dies.

I do not accompany the herald on his journey to Castle Donington. I cannot bear it. I can give Joan no consolation when she hears the news and I cannot bear to witness her grief. I can imagine it well enough, though. I imagine I can hear her screams even across the little sea.

He is buried at Rouen but then a message arrives from Joan ordering his body to be disinterred and brought home. They bring him to the Franciscan church in Stamford, his casket on the back of a cart that has taken the long road from the coast. There are two of her ladies in waiting to hold her up, Joan is unable even to stand so devastating is her grief. Her inhuman wailing reminds me of a wolf I once heard at night deep in the mountains of France.

We are all witness to it; Ned is there also. I can read his thoughts. What would it be like to have someone love you so much? All England loves Ned, of course, but no one man or woman loves him like this.

As they lower the casket into the grave inside the chapel Joan falls on her knees and tries to climb in with it. I am sorry, she says over and over. I am sorry, I am sorry. She remembers his leave-taking, and that she did not say goodbye to him, did not tell him that she loved him.

But how could she have known that would be the last time?

The women bear her grief more easily, but the men do not know where to look. They are accustomed to the sight of butchered bodies but are unmanned by such outward displays of grief. It makes them think too easily of their own end.

Joan's ladies lift her to her feet and support her as the chaplain reads the final words. Scarce anyone can hear him above the wailing she makes. None of them here have ever seen Joan raise her voice. This shocks them all. I hope they can hear her in heaven and that God perhaps feels some remorse for what He has done.

The king and queen leave, shaken. Ned lingers, perhaps he thinks to speak with her, but as she is borne past him she does not even look in his direction.

70.

Three months later

'What will you do?' the Queen says.

Joan shakes her head. 'If it were not for the children I think I should take myself to a monastery rather than endure this endless pain.'

'Have you thought of marrying again?'

'Your grace, Thomas is not yet cold.'

'It will be a salve for your grief.'

'I am still in my widow's weeds.'

'It is three months. You are thin and pale, I worry for you.'

'She does not need to marry,' Bella says to her mother. 'She is wealthy, and she is yet young. Do not listen, you do not need a husband, Joan. One day perhaps you might want to ... ' She looks up at her mother and decides not to continue with this thinking.

'There are the children to think of,' the Queen says.

'The children are well looked after. I have not been attentive since Thomas died but Blanche visits them often and their nurses ...'

'I do not mean that.' Phillipa hesitates. This is difficult. 'Joan, you are one of the wealthiest women in England, you are still young, and you are beautiful. Have you thought ... there might yet be a challenge to your married state?'

Joan looks up sharply. No, she has not considered this.

'You mean William? Has he said anything to you?'

'I believe William to be an honourable man. But there are many in his family who might be tempted to dispute ... whatever happened in the past.'

'Because of my slippery ways?'

'I do not think that.'

'But many do. Am I right?'

'You need a protector, someone who is wealthy and influential enough to protect your children's inheritance. Someone who cares for you.'

Joan looks mystified for a moment. Then she sees it all. 'Has Ned put you up to this?'

Bella looks at her mother in accusation also; the Queen contrives to look bewildered by the question but despite all her years in politics she is a very bad liar when it comes to her family.

'It's just that we know how he feels about you,' she says. 'The whole world knows how he feels. Do it for your children.'

I am sure Joan sees the sense in what she is saying. And there is this: I think that a husband who can show her kindness and affection might save her from leaping from the walls. There are many nights I have followed her up to the battlements and I worry she has thought about such a course.

Since he died she has hardly eaten, and rarely sleeps. When she does, she wakes crying. I cannot bear it. It has upset me so that I have raged and cursed along these corridors, frightening the servants who sometimes hear me and are too frightened to tell their mistress that there is a ghost, for fear the spectre may be Holand's.

'Come back to court, Joan,' the Queen says. 'Enrich your reputation, your family's endowments and its influence. Do it for the children.'

Joan looks at Bella, whom she trusts. Bella shrugs. 'He is my brother. It will make you my sister by law, not just of the heart.'

Joan, it is not disloyal, it is not selfish. Do it.

She shakes her head. I think she wants a way out of this pain as much as they do. But she would bear it, I think, if not for the children. In this, at last, she becomes like Margaret. She will guard the nest and the eggs that are in it, even though her mate can never return to it.

The silence stretches. No one speaks. Finally she nods her head, though she cannot bring herself to say the words.

'Shall I ask him to call on you?' the Queen asks her.

Another nod of the head.

'He is, after all, one of your oldest friends.'

An old friend? Is that what he is? I am glad Ned is not here, his heart would sink to hear of it.

Bella holds Joan in her arms. The Queen watches. She wonders if this is the right thing. But it is what Ned wants, what he has always wanted.

Is it the right thing? I can only tell you this: you can bend Fate to your will, if you have the power to do it, and this prince does. But if something is not yours to have, no good will come of it.

Just watch. You will see.

* * *

'You want to marry Joan?' Edward says to his son. They are alone, with wine and a roaring fire. It is late. Somewhere in the darkness an owl screeches in the woods, falling on its prey. 'But with her history, Ned ... for ten years the woman had two husbands! And there is still a question of the legitimacy of her marriage to Sir Thomas even today.'

'Yet she is the perfect choice.'

'How do you suppose that?'

'The peace treaty you have signed at Brétigny cedes us more land in France than we have ever had. It is virtually the old duchy of Aquitaine.'

'And I wish you to be its prince, as I have told you.'

'And in that you do me a great honour, father. I will not let you down.'

'I know that, but what is your point about Joan?'

'Money.'

'Money?'

'The Crown cannot afford to pour any more of the royal purse into France yet it will be expensive to administer this new duchy.'

'You will raise the finances you need from within the duchy itself, it will form an independent kingdom. That is what we decided.'

'But this will not happen overnight. At first I will have to rely on my own resources.'

'You have the largest income of anyone in England.'

'And yet my position puts even my great resources at strain. I have the largest retinue in England after you yourself, I owe money everywhere, I have recently had to borrow a further two thousand pounds from the Earl of Arundel.'

'That is because you are too generous with everyone! You give silver cups and ewers to your knights and your servants like you are tossing crusts to sparrows.'

'A reputation for generosity is no bad thing. How else do you make men loyal?'

'You may be right,' Edward concedes the point, though grudgingly.

'Taking Aquitaine will stretch my resources even further. There are few heiresses wealthy enough to relieve such a heavy burden.'

'... Except for Joan.'

'Except for Joan. Should I marry her before I leave for the Aquitaine, I will also have a consort with whom I may establish my own court.'

'But her reputation!'

'She has royal blood, she is well versed in the royal protocols of England, and she will bring with her an income of three thousand pounds a year. Think on it, father.'

'And how will we obtain permission from the Pope for this?'

'I have a plan,' Ned says, and he leans forward and whispers it. It is clear the young prince has been thinking this through for some time.

It is only when he yawns and stretches and declares himself ready for bed that the king asks him the question I would have liked to have asked from the first.

'You say it is about the money. But tell me, Ned, has money anything to do with it at all?'

The prince smiles. 'Not really.'

'You have loved her for a very long time, haven't you?'

Ned does not answer. He decides it is time to go to bed.

71.

Ned is shocked when he sees her. She sits alone in a darkened room, for even in her grief she still has a woman's vanity and she does not want a man, any man, to see her looking anything less than dazzling. But the dim candlelight only emphasises her gaunt cheeks and sunken eyes, they do not disguise it. Her ladies-in-waiting have done the best they can with powders and paint but they cannot hide what these endless months of grief have wrought on her.

Edward is not sure how to go about this; he is gruff and clumsy, that is his way. A servant brings him wine and he drinks almost the entire cup before he says anything she is likely to understand as speech.

'England has lost a fine warrior and one of its best knights,' he manages. He might as well be addressing the Parliament.

'Thank you,' Joan says.

They sit in silence for a long time, as he stares into the fire. He had rehearsed his speech all the way on the long ride from Windsor but now he cannot think of a single word to say to her.

'What will you do?' he asks her.

'I do not know. I cannot even bear to contemplate the future.'

'And yet we must.'

'Must we?'

'Joan, I have known you all my life. We have been friends from children. They say that amity can forge stronger bonds than even passion.'

Wasn't this what William tried to tell her once? She watches him fumble with his words. Joan and I both feel sorry for him, he is making such a terrible job at this. Her mind is already made up, but he is not to know this.

'You know how much I loved him?' she says.

'Do you not know how much I love you?'

'Ned, I know why you are here.'

He sits back, both relieved and a little surprised.

'The answer is yes, Ned,' she says, to put him out of his misery.

He does not seem to understand. Still he goes on with this; he tries to explain to her the benefits of marrying the prince of England, the next Edward the fourth and the most eligible unmarried heir in all Europe, as if even the dimmest pie boy in the land would not already know all this.

'Yes,' she repeats. 'I will marry you.'

Now he has what he wants, he just sits there. He imagined a struggle. He thought he should be contending with her until dawn. Joan's intransigence, after all, is the stuff of legend.

'You will?'

'Yes.'

'But why?'

'Because you have asked me so beautifully,' she says, and it is good to hear something of her former impudence in her voice.

'Do you love me even a little?'

She gets up from her chair and kisses him gently on the lips. It is such a momentous occurrence for him that he forgets to breathe. The flower of English knighthood is unmanned.

A kiss is not a lie, it is a sign of affection, and he had asked her if she loves him a little and she does, a little. That is the truth of it. It is not what he wants, it is nothing like what he wants from her, but he cannot have what he wants.

Instead, he must settle for taking her as his wife.

For myself I am just happy for her that he is here, tonight, because I know he will do his utmost to make everything alright again for her, at least for a while. Oh Ned, I know you dream hopelessly that she will love you one day but know this: if you can stop her crying for even an hour, I will love you forever.

EPILOGUE

I watch on and over her for thirty more years. Tonight, she lies sleeping in her bed, I can hear her breathing, slow and laboured. She will join me tonight, on this side. I have seen the shadow dog her for weeks now.

My watch is almost over.

In the centuries to come, when people talk about my little Joan of Kent, the first thing they will note of her is that she committed bigamy when she was just thirteen years old, as if she was some kind of temptress who thought having two husbands was a fine thing.

But at least now you know the truth of it.

What people often forget is this: that for ten years she was Queen of Aquitaine, a role she bore with both dignity and grace; that she nursed her great prince for ten years, tended to him while sickness sapped away his strength and left him wasted, a skeleton carried in a litter back to London.

Poor Ned; he mastered the French and he thought he could master Fate. Life teaches us all humility in the end. It is best to learn the lesson quickly.

So, if you remember my Joan, remember her compassion and remember also her courage, how she saved John of Gaunt in the Peasant's Revolt, giving him sanctuary from the mob. Remember how she stood by her son, the second Richard, when he rode out from the Tower to confront the ringleaders and the baying mob they brought with them.

She may look to some in our day as a modern Guinevere because of her beauty, her royal blood and tangled history. But she was so much more. Her detractors forget her steadfast loyalty and her great powers of conciliation.

England fell apart when she died, of course. There would have been no Bolingbroke, no Bosworth Field, if she had been there to cool tempers and offer wiser counsel to her son.

Tonight she takes a last painful breath and her eyes blink open wide. She sees me again, at last. 'Papa,' she murmurs. For days she has been unable to move her head from her pillow. Now she sits up from the waist and holds out her arms to the shadows thrown by the candlelight.

I cannot go to her. This time, I must wait for her to come to me.

Perhaps she remembers the last time she held out her arms to me, that day at Arundel, the little girl shouting at me to come back, come back, papa come back, and me not listening. I am sorry, little Joan, but I am here for you now.

'Papa ...' she says a second time.

She makes her crossing peacefully and then finally she is in my arms again. We are together at last. It is an embrace that has had to wait for almost sixty years.

She has left a letter with her final instructions. Ned is by now long dead and buried at Canterbury Cathedral, he has left a space for her tomb there beside him. But Joan's final testament is explicit; her bones are to be laid beside her husband, her only real husband.

Sir Thomas Holand.

We both make our last pilgrimage there before we leave this world of hurt and worry. Her grey shadow approaches his tomb. A monk shivers and scurries away, thinking he has seen a ghost. He has, of course, but one that means him no harm.

And then hand in hand we leave this place and its histories behind. Thomas Holand is not in that dank place but there in the light, waiting for her. I look around for Ned but I cannot see him. It is just the three of us now and we walk on together.

READ AN EXCERPT FROM THE PREQUEL:
"Isabella, Braveheart of France"

Boulogne-sur-Mer, France 1308

"Y̶ou will love this man. Do you understand? You will love him, serve him, and obey him in all things. This is your duty to me and to France. Am I clear?"

Isabella is twelve years old and astoundingly pretty, a woman in a girl's body. She keeps her eyes on the floor and nods her head.

Her father, the King of France, is the most handsome man she has ever seen. In the purple, he is magnificent. His eyes are glacial; a nod from him is benediction, one frown can chill her bone-deep.

He puts his hands on the arms of her chair and leans in. A comma of hair falls over one eye. He rewards her now with a rare smile. "He is a great king, Isabella, and a handsome husband. You are fortunate."

A log cracks in the hearth.

She raises her eyes. He strokes her cheek with the back of his hand. "You will not disgrace me."

She shakes her head.

"Much is dependent on this union."

Her, breathless: "I will not disappoint you."

Phillip goes to the fire and stands with his back to it, warming himself. It is the heart of winter, and this is as cold and draughty a castle as she has ever been in. She can smell the sea. There is ice in the air.

"If he has cause to reprove you, you will listen and obey him. If he is angry, you shall be kind. If he is dismissive, you shall be attentive. Cherish him, give him your attentions. Be sweet, gentle, and amiable. Patience is your byword. You will make him love you."

He stares at her. He can stand like this for an eternity; fix a look on his face as if he were carved from marble. It is unnerving.

"No matter the provocation."

"Provocation?"

"What do you know of Edward?"

"He is King of England. His father was a great warrior. They say Edward is tall and as fine a prince as England ever had." (Though it is hard for her to imagine a finer king than her father, or a more handsome man.) She has always promised herself she will have a man just like him: as fair, as strong, as feared.

"Your new husband disputes Gascony with me. One road leads to war. A less thorny path leads to the day when my grandson-to-be inherits the throne of my most ancient enemy."

"But what provocation might he give me?" Isabella says.

Phillip frowns.

"You mentioned provocation, Father."

"Did I? I meant nothing by it. Tomorrow you will be Queen of England. Remember always that you are also a daughter of France. Make me proud, Isabella."

He nods to her nurse and she is taken from the room.

She can barely contain her excitement. She has rehearsed this moment in her mind for years. A handsome prince, a throne, estates: —it is what she was born for. From tomorrow she will live her life at the side of a great king.

Happiness is assured.

* * *

Bells peal across the city. The town is hung with banners. Edward of England arrives in a thunder of hooves, his men dressed in royal livery, scarlet with yellow lions. He jumps down from his horse, his cloak swirling, and tosses back a mane of golden hair. He is like a song a troubadour might sing.

He carries himself with the loose-limbed stride of a man accustomed to having others make way for him. He is tall and blue-eyed and smiles at her with such easy charm it makes her blush. He is a man, older than her elder eldest brother, Louis, a man in his prime. His manner and bearing take her breath away.

It is love at first sight.

Her father presents her, and as she steps forward she raises her eyes, hoping to see that glorious smile again. But his attention is already elsewhere, on her father, on the bishop, on her uncle, Valois.

"We should get to business," he says.

For three days they talk about Gascony. England camps outside the town. A forest of pavilions flourishes outside the walls, as if they are besieged. There is not a room to be had anywhere; beggars and camp followers sleep in porches and gateways. The town is bursting. Isabella patrols the battlements and passages, anxious for a glimpse of him. They cannot be married until they resolve the politics of the union.

She hates it here. Boulogne is gray and cold. She misses Paris, the ceremonial, her ladies, her private *salles*, the roaring log fires. Here the draughts whistle under the doors, and the wind buffets off the sea day after day. Even the banners seem to be fading in the rain.

She closes her eyes and imagines him. He is hers. Her father was right, she is fortunate. He is beautiful, he is a king, and he is all hers.

* * *

Our Lady of Boulogne has never seen a day like this. Resplendent in a silver gown and wearing a circlet of fine gold, Isabella meets her groom on her father's arm. Isabella's hands shake; she hopes her father will think it is because of the cold. He despises emotion, which he calls weakness.

It is frigid inside the cathedral. Her breath freezes on the air.

Eight kings and queens are present; there are also mere dukes and a handful of princes. Ah, here, the King of Sicily, there the French dowager queen, all jewels and velvets, gold and shot taffeta, elbowing for a better view of the twelve-year-old bride. Everyone has heard how pretty she is. They all want to pass their own judgment.

The archbishop reads the words of the marriage. Isabella spares a glance at her father. His expression betrays nothing.

Edward studies the ceiling, his eyes on a cold bolt of sun that angles through the high lancet window. He looks faintly bored. Isabella tries to catch his eye without success.

Finally he finishes with his looking around and sees his bride; he puffs out his cheeks and raises his eyes at her. He nods at the bishop. Will this old bore never finish?

Her father frowns, but only those standing closest to him might notice. This is not the behaviour he expects from his new son-in-law. But there is no one here who might reprimand the king of England, who now stifles a yawn.

The choir sings the plainchant as they kneel on prie-dieus; the clouds of swirling incense make her gasp. The bishop joins their hands; she squeezes Edward's fingers, hoping for some response. He just sighs and returns his attention to the ribbed vault.

The marriage is contracted on the high altar. She thinks she sees her father sigh with relief when it is done, as if he had thought that even at this last moment Edward might flee the cathedral and run for his ship. The Archbishop of Narbonne sings the *"Ite, Missa missa Estest,"* and they walk hand in hand to the nave to the polite applause of every noble house in Christendom.

No one smiles as she crosses the nave, except for Edward. When they are outside, he leans in and addresses her directly for the first time: "There," he murmurs. "That wasn't so bad, was it? I thought you did rather well."

* * *

One face stands out from the others as they leave the church; he is one of Edward's men, a bleak man with a black beard and dark eyes. Even a girl as young as Isabella knows when a man is looking at her in a manner that he should not. He scares her. In that first glimpse there is a savagery to his face that is unmistakable even in a crowded and candlelit church.

Yet there is something about him that makes her glance back over her shoulder. There is something thrilling in his stare. The hairs rise on her arms.

Later, at the feast, she asks one of her ladies who he is. They do not know; enquiries are made of the English party. Someone whispers to her that his name is Roger Mortimer, and he is one of Edward's barons. Once, she catches him staring at her from across the hall. She looks quickly away and never turns back in that direction again.

* * *

Her ladies prepare her for bed. Her hair is brushed through a hundred times and arranged beneath the caul. They rub her skin with rose-scented oil, and set a fire burning in the grate.

She asks Marguerite her advice. Marguerite is married to her brother, Louis, and has already been through this ordeal. "What shall I do?"

"Whatever he asks, your grace."

"But what will he ask?"

Her old nurse, Théophania, pats her head. "Now there's no need to be frightened."

"I'm not frightened."

"You should not be a mortal woman if you were not a little frightened," Marguerite says. "But he will not come to you tonight, or any night soon."

"He won't?"

"*Ma chérie*, you are only twelve years old."

"You have not bled yet," Théophania says. "He is English, but he is not an animal."

"How old were you when you married?" she asks Marguerite.

"I was fifteen. Old enough."

"I want to make him happy."

Marguerite finds this amusing. "It is not hard to make a man happy. Be agreeable. Do not vex him. Have his children. Do as he says."

"And will he love me?"

"Love?" The smile is gone as quickly as it came. Marguerite spares her a look she has never had seen in her life: pity. "Rest your faith in God, Isabella."

When her ladies are gone, she finds the gift that her husband's stepmother has sent her, a golden silver casket with the arms of Plantagenet and Capet in quatrefoils. It is lined in red velvet. She wonders what she might put in it.

The door creaks open. She tosses the box aside and lies down again, her arms stiff at her sides. The casket clatters onto the floor.

Edward picks it up and lays it on the bed beside her. He puts his hands on his hips and studies her. "Well, you're a little on the bony side. I dare say you shall put some flesh on your bones as you grow. Pretty enough. But they told me you were beautiful."

Isabella stares at the coverlet. It bears the emblem of France.

Edward sits on the edge of the bed. He reaches for her hand, pats it. "You're frightened of me?"

She shakes her head vigorously.

"Yes, you are. Oh, I think I know what it is. But you needn't worry on that account. I'm not a monster, Isabella. The Church says we might lie together as man and wife, but I always try to put kindness and common sense before anything the pope says."

She still does not move.

"What is this you have here? Did my stepmother give you this? I would have thought the old girl might have done better. You might put jewels in it, I suppose. You shall never suffer a shortage of jewels, Isabella."

He places the casket on her lap.

A log falls from the hearth. He gets up and kicks it back into the grate.

"Do you like me, my lord?"

A broad smile. "Ah. She speaks! At last. I heard you repeat the vows in church, so I knew you were capable of it."

"Do you?"

"I hardly know you, girl. Is it necessary for me to like you? I shall treat you kindly either way."

"Are you pleased that I am your wife?"

"Of course. I need Gascony back."

"I mean -, do I please you?"

Edward frowns and sits down again. "You're queen of England, Isabella. What else is it that you want?"

She cannot answer him. She wants what her mother had; her father's endless tears at her funeral, the years of mourning. The longing. All the things that the troubadours sing about, like love and gallantry. She wishes to be a queen who is loved by the king, and that king must be someone much like her father.

But she cannot tell him any of these things, and so she says nothing.

"You will let me know if you need anything? After the festivities we leave for England. Anything you require, just speak to your ladies, and I shall attend to it." He stands up and shakes his head. "I never expected you to be so young."

"I never expected you to be so handsome."

There, it is said. He is taken aback; he laughs, then tucks the sheet up to her neck. "You should sleep now."

He makes to blow the candle out, but she stops him; tells him she is frightened of the dark. And so he kisses her on the forehead and leaves, shutting the door softly behind him. Before it closes she sees him say something to the guard and pat him on the shoulder; her father never speaks in a friendly manner to anyone less than a duke, and so this surprises her.

She sits up and retrieves the casket. She runs a finger across the velvet. "One day I will have your heart, Edward," she whispers. "One day, Edward. I promise you! One day!"

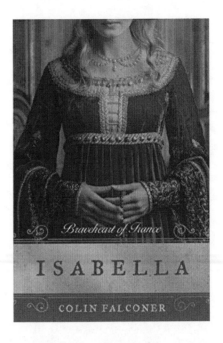

Isabella, Braveheart of France,
the prequel to "A Vain and Indecent Woman"
is published by Lake Union
And available on Amazon for Kindle, paperback or audio

AUTHOR NOTES

If this were a work of complete fiction, no competent editor would have allowed it; three times fate intervenes on Joan and Thomas's behalf and as any half-decent novelist will tell you, allowing coincidence to drive your plot is unthinkable.

Yet in life this is what happened; the Earl of Salisbury did indeed die at the Windsor tournament before he could make an accommodation with Thomas; Thomas' capture of the Comte d'Eu meant that he could make a proper legal claim to Joan at the ecclesiastical court in Avignon, just at the right moment; and Joan's brother John died of unexplained causes at the tender age of twenty-two releasing Joan to an extraordinarily lavish inheritance.

I have not attempted to change known facts or dates in any way. What I have done is surmise the thoughts and motivations of those major players in Joan's life to try and understand why things happened the way they did.

Colin Falconer

HISTORICAL

FOOTNOTES

Edmund of Woodstock and his wife Margaret had four children; John, the first Earl of Kent, was born in Arundel Castle, Sussex on 7 April 1330; the exact date is on record because John was required to prove that he was twenty-one years of age, in April 1351, in order to claim his inheritance from the Crown.

A point of historical detail that will not concern the casual reader: Joan's date of birth is invariably given as 29 September 1328, without much evidence to support it. In her brother John's Inquisition Post Mortem, taken between December 1352 and February 1353, witnesses from where John had held lands gave her age as between 22 and 26, which would place her date of birth somewhere between 1326 and 1330. These jurors may never have seen Joan and were just giving their best guess.

But as historian Kathryn Warner has pointed out, two counties gave an exact date of birth - the jurors of Nottinghamshire stated that she was '25 years and more at St Michael last'; that is, she turned 25 on 29 September 1352, which would make her date of birth 29 September 1327. The jurors of Leicestershire said that Joan was '26 years and more at St Michael last', which would make her date of birth 29 September 1326. Given the date of her parents' wedding, it is impossible that she was more than 26 years old.

There were either one or two other children besides John and Joan. The eldest son, Edmund, died as a child sometime shortly before 13 October 1331. Some believe there was a daughter, Margaret, who was betrothed to the Gascon lord Arnaud-Amanieu d'Albret in 1340. Others believe the name is erroneous, that it was Joan who was betrothed, and that the clerk called her by her mother's name in error.

We do know that Joan didn't have any other siblings alive in 1352, otherwise they would have been John's co-heirs with her.

The earliest that any of the children could have been born is September 1326, nine months after Edmund and Margaret's wedding in December 1325, and their second youngest cannot have been born any later than May or June 1329, as John was born in early April 1330 and must have been conceived in about July 1329, and Margaret would have been 'off-limits' to her husband for thirty or forty days after birthing her second last child.

Joan of Kent, then, from the evidence above, was born either on 29 September 1326 or 29 September 1327. If the former, she must have been conceived very soon after Edmund and Margaret's wedding and therefore been Edmund's twin. But this is purely conjecture.

John was baptised on the day of his birth, 7 April 1330, in the church of St Bartholomew in Arundel. James de Byne, one of the dozen jurors who gave testimony in 1353, stated that "Edmund son of the said Edmund and Brother John de Grenstede, prior of the order of Friars Preacher of Arundel, and Joan, sister of the said Edmund son of Edmund, lifted the said John from the sacred font on 7 April, 4 Edward III...".

To be big enough and responsible enough to lift their newborn brother from the font, (albeit with an adult helping them), Joan must have been older than the eighteen months that tradition subscribes to her.

* * *

As for Bella - I have used the diminutive here to avoid confusion for the reader with her grandmother, the former Queen Isabella - it may be interesting to note that she did finally marry, and that it was for love. Imitating Joan's spirited defiance and fierce sense of independence she avoided matrimony until July 1365, when at the age of thirty-three she married one Enguerrand de Coucy, a French knight being held hostage in England at the time.

He would certainly not have been her father's first choice.

As for Edward's other children, the king tried to arrange strategic marriages for his son the prince four times but each time the Pope refused to give the necessary dispensation, so it is curious that he allowed the marriage to Joan. In October 1340 and again in April 1345 a match between young Edward and Margaret of Brabant was proposed to that Edward could secure an alliance with Brabant. Dispensation was requested from the Pope, which was common enough practice among royals at the time as almost any favourable and influential match fell within the four degrees of relationship forbidden by the Fourth Lateran Council.

In effect this gave the papacy great political leverage. Since 1308 the Pope had taken up residence in a palace in Avignon, under French protection. Withholding permission from the English royal family and frustrating Edward's matrimonial plans was surety of France's ongoing support.

But Edward tried again in 1347 with another match between his son and Princess Leonora of Portugal, and as late as 1360 the widowed Margaret of Burgundy was being considered.

However, when Joan was proposed as his future bride Edward and his son acted with an intent that they had failed to display with any of the previous marriage proposals.

Although Joan was not a foreign princess there was no reason to suppose that the Pope would be any more accommodating on this occasion and lengthy negotiations would not fit into the timescale Edward had proposed for his son to assume control of Aquitaine.

The established protocol was for Edward to approach the papacy with a request for the necessary dispensation. But this time the prince contacted the Pope directly, sending his squire Nicholas Bond to attend the Pope in Rome and Avignon and his runner Picot carrying his letters, requesting politely but insistently, for formal dispensation for the marriage.

There was no immediately favourable response, and none was expected. What the prince did next was to secretly contract to marry Joan. In doing so he risked excommunication for himself and for Joan but it was an important part of the strategy they devised.

King Edward made the next move, presenting Innocent VI with a formal request concerning the prince's marriage. First, he asked for a dispensation on the grounds of his relationship to Joan; secondly, he asked the Pope to absolve the couple for having privately contracted their secret betrothal, explaining that the prince had intended to obtain the necessary dispensation later; last, he asked the Pope to formally declare all future issue of the marriage legitimate.

It was a masterstroke; Innocent was cornered. He could not withhold his consent, as he had been in correspondence with the prince for months and had not indicated that he might refuse and if he did so after Edward's formal request he would invite a breach with the English Crown.

So, on 7 September he granted the dispensations the king had requested.

In doing so, the issue of the marriage's validity was also resolved; in return a small penance was imposed for the infraction of papal rules, requiring the prince to found two chapels within a year. The remnants of that penance may still be seen in Canterbury cathedral, in the Huguenot chapel, although the masonry and decoration has gone and the pillars, bosses and roof have been whitewashed. But one of the bosses features a woman's head, her hair dressed in the style fashionable in the 1360s, held in a square-framed net close to her face. This may be a representation of Joan though there is no clear evidence of this.

But the importance of the documentation so painstakingly collected to prove the legality of the prince's marriage was thoroughly impressed on his heir. More than thirty years later, in November 1394, when Richard II was about to sail for Ireland, he ordered the Archbishop of York to take custody of a small chest containing personal documents and place them for safekeeping with the abbot of Westminster. He considered these documents so important that he had heretofore always kept them at his side. The documents consisted of eleven papal bulls related to his parents' marriage, written verification of the legality of Joan's marriage to Thomas

Holand, the annulment of her marriage to William of Salisbury, and the validity of her marriage to Prince Edward.

* * *

I have chosen to ignore the scurrilous claims of an affair between Catherine Grandison, the Countess of Salisbury, and King Edward III. To me they smack of French propaganda. They knew about smear campaigns long before it became a staple of contemporary politics. Froissart cannot be considered an impartial observer in my opinion. Gossip is not historical record.

The plague epidemic of 1348-49 reached England aboard two ships which arrived in Dorset from Gascony in the summer of 1348. It had already ravaged most of Europe, and its effects in England were equally as devastating. It spread across England within twelve months. The actual numbers who died cannot be ascertained but it is reckoned that somewhere between a third to a half of the population of England died in that period.

Ned is today more popularly known as the Black Prince, though he was not called that during his life time. The name came from Holinshed and it is uncertain how he earned the nickname; he did not wear black armour, as is sometimes believed, and the atrocities committed under his command were no better or worse than any others seen during the war. I called him Ned for ease of identification for the reader. During life he was known as Edward IV or Edward of Woodstock.

An interesting footnote: Joan was the first Duchess of Kent. There was another to follow her in our own times, a woman who would become much more famous.

But that, as they say, is another story.

To find more Colin Falconer books, head to:
colinfalconer.org.

Made in the USA
Middletown, DE
02 June 2021